FINAL BASTION ONLINE
Sages & Demons

A LitRPG Adventure

Justin Clarke

FINAL BASTION ONLINE : SAGES & DEMONS
Copyright © Justin Clarke

The following is a work of fiction. Any names,
characters, places, and incidents are the product of the
author's imagination. Any resemblance to persons,
living or dead, is entirely coincidental.

For Amanda

As sisters go, I couldn't have asked for a better one. Thanks for always caring about your annoying little brother!

P.S. The green chair is mine, as is the ottoman.

Escort Quests

Daniel made his way over towards a large table that had many different kinds of food laid out. The elves were in fine spirits and raucous celebration could be heard from all parts of the town square. As he picked up a strange looking piece of fruit and bit into it, a stray thought crossed his mind that was more panic inducing than facing off against The Nameless guild.

Oh shit! Midterms!! I haven't studied like anything and they start next week!

He thought he'd internally groaned to himself, but those around him heard his sounds of discontent and assumed it was a sound of pleasure from the delicious flavor of the bite he'd just taken.

One of the nearby elves stepped over, putting his arm around Daniel and whispered conspiratorially, "just wait till you try the apple pies down at the end there, it gives you a *very* potent tingling sensation in all the right places."

He then winked at Daniel, took a swig of his drink and went back over to his group.

Daniel's cheeks were a furious red color.

He wasn't used to interactions like that, especially when overt innuendos were involved. Putting the rest of the fruit into his mouth and swallowing it whole, he spotted Abby sitting by herself. He quickly made his way over, trying to escape from the awkward situation he'd found himself in.

Plopping himself down next to her, he gently elbowed her in the arm.

"Heya."

Abby glanced over at him absently and replied back, "Hey Daniel."

As he looked her over, he could tell that she was lost in her own thoughts, so he just sat there next to her for a while.

I know she's just an NPC, but for some reason I feel attached to her. Is it weird that I feel this way for a computer generated character? I mean, should I just ignore her and play like most others do? Even online in the wikis and forums, people don't really consider the in-game NPCs as actual people. They treat them as toys or farm them for money.

As Daniel sat next to Abby, contemplating the nature of the game's AI characters, he came to a decision on how he would conduct himself while inside the world of Final Bastion Online.

Even if other people think I'm weird, I won't let it bother me. I will treat every entity I meet that seems self aware, as if it is a true life form. I mean, honestly, what difference does it make if they are fake people or not. I want to feel good about myself and how I treat others. I never want to be like them, like Jessica or Bradley or any of them. I will always try to show others kindness first, but I won't roll over for them anymore. I won't be pushed around and bullied. I can fight them all here, so I will.. I just hope I can learn to fight them in the real world as well..

While Daniel was lost in thought himself, Abby had gotten to her feet and was now standing in front of him, staring him in the eyes.

Finally noticing her intense gaze, he tilted his head slightly and asked, "what is it?"

"I learned from some of the adults who my grandmother is. I'm goin to be like her. I want to become a Strike Maiden!"

There was a determined fire in her eyes and her fists were clenched hard as she spoke to him.

Her demeanor suddenly changed and her eyes got big and round as she asked, "will you train me?"

Daniel was taken aback.

He sat there for a moment, unsure of what to say.

Train her? Me? I mean.. I guess I could show her a few things, but I don't know if I could train someone.

He sat there for a few moments more, while Abby anxiously waffled from foot to foot.

He took a slow breath in, then said, "I won't take you on as an apprentice or anything."

Her hopeful expression melted away and she looked as if she was about to cry as Daniel hurriedly tried to mollify her. He began waving his hands frantically in front of her in an attempt to keep her from bawling and stammered out a response.

"But I will totally show you what I can while we travel to the capitol. I'm probably not any good at teaching, but I will try my best while we are traveling together, I promise!"

Her face brightened back up and she beamed a genuine heartwarming smile at him.

Daniel felt a slight tightness in his chest and a warmth wash over him as he bathed in her happiness.

I don't want to let her down.. I'll have to look online and do some research while offline to figure out what I should do first for her. She looks so excited.

Abby had performed a mini happy dance then raced off after excitedly thanking him over and over.

Daniel just shook his head and got to his feet.

What have I gotten myself into this time..

He spotted Faellintis across the square and threaded his way through the crowd towards the old elf.

"Ahh, if it isn't just the man I was looking for! Come Daniel, let me introduce you to some of your traveling companions. This is Travers and Estavold along with Mirantil and Alvira."

As Daniel looked around at the four young elfs that now surrounded him, he was surprised to find they all seemed like teenagers. Except for Estavold, who was extremely muscular and tall. They all were a good head and shoulders taller than him, but none of them were above level twenty.

Travers stepped forward to shake Daniel's forearm and said in a quiet voice, "Good to meet you, Daniel." He was a slender framed young looking elf with short cropped hair.

"Likewise." As they shook arms, Estavold cleared his throat.

"It's ess-*tahv*-old," he said with a curt nod.

Daniel just nodded back.

"Oh! It's so nice to finally meet you! I'm Mirantil, but you can just call me Mira!"

Daniel felt at a loss.

She was breathtaking.

And she was holding onto his left arm with both of her hands.

As heat flushed his face, he looked over at the other young elf girl named Alvira.

She just nodded weakly and said, "hey."

"Uhh, hello, nice to meet you all."

Daniel suddenly had a lot of saliva in his mouth and couldn't suppress an almost audible gulp.

Mira was still holding onto his left arm.

"Well, I'm glad I got to introduce you all to each other. Daniel here has agreed to escort little Abby and all of you to Aeryenous. It'll take us a few days to prepare for your trip, so take some time and say your farewells. I've got some celebration duties to attend to, so enjoy the party!"

With that, Faellintis turned and disappeared into the crowd.

Alvira and Travers quickly left as well, leaving just Daniel and Estavold standing there with Mira, who was still holding onto his arm.

Mira began tugging on his arm and started dragging Daniel with her.

"Come on! Let's go get something to drink! I want to hear about all the adventures you've been on!"

"Oh. Uhh, ok.. Ahh slow down."

As Daniel took a quick glance over his shoulder after nearly falling flat on his face from the unexpected strength of the elf girl, he saw Estavold glaring daggers at them.

Well that's not good.. He seems super upset at me for some reason. Does he like Mira or something? Or does he just not like humans?

The rest of the evening went by in a blur for Daniel.

He ate, then drank and even danced with Mira and the other elves as they celebrated their towns survival and cheered for their lost loved ones to find peace. They told stories of those who had fallen and laughed at their memories. It wasn't the type of funeral Daniel was used to. It was more like a congratulatory party where their friends and family got to move on to the next stage of their existence.

The last funeral Daniel had been to was for one of his grandparents. Everyone was dressed in dark colored suits and dresses. The atmosphere had been somber and quiet. A priest had given a eulogy as people shed tears to the sad words.

Here, for the elves, it was a goodbye, but it wasn't a sad goodbye.

Daniel had to log off before the party even ended. He'd found out that they usually spent several days merry making and cherishing the memories of their lost ones before life returned to a normal routine.

Before he went to bed that night, he spent a few hours learning about how other players trained and mentored NPCs. It all seemed about the same as if you were training someone in the real world. There didn't seem to be any special skills involved, other than having an innate ability to teach others. Daniel wasn't sure if he'd be any good at teaching, but he'd give it his best shot.

The next day, at the end of every class, Daniel approached each of his teachers and asked to confirm what he should focus on and study in their textbooks for the upcoming midterms. Each and every one of his teachers had expressed their dissatisfaction with Daniel. Exclaiming that they had already gone over this material in class and that he should pay more attention during lectures. In the end, they all provided him with some direction to focus his studies if he wanted to attain a passing score.

He saw Alyssa that morning in his first period class, but she didn't seem to pay him any mind and was wrapped up with her friends the entire time.

Daniel went back to spending his lunches in the library, finding the solitude comforting.

His previous notoriety from the clash with Jessica's guild was starting to fade. He didn't really mind that so much, since he preferred being left alone.

The next several days passed by without any incidents.

Daniel spent his time at school studying furiously and when he logged into FBO, he roamed around the nearby forests and continued working on all the quests for the townspeople of Dharesia.

He could tell that they were still preparing for the escort quest as he noticed a constant flurry of activity around the town square. Mostly around some wagons that were being constructed from the ground up and slowly loaded with all kinds of materials.

He'd spent a few hours responding to his in-game messages from Alyssa and her crew. They were mostly curious if he wanted to join back up with them for some more dungeon runs, but Daniel had to turn them down since he didn't want to miss out on this escort quest that led to a sword sage.

When he logged in on Saturday, wondering how much longer until the escort quest was ready to begin, he was met with a pleasant surprise.

Faellintis found him right away and let him know that everyone was set to depart, they were just waiting on him.

As he followed the old elf towards the center of town, Daniel found himself at a loss for what he saw being harnessed to the front of a very large covered wagon.

The creature was massive, with six legs and two thick necks with wolf-like heads on each. What really tripped Daniel up was the translucent nature of the beast. It was ephemeral and he could very clearly see elves on the other side of it attaching some ropes to it and then lashing them to the wagon.

Keeping a safe distance away from the see-through wagon sized beast, Daniel noticed a second large covered wagon behind the first. This second wagon was latched directly onto the back of the first wagon. It appeared very similar to a train in Daniel's mind.

"Daniel! Over here my boy." Faellintis called and waved as he disappeared behind the second wagon.

Daniel hurried after him.

"-yea, but do we *really* even need him? I can keep them safe. He's the reas–" Estavold abruptly stopped what he was about to say when he noticed Daniel rounding the side of the rear wagon.

Uhh, that was obviously about me. I'm starting to not like this guy.

"Now, I'll have none of that, Estavold. Despite your strength, I'm afraid you are no match for the denizens of the Aerfall. Without Daniel here, I'd never even have allowed this trip in the first place, so count yourselves lucky he's willing to shepherd you at all. This will be the first time any elf from the exiled attempt to return home."

Faellintis continued to speak to them all and gestured at the five elves standing before him. "You five are of a different generation and have not been marked as exiles, so you may freely return to our home, Aeryenous. It saddens me to see such young, fresh faces depart us, but in the knowing of your joyous return home I find my heart warmed. Stay true and faithful to each other as you make this perilous journey, the likes of which have left their scars on many of us first generation exiles. Do not stray from the wagons and use the generously provided materials to barter with so that you may start your new lives with coins in your purses and confidence in your steps."

Turning, Faellintis placed his right hand firmly on Daniel's shoulder.

"Take good care of my children Daniel. I leave them in your capable hands my boy. Lead them home, keep them safe, I beg of you."

Daniel could only muster up a nod towards Faellintis. The heaviness of the moment was getting to him and he couldn't trust himself to speak properly.

Turning back to the young elves, Faellintis gave his final instructions, "Now Abby, I want you to listen to Mirantil and the others. Do as they say and never leave their sight. Mira, Alvi, keep your eyes on her and follow Daniel's instructions. That goes for the both of you as well."

He pointed at Estavold and Travers.

"Be on alert at all times. Do not let the false sense of safety that you feel in the Aerfall be your doom. That goes for all of you. Mind your steps and stay together."

Nodding to them all, Faellintis turned and beckoned Daniel to follow him once more after calling over his shoulder, "Say your final goodbyes, you depart now."

As Faellintis led Daniel to the front of the lead wagon, he stopped at the translucent monster wolf thing and turned towards Daniel.

"This is a Volneur. It is a spirit beast that has been attached to the lead wagon. As long as the lead wagon remains in good repair, the Volneur will remain in this world. It is a very simple spirit bond so don't expect anything more of it than pulling the wagons. It will not fight for you nor can anything natural in the Aerfall harm it. Just sit there in the seat and hold the reins. It will know your intentions and will move accordingly. I would recommend having Estavold guide the Volneur. It'll give him something to do and hopefully keep his mind off of.. things."

Daniel nodded his head once more and gave a simple response, "kay."

Faellintis puckered his lips a moment and scrunched his eyes a little. Then, as if remembering something, his eyebrows arched upwards.

"Almost forgot, when you have to take your long sleeps, you should be safe in the first wagon here." He walked over and patted the side of the wooden frame.

"We did what we could to inscribe rune wards into the base. Not as good as what we put up in defense around the barn, but not far from it."

He paused a moment, with his hand resting on the wagon and gave Daniel the once over with his eye.

"Well? Any questions lad?"

"Uhh, yea, just one really. You mentioned Aerfall, what is that, exactly?"

"Ahh, the Aerfall."

Faellintis stroked his chin for a moment before speaking again.

"The Aerfall is.. it's a very large forest that spans an unfathomable distance. We are just outside the border of the Aerfall, but Aeryenous is deep inside that abominable place.

It serves well as protection for the capitol but also prohibits exploration of the surrounding areas. There is some natural enchantment that floods the place, making you feel as if you are as safe as can be, but that is a devious lie. The creatures that you will encounter the further in you go.. I.."

Faellintis visibly shivered as he recalled his own memories of the Aerfall.

"Got it, super dangerous forest. Oh, also, is there a path or a road or something that will take me to Aeryenous? I won't have to bushwhack my way through the forest, will I?"

"Hum? Oh no, there are roads to Aeryenous. The Volneur has been imprinted with the destination and will follow the roads we originally traveled to get here. The paths may have changed, but just follow this road out of Dharesia and keep to the border towns of the Aerfall until you find the crossroads. It's hard to miss them and nearly every person between here and there can help point you in the right direction, if you get lost. Aeryenous is basically a straight shot into Aerfall from the crossroads. It's not a well traveled road mind you, due to the nature of the Aerfall, so it's unlikely you'll run across any other folks once you cross the border. Whelp, looks like the youngins are piling into the wagon. Any other questions before we send you all off?"

Daniel stood there for a moment wracking his brain for any missing information he might need, but came up short. Shrugging to himself, he climbed up onto the wagon's seat and grabbed the reins and looked back over at the old elf.

"Nah, can't think of anything. You covered it all pretty well. Thanks Faellintis."

"Of course, keep them safe and stay to the roads. The Aerfall isn't the only danger you'll face out there."

Daniel softly nodded his head once more, then turned his attention towards the road leading out of Dharesia.

The Volneur jerked forward suddenly then came to an abrupt stop as Daniel shouted, "Woah!"

Alvira was in the process of climbing into the lead wagon and promptly fell off the back of it with a grunt.

"Hey! Watch it!" Came her sharp retort as she shouted at Daniel.

Estavold climbed over the seat partition from inside the lead wagon and snatched the reins out of Daniel's hands.

"Give me those."

"Yea, sorry, my bad.."

Daniel ducked his head down into his shoulders and scooted over to the side of the wagon bench.

He could hear Abby and Mirantil giggling from inside the wagon as Alvira climbed into the back with a huff.

She angrily moved around some bags of merchandise to make a seat for herself and crossed her arms then gave Daniel a stare that put a chill down his spine.

As Estavold gently started their mini caravan moving forward, nearly the entire village was spread out on either side of the road leading out of Dharesia. Estavold had his back straight as a board and waved at everyone as they passed by.

Daniel was feeling rather embarrassed about his earlier faux pas and was still hunched slightly over, trying his best to appear invisible.

He looks so obnoxious. Ugh, this escort quest sucks already.

Border Towns

It didn't take long until Abby was climbing all over Daniel. As the shouts of farewell and safe travels faded into the muted stillness that was the border forests of the Aerfall, Abby was inclined to begin her tutelage under Daniel to become the next Strike Maiden.

Looking around for a place for them to do much of anything, Daniel found himself dismayed.

The wagon is full of stuff and we're moving too fast for her to do anything alongside us. The other wagon is even more full of stuff. Maybe.. maybe we can use the second wagon's bench seat.

Abby was doing her best to shake Daniel into action, putting both of her small hands on the back of his neck and trying to push and pull him back and forth.

"Dannnnieeeellll.."

Sighing to himself, he deftly got to his feet, standing on the wagon bench and plucked Abby up and tossed her over his left shoulder in a sort of fireman carry position.

"Ekk!"

Abby shrieked and held on for dear life as Daniel nimbly made his way to the back of the wagon.

He could hear Mirantil's gentle peal of laughter behind him. It made his face flush with embarrassment.

With a soft hop, he landed on the large empty bench of the second wagon.

He tried to peel Abby off his shoulders, but she was digging her nails into his skin.

"Heeeyy, it's alright, let go, we're gonna start your training now. Ack, you have sharp nails."

She'd managed to pierce his skin and some blood was now flowing down his back, but the sting of it was extremely muted due to his pain tolerance skill being so high.

Finally, after several more seconds of coaxing, she let go and settled down on the wagon bench.

Daniel sat down next to her and surveyed the space he had to work with.

It's not much. But she's little so it's probably plenty to start with. Hmm, should we do some basic physical fitness first? Should probably build up a starting routine for her, then we can get into sword practice.. Oh! Do I still have my training swords from Henry?

Checking his inventory, he found the wooden training swords he'd used while starting his own journey in the art of sword combat.

Ahh good, we can use these when we get to–

Abby had just tried to poke Daniel in the eye and he instinctively recoiled his head backwards.

"Oye, stop that, I was thinking."

"Well. Are you done thinking yet? When do I get to become a Strike Maiden?"

"Ahh, eventually, if you train hard and do as I say."

She seemed to snap to attention at his words, her demeanor changed and she became very serious.

"Okay, what do I do first?"

"First, we need to build your body up, get you strong. Then we can start working on your swordsmanship. Physical fitness is very important, so you'll have to make sure you do your exercises even when I'm asleep, got it?"

"Yes! Whatever you say, Captain!" She gave a strange little salute with her closed right fist pressed against her heart. The motion tickled Daniel's memory.

I've seen that before.. where.. oh, the elven town guard saluted their guard captain this way when they patrolled Dharesia. That is, they used to, before The Nameless killed them.. those bastards.

Daniel snapped himself out of his negative thoughts and focused on Abby.

"Good, though I'm no captain. You don't have to salute me or anything."

"Oh. But, I want to. Is it okay?"

Her hand had half fallen down to her waist as she looked at him with big, round, sad eyes.

"Ahh, yea, I guess, it's fine if you want to, I don't mind."

Whew, she looks relieved. I'll play captain if it makes her happy. It's not a big deal or anything.

"So, like I said, first off is physical fitness. Do you know what a push-up is?"

She shook her head and from there Daniel began showing her simple exercises she could do in the space she had on the wagon bench. They went through a series of several different exercises, a few of which Daniel had looked up online and most of which he did while doing his own fitness quests in the real world every day.

He wanted to get a measure on her endurance and overall general fitness, so he kept her at these basic movement routines until she tired out. Then gave her a fifteen minute break and started over again.

To her credit, she never complained and did the best she could until her little body gave out from sheer exhaustion.

Mirantil had been trained with life and nature magic, giving her some rudimentary healing abilities, which she used for Abby's benefit.

It was good training for both of them.

Mirantil was still just a beginner with her magic, but repeated use on Abby was helping her better understand how it worked, improving her fundamental magic knowledge while also increasing her skill levels.

Travers had been sitting in the back of the second wagon and climbed his way over to them and watched for a while before finally asking Daniel if he had any tips for improving his own physical fitness.

After a brief discussion, Daniel had given Travers a few simple exercises that could help improve some of his skills. He had Travers running to the side of the wagons doing sprints from the back to the front, then slowing down until he was at the back again and dash forwards as fast as he could.

Mirantil started practicing her healing skill on moving people by using Travers as her target. She was terrible at first, constantly losing focus and fizzling out her magic. It was doubly hard to cast her heals on someone who was far away, forcing her to really explore the magic itself and how it weaved its way through the world. It didn't take long before she'd made some breakthroughs and was slinging healing magic at both Travers and Abby as they continually exhausted themselves.

Daniel had moved on to some basic sword stances and had given Abby one of his practice swords to swing around. She tried her very best at performing the swings and blocks just as Daniel had shown her. Despite her small frame, she managed to keep swinging the wooden sword around for hours.

They had departed Dharesia in the early morning and the sky had begun to darken before Abby had finally given up. He hadn't meant to push her so hard, but it just seemed she had the energy to spare.

Travers had ended his sprints several hours before and Mirantil was massaging her temples as she dealt with a mana headache from over taxing herself all day.

After another hour or so, as the stars finally made their way into the clear night sky overhead, Abby stood up once more. The fire in her eyes was as bright now as it had been that morning.

She's ready to keep going. Wow. She needs to rest though, but that determination is good, I wonder how strong she can become.

"No Abby! Demy's scales! I need to rest, my head's poundin." Mirantil agonized at Abby as the little girl began to slowly stretch her overly sore and aching limbs.

"Yea, I agree with Mira. You need a break Abby. Rest is just as important as exercise. You've also hardly eaten anything today. Get some food and relax. We'll start again tomorrow."

"Urgk."

That was all the sound she could muster as her shoulders sagged and her arms drooped low. Exhaustion had finally won out and she began to fall, face first, right off the side of the wagon.

"He-yup."

Daniel snatched her up in a princess carry before she fell and hopped over to the lead wagon. He then gently laid her down in the middle of a semi-cleared area and she promptly started lightly snoring.

"Sheesh. She should probably rest most of the day tomorrow. Didn't think she'd go so hard today."

Daniel had spoken mostly to himself, but as he looked up, he saw Alvira worriedly looking over Abby.

As he was about to turn around and find a spot in the back of the wagon to relax himself when Estavold turned his head and got Daniel's attention.

"Pssst. Check it out."

Climbing up into the empty space next to the large elf, Daniel sat down and peered ahead.

Are those lights?

"Is that a town?"

"Aye, a border town. Should be Denton's Watch, from what I'm told."

"Elfs? Or.."

"Not my kin. Humans mostly, Orcs too, according to ole Fay. He said we should be safe enough to stay there for a few days if needed. Dorran, a human, should be the leader of them."

"Cool. You want to handle the introductions when we get there? Or you want me to do it?"

The elf's grip on the reins tightened as he nodded his head towards the lights in the distance. "If you would, please, I've never spoken to anyone outside of Dharesia and from the stories told of humans, they distrust us exiled elves."

"Sure, no worries. And also, ole Fay?"

"That's just what most of us call Faellintis."

"Ahh.."

Daniel remained seated next to Estavold as the lights in the distance slowly materialized into the walls of a small, fortified town.

Denton's Watch

"**H**ail! Identify yer'selves!"

Their mini wagon train came to a halt just outside a large, closed, wooden gate. A helmeted head was poking through a small square hole at ground level from the other side of the gate.

"Ahh, Uhh-" -*Heurk*-

Daniel had to clear his throat before he could continue speaking. The anxiety from having to be prepared to speak and introduce himself to strangers had caused some flem to build up in the back of his mouth. He'd been rehearsing what he would say over and over again in his head as they'd continued their steady approach to the small town.

"Sorry, uhm, hey. I'm Daniel. We are just passing through as we make our way East. Maybe looking for some additional supplies, depending on what you guys have here."

"Ehh? Going East, you say? Ain't that nothin but the Aerfall? Why you headin that way?"

"Ohh, uhh, well no, not *directly* East. We will be following the borders of the Aerfall. I think someone told me there were strong mobs- ah, erh, monsters in there."

"Oh aye, that elf cursed forest breeds some terrible creatures, that's for sure."

The man's face was mostly hidden by his helmet, but Daniel felt his scrutinizing eyes pore over their wagons and then rest themselves on the elf sitting next to him.

"And who's this then?"

He curtly nodded towards Estavold.

Ahh, shit, I totally forgot to introduce the elves!

"Umm, sorry, this is Estavold. We are traveling together. There are four others as well. They're asleep in the wagon."

Daniel nodded his head toward the covered area behind him as he mentioned the other sleeping elves.

The man simply closed the square hole, leaving Daniel wondering if he'd said or done something wrong. It took about half a minute, but then the wooden gate started to slowly open.

A soft exhalation of relief escaped him as Estovald glowered side-eyed at him.

The guard didn't seem overly worried about the Vulneur. I wonder if these things are common around here.

Once the gates were wide enough for the wagons to fit through, Estovold slightly adjusted the reins and they slowly made their way past the wooden barricade that surrounded the small border town.

The gate guard was standing next to several other guards, all of them wearing the same full face covered helmets and full body chainmail.

He nodded at Daniel as they passed and called out, "Welcome to Denton's Watch. Don't go causin any trouble. That goes doubly so for that elf. In the center of the town square there's an obelisk and the inn is right by it."

With that, he abruptly turned around and joined back into the ongoing conversation between all the other guardsmen.

Daniel turned towards the elf and smiled.

"Well, that was easier than I thought."

Estavold sneered back at him, "What's so hard about saying hello? It's not like they would have turned you away."

Daniel was taken aback by the sudden harsh tone. He felt himself shrink down a little, turtling up and putting a wall in between himself and his emotions. He did this instinctually, just out of habit, and hunched his shoulders as he watched the ground pass beneath them.

Nothing more was said until they reached the square.

Estavold grunted and called back over his shoulder to the others, "We're stopping here, get up and help secure the wagons."

Daniel silently got up off the wagon and made his way over to the obelisk that was smack in the middle of the town square.

A bind stone. I definitely need to bind here.. Just in case. I think the last place I bound was waaay over near Eliswin. That elf town didn't have a bind stone either, so I'm actually lucky to have found one before getting killed. Oh man, I would probably have failed this escort quest if that happened.

Without any further hesitation, Daniel placed his palm on the bind stone and felt the warm, tingly, sensation flood his body as he bound himself to Denton's Watch.

Whew, safe! Now to explore.. Or, should I find a safe place to log out for lunch?

Checking his internal clock, it was a little after eleven in the morning, Earth time.

Definitely time for lunch.. Just gotta find a safe place to rest.

Making his way back over to the inn, the elves were busy securing the wagons in a large, empty fenced off area attached to the side of the building. The Vulneur was placidly standing still as Daniel looked it over for the hundredth time.

It's just so weird how I can see through it. Can I touch it? Or will my hand pass right through?

Daniel contemplated the pros and cons of attempting to pet the Vulneur as he stepped into the inn. To his left was a reception desk with a staircase going up to the higher floors and off to his right was the main floor of the large building. Tables were scattered about with a bar along a back wall.

No fireplace. In all the books I've read, there was always a cackling fire, offering warmth to the weary travelers. I wonder if it snows here at all?

It was dark and nobody was around.

Daniel just stood there dumbly, unsure of what to do or how to get the attention of someone that worked there. He was looking all around for some sort of bell or sounding device to let them know he was there, but he couldn't find anything to ring.

Alvira walked in behind him, took a quick glance around, then promptly stepped over to the wall beside them and banged loudly on it several times.

Ahh, I guess that will work too..

Sure enough, less than a minute later shuffling sounds could be heard then a small light was floating their way coming down the stairs.

A disheveled older gentleman came to a soft stop at the base of the stairs, his eyes slowly going from slightly glazed to a bit more focused as he looked the two of them over.

"Can I help ye?"

Alvira elbowed Daniel.

"Ohh, uhh yea, we need some rooms for the night."

The man quietly nodded and made his way behind the reception desk and asked, "How many and for how long?"

Daniel looked back over at Alvira with a questioning look on his face.

She rolled her eyes at him and said, "Two for us, boys in one and girls in another, you might want a room to yourself though, seems Estavold doesn't like you much."

He pursed his lips for a moment, then turned to the man behind the desk.

"Three rooms, for one night, please."

Again, the man quietly nodded, gathering parchment and scrawling some notes on them.

"Third floor, first three rooms on the right are yours. Six gold a night for all three."

Daniel stepped up to the desk and pixelated six gold coins from his inventory. A small smile played on his lips as he watched the miniscule pink pixels dissipate after materializing his money.

I wish I could do that in the real world.

The man scooped up the coins then turned and went back upstairs with his light in tow, leaving both of them drenched in darkness once more.

Alvira turned and went back outside, calling over her shoulder that she would let the others know and that he should take the first room.

Making his way to the third floor, he found himself in a long hallway with several doors on both sides. Going to the first door on his right, he experimentally tested the latch.

It was unlocked.

Carefully, he opened the door and peered inside.

Empty. Whew, guess these lock from the inside?

Closing the door behind him, he couldn't seem to find a way to secure the door. Shrugging to himself, he just walked over to a side wall and slumped down to log off.

I'm bound here, so even if I get ganked while offline, it's not like I'll have far to walk.

As Daniel stretched from the long session and used the restroom, he strained his senses to try and hear if his parents were home. Nothing but silence greeted him.

Shuffling through his fridge, he made a simple sandwich. While eating, he gazed around his dining room with sightless eyes. The outside world seemed so dull and normal to him. He was robotically going about his tasks, eating and then changing into some work out clothes to get his fitness quests done.

Before he knew it, he was back in his room, getting ready to log back in. As he laid down and turned on his gear, excitement about meeting a sword sage filled his thoughts.

When he opened his eyes, it was with a startled yelp.

Mirantil was sitting directly across from him and was knee to knee with him, leaning towards him with only a few scant inches between their noses.

She jerked back in surprise as well, a slight blush coloring her cheeks.

Butterflies

Daniel felt his own blush creep onto his face.

She was so close! Why is she in my room?!

Suddenly, a nervous churning pulsed in his stomach. This was different from the anxiety he would feel when at school. A bit of adrenaline flushed his system and he felt his throat constrict slightly as he watched her settle down from her own sudden surprise.

What.. my heart is beating so loudly, I can feel it in my ears!

It took several moments for Daniel to get a handle on his raging emotions. A rough mixture of fear and excitement were at war within him. He did everything he could to keep his facial features neutral, doing his best to suppress any outward emotions from surfacing.

Mirantil was intensely staring directly into his eyes the entire time.

When Daniel finally mastered himself enough to speak, he lamely said, "Uhh, hey.."

Gah! My voice cracked when I said that!

She gave him a crooked smile, while continuing to bore into him with her piercingly blue eyes.

As he sat there in awkward silence, Daniel felt like he was sweating, even though avatars in Final Bastion Online didn't actually secrete anything.

Finally, Mirantil lazily stood and let out a small stretch before doing a half spin. Looking back at him with her head tilted toward her shoulder, she gave him a bright smile.

Playfully, she exclaimed, "Show me around town!"

Heart hammering in his chest, Daniel practically leapt to his feet, nodding his head a bit too enthusiastically, giving himself minor whiplash.

"Yea, for sure!"

He followed her out of the room like an excited puppy and down the stairs, then outside.

Walking out into the pre-dawn light, Mirantil turned towards him and crooked her arm out for him.

Heart thundering and a face that was redder than before, he hooked her proffered left arm with his right elbow and they started walking arm in arm across the town square.

Passing the bind stone, Mirantil started softly humming to herself.

A soft breeze kicked up and Daniel could smell the dirt road they walked along. Mixed in with the typical smells was her scent as well. He got hints of lavender and surprisingly pumpkin spice. He was only able to pick those smells out because of all the different types of candles his mom would bring home and burn in their living room all year long.

She smells so.. Wonderful..

Daniel felt his chest tighten up a bit at this thought. His emotions started to riot once again, forcing him to struggle with himself to try and remain mostly impassive as they walked.

"-nking about?"

Shit, I missed the first part of what she said. Was she asking me what I'm thinking about?

"Umm, sorry, what was that?"

She laughed lightly and said, "I *asked*, what it was you were thinking so hard about over there."

"Ahh, I.. uhmm, ju-" *-Heurk-*

He had to clear his throat as his voice kept cracking after every other syllable.

"I was just thinking, uhh, that you smelled like lavender and pumpkin spice."

"Hah!" She snorted a small laugh.

"I know what lavender is, but what is pumpkin spice?"

"Ohh, ahh, good question, I don't really know myself."

Her eyebrows scrunched together as she looked over at him with a playful frown on her face.

She looks so adorable! She's so pretty.. What the heck is happening?!

Daniel's forward motion was partially arrested by the silly look she gave him.

She lightly tugged on his arm with both of hers as she chided him.

"How can you say I smell like something and not even know what that *thing* is? What if it's a terrible thing, like sour fruit juice?!"

He just let himself be led along by the elf he found himself wildly attracted to, with a smile plastered on his face that seemed impossible to remove.

"Well? Is this pumpkin spice a *good* or bad smelling thing?"

She glared at him, then poked him in the chest as he just walked along beside her without answering, his smile growing wider by the second.

She punctuated her next statement with an increasingly aggressive poke after each syllable.

"An. Swer. Me!"

"Ow. Hah, okay okay."

Daniel had to grab her right arm since she was swinging a closed fist in his direction.

She growled at him and they play-fought each other for a few minutes, giggling at each other, until a passerby coughed loudly.

Feeling his cheeks flush out of embarrassment and also for some reason out of breath as well, Daniel just stared at Mirantil. It was as if his mind had shut off completely. He was just simply there, existing, happy, enjoying and savoring this brief moment as he watched Mirantil shyly look over at him with her own cheeks flushed and her thumbs fiddling, with her hair in slight disarray as it fell about her face.

He watched as the look in her eyes went from lightly embarrassed to something else, something he wasn't quite sure about, as she rested her gaze on his chest.

Daniel hadn't been blessed with many friends in his life, nor had he any experience with romance, but the look this elven girl was currently giving him triggered some dormant biological desire that overwhelmed him.

Without thought, Daniel had taken a half step forward and wrapped his arms around her.

As his mind finally caught up to what he was doing, his brain scrambled to assess the potential damage he may have caused. He was able to register that she was at first surprised but then accepted his sudden embrace.

Relief flooded his mind and caused his arms to sag slightly from being so tense a moment before. Then the awkwardness of having no idea what he should do next had him tensing up once more.

Luckily for Daniel, Mirantil took control of the situation and leaned down, giving him a light kiss on his cheek, then pushed away while pulling on his arm.

A bubbly giddiness was bouncing around inside him. He felt like he was just floating along behind her, as if he wasn't even anchored to the ground.

She pulled him closer so they could walk side by side once more. This time, hand in hand instead of arm in arm. She was lacing her fingers between his when she started the conversation back up.

"I'm still waiting for an answer about pumpkin spice."

"It's a good thing, I promise. It's like a special holiday spice that is super popular. It always reminds me of fall and good memories. Now, the best memory I have."

She squeezed his hand affectionately.

"What's fall?"

"Oh, uhm, when all the leaves fall off the trees and winter starts."

"What?! All the leaves fall off the trees? Like all trees?"

"Ahh, yea? Is that not a thing here?"

"Of course not! Well, I mean if it is, *I've* never seen anything like it. Demy's scales! I can't even imagine such a thing."

They walked in silence for a bit, both of them lost in their own thoughts.

As they turned onto the next street, the town square was visible ahead and there was a steady bustle of activity happening with street vendors setting up for the day and a village crier calling out the latest happenings of the town.

"Do the trees die when their leaves fall off?"

Daniel had been distracted by all the comings and goings happening in the square ahead and it took him a minute to register the question he was asked.

"Hmm, no, when spring rolls around all the leaves grow back. Oh, uhh, spring is just the name of the time of year when winter is over."

"So the leaves just decide to fall off then grow back after this winter time is over?"

"Yup, winter is when everything gets really cold and in lots of places snow falls, blanketing the world in white. I've only really seen heavy snow once-"

Daniel froze in his tracks.

"What? What is it? What's wrong?"

The worry in her voice was evident as Daniel stood motionless and rigid beside her.

They had just arrived fully into the town square when Daniel spotted two familiar faces making their way across the busy thoroughfare.

It's them, The Nameless.

The Burden of The Strong

"Daniel, what is it?"

It doesn't look like they've spotted me. I remember those two, they were part of the first group who attacked Dharesia. The one walking in front was the magic chains guy. Do they know about the others? Is Abby safe?

"We need to get back to the inn."

"Okay, but please tell me what is wrong."

"See those two guys walking past that street crier person?"

"What? Who.. I don't-"

The sharp inhale of breath was enough for Daniel to surmise that she recognized them as well.

Her grip on his arm became like iron.

Together, they quickly and quietly made their way back to the inn where the others should still be.

I don't have my mask on.. Shit! I haven't been wearing it since I took it off for that celebration in Dharesia.

When they finally reached the front of the inn, Mirantil bolted into the front doors while Daniel made his way around towards their wagons.

On the way, he slipped his mask on, feeling instantly better, the mask offering some psychological comfort while being worn.

The wagons look ok, the same as how we left them. The Vulneur is placid as ever. I'll just keep watch down here until the others come down, shouldn't be too long now.

Daniel's assumption was correct. The others quickly assembled and they all worked together to get the wagons tied to each other and led the Vulneur out of the fenced courtyard.

It didn't take long for them to reach the same gate they entered through. The tension among the group was taut, all of them on high alert, scrutinizing every person that crossed their path.

The gate was open, so they just led the Vulneur through and out onto the dirt road.

Following the path, then cutting left so as to keep along the borders of the Aerfall, they spotted a travel worn road matching their direction and had to navigate a bit around some uneven terrain until they were on the road itself. Once their wheels hit the packed ground, Estavold let the Vulneur loose and their wagons started to rattle uncomfortably as they fled Denton's Watch, leaving a literal dust trail in their wake.

As they pushed their wagons hard for several long minutes, the heavily deforested area around Denton's Watch was slowly being replaced with forest and trees once more.

While looking over all the elves holding on tightly in the back of the lead wagon, Daniel saw hesitant smiles start to emerge. Glancing over at Estavold, they shared a look. Visible relief could be seen on the large elf's face.

Daniel opened his mouth to speak, "I thin-"

A sharp tingling sensation began to emanate just above his left ear as his Attack Prediction skill triggered.

Memories of a dark pit filled with snakes constantly trying to bite him wisped across his mind.

Without thought, Daniel materialized his currently equipped sword into his left hand and protected his head.

TINK!

The metallic sound of metal striking metal echoed out as an arrow went spinning past his head.

Glowing orange and red magic sigils could be seen covering the road up ahead of them.

In a panic, Estavold jerked hard to the right on the reins, the Vulneur turned sharply causing the wagons to jackknife and flip, spilling their contents and the elves across the road and off to the side.

Daniel was sent flying straight into the glowing circular magical trap.

A pillar of superheated flames sprung up around him, obscuring him from all angles.

As adrenaline filled his body, Daniel flared his aura to accelerate his mind's processing speed. He'd spotted a nearby tree that was outside of the trap's circle and the large branch that filled his vision looked sturdy enough for him to stand on. Using a lightning step, he clung tightly to the safety of the tree after narrowly escaping the trap spell.

Standing rather high up and slightly away from the intense pillar of fire, he could feel the incredible heat from his newfound perch.

Damn, not sure if my aura could have protected me from all that, even if I went full power.

Spotting the wagons below, he saw the elves gathering together near the first wagon and the always placid Vulnear standing calmly while both wagons had tipped over. The straps looked strained and slightly broken from his vantage point, but to his immense relief the elves all seemed perfectly fine, except for their facial expressions that had them looking emotionally rattled.

As the fire trap sputtered and died, well over a dozen players stepped out from the trees surrounding the road way.

"Did we get'em?"

Daniel could hear one of them call out laughingly.

"God damn, that's one helluva barbeque."

"I don't smell any smoked meat!"

"It probably just incinerated the dude, those flames were hot as shit, I could feel em from way over there!"

The group approached the scorched ground where their trap had gone off, then started heading for the elves.

Shit. Can't have that.

Daniel let himself fall head first over the side of the tree until he was horizontal then pushed off from the base of the branch, rocketing himself right into the center of their formation.

Two of them were pixelated into nothingness before a startled cry went out.

"Rings!"

A third one was cut in half, both parts of his body turning to millions of pink pixels.

The fourth one went flying off to the side as a spherical bubble popped up around him just as Daniel struck.

Despite the sudden unexpected resistance, Daniel didn't stop. He kept moving among them, blasting away with lightning enhanced strikes.

Instead of cutting them to pieces, they were simply bounced around inside their protective bubbles, getting back up moments later none the worse for wear.

One of the players getting up on his right called out, "looks like they work!" The rest started softly laughing, pulling out weapons and charging skills and spells up.

The chain magic wielder stepped forward then.

"What brings you out this way Daniel? Doing some kind of Escort Quest or something with those NPCs?"

He used his left thumb to point at the gathered elves.

"I didn't think you'd noticed me in town this morning."

Daniel was shifting his stance slightly, trying his best to keep an eye on all the players that were now encircling him.

Those shields are a problem, might have to try cycling different mana types into my blades and see if any can cut through.

"This morning? Ah naw man, we saw you last night. Been watching you since and calling in some friends is all. Guessing you saw us and got spooked."

"Brodie, the rings won't last, hold him here and we'll go kill his elves."

Several players turned and bolted, running straight at the panicked group of elves.

Motherfu-

Chains erupted from the air, tightly binding Daniel to the ground.

His lightning step was still on cool down so all he could do was blast his aura out to try and stop them while he frantically flicked his wrists, desperately trying to cut his bonds.

All of their shields flared as his lightning aura swept outwards, but it did nothing to slow them down.

He did feel the magical chains dissipate from his aura attack. Launching himself in the air, he flew over players, spells and all as he landed directly in front of Abby and the others.

"Stay directly behind me!"

He hoped they heard his shout over all the clamor.

Crossing his blades, he flared his aura out once more while focusing on forming it into a cone shape to try and encompass everyone running at them. With so much force and directed concentration, it started to rapidly drain his health.

A surge of visible lightning as thick as a dragon's breath attack swept over the onrushing players.

The tips of little bubbles of light could be seen bobbing up above his surging lightning infused aura attack.

He'd never used his aura this way before, although he'd done something similar when the Griffon had used its own lightning attack on him. He had survived and the whole ordeal had given him a great amount of confidence in the strength of his aura since it had been a raid boss attack after all.

He kept the pressure on, as the little light bubbles seemed to be stuck, unable to push forward through his surging lightning aura.

Unfortunately, his health would not last for more than fifteen seconds, at best.

As he was preparing to halt his attack, a hand was placed on his back and healing magic swept through him.

Mirantil! She's healing me! Maybe we can keep them all back until those shields run out of juice.

His health jumped back up, but then drained back down once more. It became a constant struggle, Mirantil fighting to keep his health up while he continued to blast his aura out, killing himself in the process from the lightning damage it was causing him.

BASE LIGHTNING RESISTANCE - LEVEL (653)
BASE LIGHTNING RESISTANCE - LEVEL (654)

He watched as his health yoyo'd and his lightning resistance continually improved. All of his lightning related skills and even his lightning aura skill itself leveled up. His mana consumption was almost non-existent, as his ability to draw lightning magic into his body was extremely high as well. The strength of his aura was based on its skill level and his willpower to drain his health and deal with the pain of it all. As long as Mirantil kept his health up, he could keep the attack going.

This is some good training, might be able to hit master ranks if I can keep this up.

He felt Mirantil sag against his back, a feeling of dread welling up in his stomach.

She's out, and they are all still alive, protected and safe in those stupid bubbles.

As Daniel prepared for the worst, he watched his health drain once more past the halfway point and continue down.

POP!

"Aarrghh-!"

One of the bubbles had popped and the player inside was swept away by Daniels cone of lightning.

Daniel kept an eye on his health as he watched more light bubbles pop.

Shit shit shit, this is gonna be close..

Just as his health hit the five percent mark, the last three bubbles popped and those players were swept away, pixelated into nothingness.

Daniel cut off his aura and surveyed the aftermath of his reckless aura attack.

The constant brightly flickering lightning had left after images in his vision, taking several moments to clear up.

There was nothing left of the players, just the little system generated loot bags full of coins on the ground. A cone of charred earth extended outward from Daniel all the way to the scorched magical trap in the middle of the road.

Turning to take in the elves, there was a mixture of emotions visible on all of their faces. Estavold seemed to be annoyed, while Abby looked absolutely awestruck. Travers was continuously shifting his eyes to the forest around them, ever on alert, while Alvira looked to be afraid of Daniel.

Mirantil had fallen to the ground and looked up at him with relief and a tired smile.

He reached his hand down and helped her up to her feet.

"Thanks for the heals, I wouldn't have been able to keep that up for long without you."

"Of course. You've saved us again, thank you Daniel."

"Saved us? This was his fault in the first place, Mira!"

Estavold stormed off and started trying to turn the wagons up right. Travers quietly moved to help him. Alvira grabbed Abby's hand and pulled her away to give them room to work.

"That was the most amazing thing I've ever seen! How did you *do* that Dani- *Cap*tain?"

Abby was trying to break away from Alvira and run over to pester Daniel with questions.

Daniel turned back to Mirantil, placing his hand on her shoulder, "Got one more heal tucked away in there? I'm really low on health right now."

She nodded and gently pressed her hand on his chest, channeling what little power she had left into him. It pushed his health back up over forty percent, but she was completely spent.

He half carried her over to Alvira and Abby who was continually squirming in the older elfs grasp.

Daniel kept an eye out as the other two went about fixing the wagons and loading all the spilled equipment. When they were finally ready to get moving again, he quickly went around and looted all the dropped coin bags then hopped up into the wagon.

For the rest of that entire day, the group was silent for the most part, aside from Abby, as they tried to put as much distance as they could between them and the site of the ambush.

When they neared a town, Estavold steered their wagons around, giving the small settlements a wide berth.

It was coming up on dinner time for Daniel, and he needed to log out. It was still daylight out in the game, but by the time he would be able to log in again nearly a whole day would have passed since time moved twice as fast in Final Bastion Online.

Daniel spoke softly to Estavold, "Hey, I uhh, I need to go to sleep for a bit."

The large elf looked over at him and just curtly nodded.

"You, ahh, you plan on stopping or anything? Or you just gonna keep driving past all the border towns?"

"We'll keep to the roads for now, how long?"

"Hmm? How long for what?"

The elf let out a frustrated breath, "How long will you sleep for?"

"Ohh, ahh, umm, probably a day, maybe a little less."

Again, the elf just nodded and went back to focusing on the road ahead.

Shrugging to himself, Daniel climbed over the wagon seat and made his way to the back of the wagon, intending to jump to the second wagon to log out.

A hand reached out and grabbed his leg. The hand was attached to a tired looking Mirantil. Despite her obvious weariness, she smiled up at him.

"Where do you think you're going?"

"Oh, uhh, I was going to go log- err sleep, I was going to go sleep, in the other wagon."

She scooted over to make room for him and patted the space next to her.

With only a slight hesitation, he sat down and got comfortable.

"Crazy day, huh?" He asked as he glanced sideways at her.

"Mmhmm." Was all she said as she rested her head on his shoulder and closed her eyes.

Guess I should probably just log off, don't want my parents getting upset at me for missing dinner or anything. But.. maybe I'll just sit here for a few.

Daniel closed his eyes and pretended to be logged out for a while. He was acutely aware of each breath she took and the feel of her head on his shoulder. As he inhaled the wonderful smell of her, a smile crept across his face. It took considerable effort on his part to force himself to actually log off.

Lazy Stressful Sundays

Making his way to his bathroom, he could hear the television on and his parents having a conversation. As he looked at himself in the mirror, all of the interactions between him and Mirantil played on repeat, over and over in his head.

I can't believe she kissed me! And I just grabbed her, put my hands around her! What WAS that! I think she really likes me! This is so crazy, she's so hot! What the heck!

Daniel took his shirt off and started flexing his muscles in front of the mirror. Striking up poses he'd seen popular athletes use in sports magazine photos. He then tried to look as sexual as possible, putting both his hands on his head and turning his body at an angle.

Ohh yea, you like that Mira? I'm the shit, baby! Look at me, I'm just too sexy for this world.

He started thrusting his hips aggressively, while chanting in his head.

You. Can't. Handle. All. This. Boo. Yah.

A noise just outside the bathroom door startled him something fierce.

With a speed driven by horrific embarrassment, he put his shirt back on and washed his hands.

When he walked into the living room, his mother was bustling about while his father was watching the news.

"Hey sweetie, dinner will be ready in a bit."

"Okay, cool. Want me to help with anything?"

"Hrmm?"

His mother paused what she was doing and looked at him. She was able to read him like an open book. With a small smile on her face, she beckoned him over.

"Sure, why don't you come help peel the potatoes."

Prepping some chicken to bake in the oven, she watched as Daniel set up a potato peeling station by dragging the trash can over to a chair and setting some potatoes on a plate next to him. As he methodically began to peel, she couldn't help herself and had to find out why he wouldn't stop smiling.

"So, how was your day, sweetie?"

"Ohh, uhh, fine."

"That's it? Nothing good happen today?"

"Hmm? Uhh, I mean yea, I ran into some people today that tried to grief me, but I crushed them."

A feeling of smugness blossomed in his chest at the thought of how much stronger he was than most of the other players he'd encountered in Final Bastion Online.

"And that's it? Just some battle or whatever, that's all that happened?"

His smugness was instantly replaced with caution.

Oh crap, I can't let her find out I'm getting involved with a game character, she would lose her shit.

"Yea, they were part of the big group that tried to take me out a while back. At least in there I have the strength to put them down, out here I'm weak."

Brushing up against the almost taboo subject of his bullying did the trick and had his mom quickly changing the direction of their conversation.

"How is the studying going for your midterms?"

"It's going good. I've memorized most of the study material, so I'm feeling really good about them."

Well, I've read most of the study material, so I probably won't fail any tests..

Their conversation continued on, mostly around mundane everyday things. Errands to run and things needed while at the store during their next visit.

Finishing up with their nightly routine, Daniel was doing his best to calm his racing mind as he tried to drift off to sleep. The thought of his other self lying next to Mirantil had him fighting the urge to log back on. He wasn't sure when it finally happened, but sleep overtook him and his alarm had him rolling out of bed the next morning.

Loading into Final Bastion Online, he was surprised to find Mirantil at the reins of the Vulneur with Travers sitting next to her. Estavold was snoring softly across the wagon from him and Alvira was also sitting with her eyes closed. Abby was quietly fiddling with some of the random pieces of equipment they had in their wagons.

He got to his feet and did a little stretch.

The sudden movement startled Abby, causing her to yelp in surprise.

Alvira, Mirantil and Travers all whipped their heads in his direction, tensing up. As they registered that it was just him getting up, they all relaxed. Alvira just closed her eyes again and Travers turned back around, focusing once more on the road in front of them.

Mirantil's gaze lingered on him for a moment more, a soft tired smile playing about her lips.

Heat flushed Daniel's cheeks and he noticed his mask was somehow off, lying next to where he logged out. Bending down to pick it up, he quickly put it back on.

"That's weird.."

"What's weird?" Abby piped up.

"Uhh, just that my mask was off, thought I left it on when I log- went to sleep."

"Oh, Mira took it off. When I asked her why she said she liked watching you sleep."

The tiny little elf girl shrugged her shoulders and went back to playing with what looked like a woven basket.

"Abby!" Mirantil had turned around and looked embarrassed as her eyes flashed in his direction. She quickly turned back towards the front and seemed to focus intensely on the reins in her hands.

Daniel stepped his way carefully towards the two elves sitting on the drivers bench and peered out ahead of them. The thought of Mirantil taking off his mask to watch him sleep made his gut squirm in nervous excitement. Looking ahead, the scenery looked much the same, trees and large bushes, though not tightly packed or anything, with plenty of light filtering in through the gaps. The road seemed a bit more well maintained, but otherwise still a hard packed dirt path, large enough for two wagons to pass each other if needed.

I wonder if there are wagon driving rules, like stay to the left or right or something. We're kinda in the middle of the road though. Wonder if there's been any traffic on this road while I was offline? They all seem so jumpy.

"Everything going okay?" Daniel quietly asked the pair.

Travers nodded softly, while Mirantil answered back.

"Yea, so far. Haven't run into anymore of those terrible guild people, but we've run across a few different traveling caravans. They were all humans and a few orcs, never seen orcs before, besides those who attacked us from that Nameless guild."

Travers, who had been nodding along, added, "they were asking a lot of questions, especially the orcs."

"Too many questions." Mirantil bobbed her head.

"Ahh, is that what's got you all on edge?"

"That, and you being asleep. How was your rest? Sorry for taking your mask off.. I.."

Daniel rested his hand on her shoulder. He felt her stiffen at first, then relaxed at his touch.

"It's fine, you can take it off anytime you want. I had trouble falling asleep at first, but I'm good to go, feel completely refreshed."

"That's good! What was giving you trouble?"

Mirantil's innocent question had Daniel's cheeks blushing a furious red.

Cause I was thinking about you all night!

"Ahh, nothing really.." He felt a great deal of relief knowing his mask was hiding his face.

Mirantil reached a hand up and snatched his mask off.

"Hey!" He squeaked in surprise, his voice cracking slightly.

A mischievous smirk covered her face as she glibly offered him back his mask.

"Your face is awfully red for thinking about nothing."

Feeling like prey caught in the jaws of a predator, he took a deep breath and as calmly as he could, retrieved his mask.

"Hey! Watch out!" Travers called out a warning.

They had drifted towards the left side of the road and a slight turn was coming up.

"Whoops." Mirantil whispered as she turned back to the reins and corrected their course.

Travers just rolled his eyes.

Looking around to try and find something to occupy himself with, Daniel's eyes landed on Abby.

Feeling his gaze, she slowly stopped playing with her basket and ever so slowly raised her head until she was looking him eye to eye.

"I'm surprised you haven't been bugging me to train. Don't you want to be an Elven Strike Maiden?"

"Ah, uhh, well.." Her eyes suddenly got as round as dinner plates as she looked up at him.

"I don't think I'm ready to be a Strike Maiden just yet. Is it okay if I stop training?"

Her little voice was practically trembling.

Daniel couldn't help but smile down at her.

She is just so freakin adorable.

"It's okay Abby. You have a ton of potential and can absolutely become a Strike Maiden if you set your mind to it one day. You can do anything. I believe in you."

He first saw relief wash across her face, followed swiftly by concentration, then pride mixed with a big, bright smile.

Daniel felt that warmth once more, deep in his chest.

I want to protect her.

That one thought echoed across his being. It felt a little alien at first, like it was coming from outside himself, but soon he felt the thought radiating within him. He dismissed the strange sensations and was about to turn and head off to the second wagon when Travers got his attention.

"You mind taking over watch for a bit, I'm weary to my core."

"Ah sure, I can do that man, go rest up, I'm good for the rest of the day honestly."

Without another word, Travers got up and made his way to an empty space in the back and was snoring softly within moments.

Daniel climbed over the bench and sat down.

"Here."

Mirantil handed over the reins to him as soon as he was seated. He took them without complaint.

She looks totally wiped out.

"You can go rest up as well if you want, I got this."

Shaking her head, she scooted over closer to him and rested her head on his shoulder.

"No, I'm fine right where I am."

The smell of lavender and pumpkin spice tickled enticingly at his nose. He took a long, slow deep inhale, fully enjoying the feel and smell of the woman resting her head on him.

This. Is. AWESOME!

Daniel did everything he could to remain as still as possible. Doing his absolute best to be the greatest headrest that had ever existed.

The rest of the day passed in companionable silence.

Time flew by and before he realized it, night had fallen and the stars were out. A bright blue moon could be seen lighting the dark sky. At first, the darkness was concerning, until he remembered his mask had vision enhancements. The elves had excellent night vision, so they were unperturbed by the darkness, but Daniel's human sight was clearly lacking without magical assistance.

With his mask on, they safely rode on into the night. Passing by another town with twinkling torches lighting up their walls and rooftops, Daniel led them further onward. He was glad that the roads seemed to line up and head in the direction he thought they should be traveling. Daniel had no idea if he was going the right way and just kept them moving down the road.

A game notification popped up, letting Daniel know he'd been logged in for an extended period of time and that he should log off to take care of his true physical needs.

Guess it's lunch time. I should only be gone for an hour or so.

He shifted in his seat, stirring Mirantil awake.

"Mmmm." She mumbled softly next to him.

Damn, I hate having to wake her up.

"Uhh, hey, I need to rest for an hour or so."

"Ohh, is it that time already?"

Daniel could hear the sleepiness in her voice.

Looking over his shoulder he saw a pair of eyes blazing hatefully in his direction.

Estavold. Bleh, what's his deal?

Sighing internally he beckoned the large elf, motioning at the reins in his hands.

Seeing that the angry looking Estavold was getting up, Daniel started to shift once more in his seat, waking up Mirantil.

"Hey, make some room, Estavold is gonna take over."

"Hmm? Mmmhmm."

Was that an okay? Is she even awake?

Mirantil groggily climbed over the drivers bench and made for an empty space in the back of the wagon.

No words were said as the reins exchanged hands.

Daniel simply followed after Mirantil and sat down next to her. She snuggled up to him, curling her body around his.

Frozen for a half minute, Daniel just lay there, feeling her up against him. He debated with himself, whether or not to actually log off or just stay here instead. The log off warning popped up again and a frustrated Daniel logged himself out of the only place he really wanted to be.

After using the restroom and scarfing down a quick lunch, he bolted back to his room, completely foregoing the typical daily workout routine. This would be the first day he actually failed to complete his daily workout quests since being given that token from Henry, what felt like ages ago to him now.

Logging back in, he found himself in paradise.

His mask was off again, lying off to the side, with Mirantil snuggled up on his left. He felt her soft breath on his neck as she lay peacefully asleep.

He felt his left arm go slightly numb, her weight pressing down on it and cutting off the circulation in that arm. He didn't care. This was the most amazing experience he'd ever had in his entire life. His mind was racing as he felt parts of him stir with exhilaration.

Just as his mind was about to start treading some dangerous waters, the wagon came to a screeching halt.

To Help Or Loot

Mirantil was slammed into Daniel's side and all the miscellaneous things inside the wagon bounced around wildly.

Daniel was on his feet and zipping to the front of the wagon moments later. What he saw was mostly just confusing at first.

Concerned they were under some kind of attack, Daniel was partially in a combat stance, looking for foes to defend against. All he saw was some overturned wagon on the far side of the road with some bulbous rags tumbled about.

"What is it?"

Looking at Estavold, all he could see was an almost furious look on the elfs face as he just sat there like a brick wall, staring straight ahead.

Travers was now right behind Daniel, peering out with extreme alertness.

"Why did we stop Esty?"

Gesturing roughly toward the overturned wagon, he finally responded, "I heard someone calling for help over there."

This freaking guy..

"Well why didn't you say so?" Daniel let out in frustration and jumped out of the wagon, heading over to the crash site.

"I did, say so, that is."

Travers seemed to lower his alert level and climbed out of the wagon, followed shortly by the others. Estavold, sitting firming on the wagon bench, kept staring straight ahead with a deep frown coloring his face.

"What's rammed up his backside?"

Alvira sneered as she caught up with the others.

Travers just shrugged his shoulders while Mirantil grabbed Abby's hand and looked concerningly over at Estavold.

"He.. help.. me.."

A soft voice seemed to drift from the pile of rags next to the overturned wagon.

Rushing down to inspect the injured person, Daniel carefully peeled back the torn up cloth.

What greeted him was a human man, likely in his seventies with graying hair and a tanned, wrinkled face. A face that was covered in blood.

"Mira!"

Daniel called for her but she was already there, kneeling on the other side of the man with a hand pressed down on him.

Looking up at Daniel, she had a sorrowful look on her face as she shook her head.

Seeing a worn hand struggling to lift itself, Daniel reached out to hold it as he was suddenly consumed by the dying man's eyes. They held his complete attention as a momentary spark of life filled them.

"Pl.. please.. Can you .. take th .. take necklace."

He was pulling Daniel's hand up towards his throat.

"Take to my .. to .. niece."

"Okay, you got it, I'll take your necklace to your niece."

Daniel could see the moment the man died.

It was extremely unsettling as he watched the life that had once been filling the man's eyes simply disappear.

"Shit, wait, where is she? Who is your niece!"

It was too late, no more answers would ever come from this man. Not from his words at least.

Daniel shifted the fabric around the man's throat and found an extremely gaudy looking necklace.

Alvira's sharp hiss had him flinching away from it. He had been seconds away from grasping it in his left hand.

"What? What is it? Is it cursed or something?"

Alvira just looked at him with annoyance.

"No, well, I don't know, it could be, but the jewel on it. Those are known as heartstone gems. They possess the power of souls. Who was this man?"

Daniel looked over at Mirantil, confusion etched across his face.

"The power of souls?"

She looked just as confused as him and shrugged her shoulders.

Alvira made a *tck* sound, "It's incredibly valuable. Some say they are worth half a kingdom in ransom. Faellintis had a small one that was given to him to protect the exiles. This one is three times the size. It's worth is incalculable!"

"Can I have it?"

Abby's beseeching eyes looking longingly at Daniel.

"I'm afraid not Abby, I told this man I would get it to his niece, whoever that is, and I plan to try my best to keep my word."

Carefully, Daniel lifted the gaudy looking necklace off the man's chest and slid the chain from around his bloodied head. As soon as it was free of the man, it vibrated slightly and Daniel received a system message.

NEW QUEST (SECRET UNIQUE):
THE HEARTSTONE GEM NECKLACE
RETURN THE HEARTSTONE NECKLACE TO THE NIECE OF
THE MAN WHO ONCE OWNED IT
REWARD: VARIABLE
PENALTY FOR FAILURE: UNKNOWN

A secret AND unique quest? What is this all about? How am I supposed to figure out who his niece is? Gah!

After placing the necklace into his inventory, he carefully started rummaging around in the man's shredded clothing, hoping to find a clue.

"Yuck, you humans are disgusting. Looks like he had some decent valuables in his wagon. Since you're pilfering his corpse, you might as well pilfer his other treasures as well."

Alvira huffed and turned on her heel, heading back to the wagon with Abby in tow.

Mirantil was giving him a searching look, and he suddenly felt the extreme urge to defend himself and his actions.

"Wait, it's not what it looks like, trust me, I got a special quest when I picked up the necklace. I'm just trying to find clues as to who his niece is, that's all, I promise!"

The look she gave him was borderline unapproving.

"Do what you must, I'll be back in the wagon."

With that, she got up and left him alone with the corpse of the old man that was, for some reason, not turning into millions of pink pixels and dissolving into nothingness.

That's kind of weird. I think this is the first time I've ever seen a dead body. Like ever. I thought they were supposed to smell? Maybe the game system is trying to keep it as un-horrifying as possible. He does seem to be all wrapped up and covered, with just a few red stains on his blue clothes.

Finding nothing on the man himself, Daniel stood up and went over to the contents of the wagon. He found lots of daily supplies and a few boxes of artifacts that looked incredibly valuable.

He was no curator of antiquities or lost treasures, but these things looked like all the other kinds of immensely valuable relics that heroes and heroines in movies found at the end of their action packed adventures.

Sifting through one last box, he finally found some papers and let his translation abilities go to work. The in-game mechanics of being able to read and understand any language were extremely helpful for quest progressions for all the players.

Only two pieces of information seemed all that relevant. The first was an estimated value of all the relics in the chests and the second was related to the man himself, or at least his destination anyways.

Apparently, the treasures had been found in a lost dungeon deep in the Aerfall and the man had estimated their value to be in the hundreds of thousands of platinum. He was returning them to Eliswin as he had been on some kind of diplomatic mission to Aeryenous when he made a pit stop and found the lost dungeon by happenstance.

After reading the correspondence, his quest was updated.

QUEST UPDATE:
THE HEARTSTONE GEM NECKLACE
RETURN THE HEARTSTONE NECKLACE TO THE NIECE OF
THE MAN WHO ONCE OWNED IT. HIS LAST DESTINATION
WAS ELISWIN AFTER PERFORMING DIPLOMATIC DUTIES IN
THE ELVEN KINGDOM OF AERYENOUS.
CHOICE POINT:
CLAIM THE TREASURES OF THE LOST DUNGEON FOR
YOURSELF OR BURY THE TREASURES ALONG SIDE THE OLD
MAN
REWARD: VARIABLE
PENALTY FOR FAILURE: UNKNOWN

Choice point? This is one of those branching quest lines that are dynamic and change based on my decisions! That treasure is worth hundreds of thousands of platinum. I could buy ANY piece of gear that I wanted, SEVERAL pieces of the absolute best, in fact.

Daniel paused and looked himself over.

He was still wearing that newbie armor he'd gotten from Eliswin. The only worthwhile piece of gear was his mask, which had scaling stats on it. Everything else was extremely basic and meant for someone of a much lower level than him. His swords were an exception, as they had been gifts from Henry.

Travers came over and got his attention.

"You good here? We need to get moving soon."

"Ahh yea. Well, this is actually gonna take me a little bit."

Daniel looked apologetically over at Travers.

The elf just shrugged his right shoulder.

"We're gonna move on ahead, this area isn't all that safe, pushing so far into the Aerfall as it has. We should be close to the Path of Ellis. From the confusion on your face, you've no idea what that is. It's just the big main road that leads straight into the Aerfall, to the gates of Aeryenous itself. Make a left when you get there, it has magical protection for travelers."

"Ahh, gotcha, kay, I'll catch up as soon as I can."

As Daniel contemplated his choice point, the wagons started up again and took off down the road. From his standstill position, it looked to be moving incredibly fast.

Geez, hope I can actually catch up to them. We haven't been attacked by anything or anyone for a long while.. And if that road has some kind of protection, they should be safe. Probably.. Damn, I better do this quick and catch back up with them.

Daniel stood alone on the empty road, envisioning all the new and powerful gear he could purchase with hundreds of thousands of platinum.

Looking at his meager savings so far, he barely had enough money for basic supplies. He didn't even come close to being able to afford any gear that was actually his level. The player raid on Dharesia had really skyrocketed his level. Not that levels even mattered all that much in his estimation.

His eyes kept shifting over to the boxes full of loot.

It's not like I have any tools or anything to bury it all in the first place..

A shovel and a pickaxe suddenly caught his eye, piled in with all the other random survival gear.

Shit.

Taking a deep breath, he let out a long, suffering, sigh and got to work digging a larger than necessary grave off to the side of the road under a particularly vibrant looking tree.

It didn't take long, using his aura and smashing stubborn rocks into dust with his booted, lightning infused feet.

He gently laid the old man down in the center of a hole that was taller than he was. Around the man he placed the boxes full of priceless relics. He even placed most of the random survival junk at the base of his feet. In a strange sense of poetic artistry, he put the lantern next to the man's head and removed one of the glimmering artifacts and placed it in his hands, held across his chest.

Now he looks like a legendary explorer, off on his final adventure.

Snorting to himself, Daniel climbed out of the hole and started filling it up with dirt. Once he was done, all that was left was the empty overturned wagon and the shovel.

Taking one of his swords out, he pierced a hole into the ground and the head of the grave and stuck the shovel into it, shaft first so the metallic head was all that remained on the surface.

Moving over to the wagon, he grabbed a bunch of the broken pieces of wood and placed them in his inventory, then focused his aura into a cone and obliterated the rest of it into nothingness with a lightning surge.

It cost him a quarter of his health, but he figured it was worth it.

Hopefully this way passersby won't see the debris and end up grave robbing the poor guy.

Inspecting his work one last time, he bid farewell to the unknown man and cranked up his aura while burning a lightning step to try and catch up to the others as fast as possible.

Despite his earlier misgivings, it didn't take more than a handful of minutes to catch up to the elves. Once they had made it to the Path of Ellis, they'd dramatically slowed their pace. As Daniel happened upon the beautifully paved road that was engraved with glowing sigils, he felt a slight magical pressure wash over him after stepping a foot down. He gazed down at it in wonder as he jogged along before spotting his caravan in the distance.

Running up to the driver's seat, he waved to Estavold, then dropped back and hopped up into the back, where the others were all sitting around chatting.

"Hey! You made it back quickly, everything went alright?"

"Hey Mira, yea, no issues, ended up burying the old dude so it took a bit."

"Oh! You put him to rest? How thoughtful of you!"

She clapped her hands together and smiled warmly at him.

Alvira cut in, "It's the least you could do after taking all his treasure."

"Ahh, well, I buried it all with him, actually."

Daniel was rubbing the back of his neck forlornly, pained at the thought of losing so much potential money.

"Truly?" The quiet surprise in Alvira's voice brought Daniel up short. A look of intense hopefulness from her just confused him even further. Mirantil saved him from having to think on it as she grabbed his hands.

"Your hands are covered in dirt. Here, let me clean them."

Before he could so much as lodge a protest, she was pouring water over a cloth and rubbing his hands and arms clean of the dirt.

In the back of Daniel's mind, he registered that she shouldn't have needed to clean his hands, they should have already been clean on their own, quite some time ago as a matter of fact. The game kept all player characters' bodies in a fresh state after a few minutes of being out of combat, so while he was catching up to them the dirt was supposed to have pixelated away. He didn't give it much thought as he thoroughly enjoyed her ministrations.

It wasn't long after that until Estavold was pulling their wagons off the side of the road and into a small clearing surrounded by a few small buildings.

As they all got out to stretch their legs, Daniel approached Estavold to ask him why they had stopped.

"This is a protected camp site for travelers. See the runic script on all the buildings? They are meant to keep the monsters at bay and allow us to rest."

"Oh, cool. How long are you planning to have us rest here?"

The large elf paused and looked the others over for a bit before responding.

"We are worn and not at all used to such harsh travels. I would like to rest here at least for a day. None of us know how much farther it is to the capitol, but we all feel the magic of this road and its call of safety and shelter rings in my ears. So, a day at the least."

Without another word he disappeared inside one of the buildings, leaving Daniel to his thoughts.

Tumultuous Troubles

As Daniel wandered over to explore a neighboring building, he contemplated what the large elf had said.

A day? Hmm.. I'm gonna have to log off here in a bit, probably just before nightfall. And since Monday is a school day, I won't be able to log on until after class. I guess it's a good thing they are taking a day off. I'll be stuck at school while they rest up here. I hope they won't run into any trouble while-

His inner thoughts were interrupted by a warm embrace.

Mira.

He had gotten a whiff of her scent right as she wrapped her arms around him, recognizing it immediately.

"I'm going to step away with the girls for a bit, but I expect you to be here when I get back. You promise to wait for me?"

At first, Daniel laughed at her antics. But her embrace lingered and he started to feel awkward. Then her arms squeezed tighter and she breathily spoke in his right ear.

"Well?"

Suddenly, as if a switch was flicked, he understood that his relationship with Mirantil was about to mature.

All those television shows, and books he'd read, as well as things he'd seen on the internet that his mother would have surely punished him for, coalesced into understanding.

"Uhh, yea, of course I'll be here, I promise!"

The mix of adrenaline and his flip-flopping gut caused his voice to crack more than usual and sound much too high pitched for Daniel's liking.

She snuck in a kiss on his cheek then flitted away through the open doorway, calling over her shoulder, "see you soon!"

Daniel's mind was racing, his heart hammering.

Oh my gawd! What the heck! Calm down stomach, don't you dare puke! Don't even think about it!

With his stomach doing somersaults and his thoughts marching off in a hundred different directions all at once, he began to get that floaty feeling once more.

For the last several minutes, Daniel had been pacing vigorously back and forth in the empty building. The only light coming from the unobstructed doorway, spilling across the floor and casting most of the room in dark shadows.

A scuffling at the entrance had Daniel whirling around.

His stomach had been churning so nervously that he nearly vomited on the floor from the overwhelming mix of anxiety, panic, fear, excitement, desire and the unexpected sound giving him a fright.

To his immense relief and utter disappointment, it wasn't Mirantil that was standing in the doorway.

It was Estavold.

"What's up man?" Daniel said a bit more rudely than he'd intended to.

He was considering whether or not to apologize when Estavold stepped further into the room and crossed his arms.

"I.. ahh.. I need to tell you something. Look. I mean, listen. It's just, I need to apologize to you. I've been treating you poorly since the first day that we met. There's a reason for it, and no, not because you're human. I hold no grudges against other races. I.."

He had his arms out, as if beseeching Daniel for something.

"It's okay man, you can tell me. What is it?"

"Well, the simple truth of it is this. I'm in love with Mirantil. I have been for a very long time. We, us elves, well, we feel emotions much more strongly than humans do, and they resonate within us, warping our very natures. The jealousy I have for the affection she shows you has twisted my mind and caused this hatred to manifest. It's changed me. I'm not the elf I should be, I have fallen far from grace. I come here to beg a favor from you. With an open heart, I plead with you, please reject her affection. She is all I've ever desired in this life. I cannot live without her by my side. My very being calls so desperately out to you. Will you do this for me? For her? You are a person who is not truly of this world. You must see that. It could never be! You and her. It *should* never be, for her sake."

Estavold took a slow, small step closer, both arms opened wide with a pained expression contorting his face.

"Please, will you do this, will you save her from herself, will you set her free? For me?"

Daniel was mentally rocked.

His mind didn't seem to want to work at that moment.

All he could do was fall back on old habits.

With eyes partially glazed, he nodded his head.

"Uhh, yea, sure man.."

The relief flooding from the elf was palpable.

"Oh thank the heavenly stars, I am very relieved to hear that. Thank you Daniel! Thank you so, so very much! You are doing such a wonderful thing for her. I know she will be grateful to you once she realizes it! Bless you."

As the elf turned and left, a small part of Daniel noticed the slight pep in his step.

Walking over to the back wall, he just slumped down to the floor. Numbness washed through him and he suddenly had the urge to cry. He was overcome with self recrimination.

I should have known better. He's right, I'm not even from this world. There's no way she would actually want someone like me. What was I thinking?

Wallowing in self pity, Daniel remained sitting there, slumped along the wall, shoulders hunched as he closed in on himself. Estavold had come on so strongly and was resonating with some kind of powerful emotional control that had overwhelmed Daniels fragile sense of self. He'd received a skill up during the conversation but was far too depressed to bring up his notifications to care.

With a heavy heart, he was preparing himself to log off.

I don't deserve to see her again. I should log off before she gets back. It's for the best after all.

A needle of curiosity was picking at his brain. Before he could let himself log off, he wanted to know what skill he'd leveled. It was a morbid type of curiosity, what could possibly have improved while his heart was being ripped asunder.

MENTAL FORTITUDE - LEVEL (12)

That's the skill I got when the Griffon took over my body with a fear spell. Why did it go up just now? Estavold.. Did he.. What THE FU-

"Hey!"

As Mirantil bounced into the room, the bright, cheerful smile melted from her face the moment she set her eyes on him.

"What happened? What is it?"

She rushed over to him, kneeling down on the ground next to him as she grabbed his hand and looked him over.

He reached up to rub at his eyes with his other hand because it was hard to see clearly, for some reason. As he wiped his hand across his face, he felt the tears that were falling, just now noticing he'd been crying, evidently for quite some time.

"I don't.. I.. we.. we shouldn't.."

He couldn't bring himself to say it out loud. Even though his emotions were screaming at him to tell her, he couldn't speak the words.

MENTAL FORTITUDE - LEVEL (13)

His mind was a swirl of chaos.

Why am I getting those skill ups? Everything feels so wrong inside of me. What's happening to me?!

Mirantil's eyes practically glowed with power as she held his hand and delved deep into his emotional core. He felt her vibrating slightly and as he watched, her entire body was outlined in a soft glow.

"You have some kind of curse affliction! Hold still."

She looked otherworldly to him, like an avenging Angel come down from some high heaven above, as she scoured his soul clean.

It was over in the blink of an eye.

She was out of breath as she sagged down to the wall beside him, still holding tightly to his hand.

Daniel suddenly felt normal again. As if the past hour had been nothing but a hazy dream. He barely remembered Estavolds speech. But he clearly recalled the emotions behind it.

"That *fucking* asshole."

"What?"

Still taking deep breaths, she looked over at him. Worry lines still etched across her face.

"Estavold, he hit me with some sort of emotional or mental attack."

"Wha- Why?"

"He wanted me to reject you, said something about how I should set you free and that we don't belong together."

She let out a half scream of frustration.

"He *always* does this! Always getting in the way! It's so aggravating! He knows I don't care for him in the same way he does for me! We've spoken at length about this. You have to understand this, I cherish my friendship with him but we are and will be nothing more than that. I.."

She trailed off as she looked back over at Daniel.

He felt riveted by her words. Something in the air made this moment feel extremely significant.

As her face filled his vision, she turned slightly and leaned in closer to him.

"I'm in love with you Daniel."

His stomach dropped out of his body.

Then she leaned further in and gave him his very first kiss.

It was over in a flash, leaving them both breathless.

"Wow, I, uhh.."

PARENTAL ALERT:
DAILY PLAYTIME LIMIT REACHED
FIND A SAFE PLACE TO LOG OUT: 00:09:58

FUUUUuuuuuu-

"What is it now?!"

"I have to find a safe place to rest within the next few minutes."

"So soon?"

The disappointment in her voice ate at his very soul.

"Yes, but, I absolutely promise to return as *soon* as I can!"

Desperation laced his voice as he looked apologetically over at her while grabbing her hand in both of his.

"Grawww! Fine! I can't believe you're making me wait! It better be worth it."

With that, she tackled him to the ground and kissed him once more before leaping to her feet and sweeping out the open doorway.

Daniel watched her go, feeling like he was floating six feet off the floor.

The parental alarm blared again, so Daniel just logged off where he was pushed down by the woman he would later refer to as his first love.

Mondays

Rushing to relieve himself after holding it in all day, Daniel found himself once more critically eyeing his body in the bathroom mirror.

Ohh man, what the heck is happening between us?

He wrestled with himself and his feelings toward Mirantil. As he stared at himself in the mirror, he replayed several of their conversations over again in his head.

Thoughts of what his classmates might say if they ever found out about him liking a computer generated character in a game had him getting embarrassed all over again. Standing there, staring at himself in the mirror wasn't doing him any good, so he decided to hop in the shower for a bit.

It took an hour long shower for him to settle his feelings down. He didn't care what anyone else would say about him and Mirantil. It's not like he had any real life friends anyway. Although, for some reason, he was extremely averse to having Alyssa find out.

He could barely catch a wink of sleep that night. His thoughts were revolving around his first kiss and what she said afterwards.

I'm making her wait? Wait for what? .. What is supposed to happen when I log back in?!

All day in class, he spent his time furiously looking for any outdoorsy activities or festival-like happenings going on around town. He was desperate to find something to keep his parents busy while he was logged in. His fantasies were going wild with speculations around what might happen when he met back up with Mirantil. If even a fraction of what he was daydreaming about came to pass, he had to make absolutely sure his parents would be too busy to check his player feed.

If they found out about his relationship with an in-game AI character, he'd be banned from playing instantly and permanently.

The risk was great, certainly, but the reward..

I can't even begin to guess at what she meant, cause there is no way she means what I hope.. And dread.. Oh man. Is this really happening? There's no way, right? I'm totally not reading the situation properly. That has to be it. But.. She said she loves me.. And.. and we KISSED AND EVERYTHING ! Oh my gaawwwwddd..

He felt like his entire face was going to melt off from how embarrassed he was from all the thoughts swirling around his brain. Every time he saw her face in his mind's eye, his heart began to hammer against his chest. When that would happen, his embarrassment would compound and his face would get even more flushed, forcing him to dart panicked glances at all the students sitting around him to make sure they didn't notice or hear his pounding heart or catch on to his sweaty, embarrassed, state.

He would do everything in his power to make sure his play time went undisturbed that evening, just to be safe.

His determination paid off when he stumbled across a special winery event that was going on that very evening at a local arts studio.

This is perfect! Mom loves to paint and both my parents enjoy wine. I have to text her this right away.

As luck would have it, his mother jumped at the chance to drink wine and paint pictures with his father that evening.

With his parents properly occupied, Daniel was feeling elated at his success. His classes were mostly dedicated to study sessions, preparing the students for the upcoming tests later that week, but he was far too preoccupied to pay much attention to anything. Spending most of his time doodling in the sides of his textbooks, Daniel counted the minutes on the clock until school was out.

Racing home, he ran to his room and threw on his FBO kit. This would be the second time he skipped out on his daily workout quests. He had much more important things on his mind.

As the world around him came into startling relief, he found himself lying on the ground in that same building he'd logged off in.

Getting up to stretch his legs, he made his way out into the bright sunlight. The wagons were still there with the Vulneur patiently latched to the lead cart.

The rest of the camp seemed eerily silent.

A rustling off to his left caught his attention. As he moved to investigate, a panic stricken Travers emerged from the shrubbery.

"Your back, thank the heavenly stars. There's trouble, they need your help, come quick."

Without another word, he turned and bolted back into the forest with Daniel hot on his heels.

He seemed really upset, oh damn, I hope Mira's okay..

Anxiety and uncertainty left Daniel feeling ill at ease.

After just a few minutes of racing through the towering trees, they came upon some ruined buildings. Only a few walls remained standing as nature did its work to reclaim the land.

"Over here."

Travers led them into one of the dilapidated structures and down an interior stairwell that led into a chilling darkness.

At the bottom of the stairs was a large metal door.

Just to the right of the door, a dull crystal was embedded in the door frame at waist height.

Travers placed his hand on the crystal and disappeared.

Is this a dungeon?

Following the elfs lead, he placed his own hand on the crystal and a system prompt appeared.

SELECT A DUNGEON INSTANCE:
ABANDONED LABORATORY - (UNIQUE: PLAYER LOCKED)

Moments later, Daniel materialized inside the dungeon that was constructed just for him. Worry was turning his stomach into knots. As he assessed the room, on high alert for threats, the dread he'd started to feel on the run over began to spread exponentially inside his chest.

Alvira was furiously moving strange patterned stones on the ground into different alignments, cursing to herself, then starting over again.

Estravold was off to his right, pounding on an empty glass container that was large enough to hold a person in. Travers had joined him in trying to smash the empty tube.

Abby was inside one of the glass containers, slumped to the ground as she struggled to breathe.

Mirantil was in a glass tube container next to her.

She seemed to be faring a bit better than Abby, but it was obvious she was supplementing herself with sporadic glows of healing magic.

With a new found type of fear constricting his heart, Daniel lightning stepped over to Mirantil's glass prison and placed his left hand upon it. He started surging his aura and equipped one of his swords in his right and channeled lightning down the blade's length.

"STOP! YOU IDIOT!!"

The outburst from Alvira arrested his strike.

He whirled on her and demanded to know what was happening.

"Why did you stop me! What is all this?!"

His voice sounded shrill and panicky and he mentally chastised himself for even caring about how he sounded while the others were in apparent danger.

Alvira began shouting at him in frustration.

"Look at the base of the glass tanks! Do you see those blue glowing magic sigils? That means they are powered by some sort of enchantment. The stones here are some sort of key that I've been trying to figure out. There's some strange metal tablet on the wall over there, but I can't understand it. We've already tried busting one of the tanks that had some remains in them. The moment the glass cracked the entire sealed chamber inside was flushed clean and sterilized, leaving nothing behind, not even motes of ash! Those idiots over there are trying again, but breaking through the tanks will only kill them! What's worse is there appears not to be much air in the tanks, so they will suffocate soon if we don't figure this out!"

Daniel matched her volume as he shouted back.

"How did they even end up in there in the first place?!"

"I don't KNOW! JUST HELP ME!"

She turned back to the four stones, each with their own patterns.

New Quest (Unique):
Save them!
Solve the riddle of the stones and save the elves before the auto sterilization enchantments trigger

Time Remaining: 00:04:23

Reward: Variable

Penalty for Failure: Automatic quest failure for the following active quests: **The Hunt for Sword Sages**

"GOD DAMNIT!"

Daniel's shout caused all the elves to briefly look at him, before furiously returning to their own attempts at trying to save their trapped friends.

He ran over to the plaque on the wall as he shouted over his shoulder to the rest of them, "We only have four minutes until those sterilizing enchantments activate!"

"WHAT?!"

Alvira leapt to her feet and grabbed the stones.

She was hastily arranging them on a raised pedestal beside one of the empty glass containers.

Daniel read the wall mounted plaque as quickly as possible.

Access to this laboratory is restricted to authorized personnel only. Intruders will be subject to fines and imprisonment of up to 10 years. All test specimens must remain confined to their assigned containment device. In the event of a breach of the containment devices, protection measures have been incorporated to prevent catastrophic loss of life. If confinement in one of the containment devices happens in error, use the designated emergency keys in the following sequence to open the containment device. Keys will be consumed during the first use and administration must be notified in order to produce another set of emergency release keys

Underneath the panel was the sequence of the keys and where to look on them to identify which sequential step they were meant for.

Daniel turned back to Alvira, expecting her to still be sitting on the floor with the stones, only to realize with mounting horror that she was about to use the only set keys they had to open an empty container.

"Alvira! NO! STOP!"

Daniel had managed to prevent a colossal misstep and raced over to grab some stones off the pedestal.

After catching his breath, he grabbed the others and placed the stones on the floor in front of the two containers in the correct sequence. Then he looked up at them all and motioned for them to gather around.

"So, according to the instructions over there, we only have one set of keys, and they will be consumed when we open one of the containers. If we attempt to break them, the containment devices are set to destroy whatever is in them. We only have .. just over two minutes to use the keys on one of the containers. But then the keys are gone and we need some kind of authority figure over this place to make a new set of keys."

He left it at that, allowing the others to absorb his words.

Estavold was the first to speak, "Save Mira!"

"What?! No, we *must* save Abby! She was entrusted to our care!"

Alvira and Estavold then got into a heated argument as Travers just stood there silently, sadness marring his otherwise intensely alert eyes.

We're running out of time. Is there no other way to save them both? There has to be a way, the quest said to save them both!

At the one minute thirty mark, his quest updated.

Quest Update:
Save them!

SOLVE THE RIDDLE OF THE STONES AND SAVE THE ELVES
BEFORE THE AUTO STERILIZATION ENCHANTMENTS
TRIGGER

TIME REMAINING: 00:01:26

CHOICE POINT:

USE THE KEYS TO SAVE ABBYZAEL AND RECEIVE A BONUS
REWARD FOR THE FOLLOWING QUEST: **THE HUNT FOR
SWORD SAGES**

OR

USE THE KEYS TO SAVE MIRANTIL, NO ADJUSTMENTS
MADE TO THE QUEST REWARD FOR THE FOLLOWING
QUEST: **THE HUNT FOR SWORD SAGES**

REWARD: VARIABLE

PENALTY FOR FAILURE: AUTOMATIC QUEST FAILURE FOR
THE FOLLOWING ACTIVE QUESTS: **THE HUNT FOR SWORD
SAGES**

Fuck. Fuck! FUCK!

Daniel was emotionally shredded. He had no idea how he could make such a terrible decision. At this point, he wasn't even thinking about the quest rewards. His romantic feelings towards Mirantil warred with his overwhelming instinct to protect Abby.

As he looked at them both, their struggles to remain conscious as the air slowly ran out, his legs felt like they were fused to the floor. Mirantil's eyes looked desperately, pleadingly, at him while Abby's were continually fluttering as her tiny body did its best to keep her awake.

His heart ached.

The runes started to flash menacingly.

In a frenzied panic Daniel scrambled to pick up all the stones and check his timer.

Thirty seconds left.

The others behind him became deathly silent as they all held their breaths.

Hollowly, Daniel stepped forward and placed the stones in the correct sequence on a raised pedestal. With a hiss, the glass container pressurized with the outside air and then pixelated into nothingness.

Daniel turned with agonizing slowness to look into the still sealed containment device.

As his eyes met Mirantil's, bile rose up in his throat.

The absolute betrayal he saw there made him sick.

Bright, flashing sigils started flaring inside her container and her scream had Daniel on his knees, puking his guts out.

With an abruptness that took them all by surprise, the entire facility went dark. For several seconds Daniel thought he might have blacked out. Realizing for the first time that there had been a soft light being emitted by magic sigils carved along all the walls that had been providing them all with enough light to see by, Daniel slammed his mask on.

It was pitch black, but with the magical enhancement vision turned on by his mask, he was able to see everything in shades of gray.

To his utter relief, Mirantil was still sitting in the containment device, with her arms wrapped tightly about her knees.

Without hesitation, Daniel flew at the container with his swords and shattered it to pieces.

The light he was emitting from his lightning aura and charged swords provided the others with an eerie light that cast shadows dancing all about from the flickering lightning.

"Mira!" Estavold shouted and rushed to help her out of the death trap.

Alvira had Abby tucked safely in her arms as they all fled the abandoned laboratory.

Estavold had rushed Mirantil to the exit before Daniel had a chance to check on her himself. Once they were finally outside though, he burned a lightning step and blocked their path.

Taking his mask off, he reached out to her slowly.

"Are.. are you okay?"

The look on her face was heart wrenching.

Sadness, disappointment, betrayal.

Daniel could somehow feel these emotions pouring out of her as she looked at him. The frown and puffy red eyes that welled with unshed tears hit Daniel harder than any punch to the gut he'd ever received.

"I.. need time.."

This was all she said to him as she wrapped her arms a bit more tightly around herself.

Estavold led her around him and left Daniel standing there, arm still half hanging in the air.

What.. happened? This.. I.. what do I do?

Bereft of any guidance, Daniel felt like he was stranded out at sea. He had no idea what he could do to fix things, to get them back to the way they were. He didn't even know if that was possible now, not after all those emotions she was pushing out at him.

Feeling such heartache, something he'd never known before, he numbly made his way back to the camp with the others. They were all getting ready to depart, having had their fill of this place.

The girls all huddled together in the back of the lead wagon while Estavold was holding the reins and guiding the Vulneur out towards the main road. Travers, ever the watchful scout, was sitting next to Estavold, busy scrutinizing their surroundings.

They hadn't even waited for him to catch up.

He silently hopped onto the second wagon's seat and forlornly watched as Alvira did her best to console Mirantil as Abby just sat nearby with eyes as big as saucers.

As their mini caravan began to travel at speed down the Path of Ellis, the edges of a morbid sense of humor sunk its teeth into Daniel's psyche.

Well THIS wasn't exactly how i'd planned to spend my evening. I bet the game would never have even allowed anything to happen since I'm underage. I HATE all these restrictions on minors. I just want to be an adult already..

His mind devolved into fantasies of him and Mirantil.

For a while, he let himself play in his mental dreamland.

It was with complete surprise that barely an hour later the elven capital of Aeryenous appeared before them.

None of them had expected to have been camping so close to their destination. Daniel rocked back in his seat and did an actual face palm.

We were less than an hour away this whole time?

A sudden bout of soft laughter overtook him.

Once he settled his rattled mental state, he took another long look at the elven capital.

This place is definitely bigger than Eliswin. Holy moly. It's more like a megalopolis. I could get lost for months in there.. That actually doesn't sound like such a bad idea honestly.

Daniel's emotions were still a bit raw from the whiplash he'd gone through that day.

Guess I better put on my mask. No more taking it off.

Slipping his unique piece of gear on his face, he toggled the zoom function to get a better view of the massive city looming ahead of them.

There was considerably more traffic on this road than any of the others they'd traveled. Something Daniel was just now registering. He'd been so wrapped up in himself and Mirantil that he'd hardly paid attention to anything else at all. He silently admonished himself to pay more attention to his surroundings. Environmental awareness was one of those unlisted skills Henry had tried to drill into him during training.

Seems I wasn't as good at that as I thought I was. Oh man, these past few days feel kinda hazy. Hormones are scary..

Daniel started working harder on actively paying attention to all the goings on of those around him. He felt his mind continually drift back to Mirantil and his emotions would spiral downward. The struggle to focus and not get swept away by his building depression was becoming a bit easier to manage as he buried his heartache and did his best to ignore it.

Aeryenous

Sitting in line, waiting for their turn to cross under the massive walls that protected the elf city, Daniel ran his eyes along the enormous, silvery glimmering gates arrayed before them.

He spotted magical glowing sigils all along the doors. The entry arched upwards at the middle, which had to have been in the range of five stories, at the very least. Daniel wasn't the best at judging heights, but the wall was easily double the height of the doors at their peak point in the middle.

It was staggering to him, the scale of it all.

The line to get into the city took them longer than the trip from the campsite they had used.

Are they checking all the wagons or something? It hardly took any time at all to get through the Eliswin gates.

Daniel's questions were answered as he peered around their lead wagon and watched the group ahead of them go through an extremely thorough inspection before being let into the city. All of them were forced to sign some magical document that verified their identity in some way after their luggage was examined.

Finally it was his turn.

Waiting patiently on the second wagon, Daniel let Estavold take the lead here. He hadn't even offered. None of the elves had spoken with him at all since they'd departed the disastrous dungeon. As he sat there, he listened intently to their conversation.

"Hello. Point of origin and nature of your business in Aeryenous?"

An elven guard wearing silvery armor that was accented with gleaming gold relief, stood to the side with an eight foot spear pointing into the air.

Several other elven guards approached the wagon and spread out, planting four dull silver staffs into the ground placing the lead wagon inside their rectangle. A soft blue light hummed and the entire wagon was encased in this magical glow that dissipated after a few seconds. They then moved on to the wagon he sat in and performed the same scan. As the blue magical light encased him, he felt absolutely nothing.

Kinda like a magical metal detector? Cool.

Estavold had been straight to the point in his conversation with the guard holding the spear.

"We are from Dharesia. We come to Aeryenous to build a new future for ourselves."

"Types of merchandise?"

"Traveling supplies and miscellaneous trade goods to sell."

The four guards doing the scanning returned to the gate and one of them called out as they passed, "All clear, Sir!"

"Very good. Please disembark from the wagons and line up to the side."

They all got up out of the wagons and stood to the side in a haphazard line.

Estavold was in the front followed by Travers then Mirnatil with Abby in between her and Alvira.

Daniel was at the back, too far away from Mirantil to try and strike up a conversation, not that he wanted to.

"Place your hand upon this gem first then sign here please."

Estavold complied without question. The guard nodded and instructed him to step aside to make room for the rest of us.

Travers was the first to ask any questions.

"What is the gem for and what am I signing, sir?"

The armored elf seemed to approve of Travers question with a small smile and responded, "The gem confirms if there are any active bounties against you and signing this document marks your agreement with following all the laws and regulations within Aeryenous and consenting to subject yourself to the punishments we deem appropriate for any violations levied against you."

"Who determines the punishments?"

"The judiciary officiants are responsible for such things and are bound by law to perform their duties in an unbiased manner."

"Can anyone levy violations against another?"

The smile faded from the armored elfs face as he answered in a stern manner, "Only the city guard can levy violations against a person. Citizens are allowed to request an inquiry against another but the city guard are ultimately held responsible for keeping the peace and levying violations."

Without another word, Travers placed a hand on the crystal and signed the document.

The others all followed suit, with Alvira helping to lift Abby up so she could do the same.

Feeling a small bit of anxiety worm its way into his gut, Daniel placed his hand on the gem.

It's not like I have any bounties against me here, the one The Nameless placed on my head was player generated. It shouldn't be in effect here.. Right?

Seeing that the gem remained unresponsive, Daniel signed the document and stepped aside as a small sliver of relief warmed his spine.

"Very good, welcome to Aeryenous. Please proceed through the gates. If you have further questions, there is an information center just down the main roadway. Have a pleasant day."

Understanding the dismissal for what it was, they all climbed back into the wagons and made their way past the monstrously thick gates and into the city proper.

The avenue was extremely wide, allowing for plenty of room for them to move forward. Estavold pulled their wagons over once they reached the information center.

Once more, they all climbed out and made a haphazard circle.

At first, no one spoke, then a shrill scream of excitement followed by Abby running off had them all turning in concern at the commotion. Just down the road, a magical theater show was taking place. Several elves were dressed up in all kinds of striking colors and used some sort of magic to make glowing little constructs move about on a stage. A little elf looking doll was wielding a staff and blasting off tiny fireballs at some kind of tiny rock monster.

Abby had raced over to join the small crowd of watchers with a put upon Alvira swiftly following after.

Daniel let out a soft chuckle.

Ahh, to be innocent and young. I miss the old days of last week..

Snorting at his own joke, he returned his attention back to the others.

Travers was the first to speak, "We need to figure out where Gwenithe's household is, then we should get Abby there. After that, we can figure out what to do with the wagons."

"Yea, hopefully they will let us stay there, if not we can get some information on places to stay. I'll stay with the wagons Trav, you go inside and see what you can find out." Estavold gestured back toward the wagons as he mentioned them.

"I'll go with you." Mirantil quickly added as she bolted for the door near them. Travers followed a moment later, tossing a brief glance at Daniel.

Mentally shrugging, Daniel walked over to the magical puppet show. The awkwardness between him and Mirantil was getting worse by the minute. It was making him feel very self conscious and uncomfortable. He wanted to just get away from them all, so finding Gwenithe as soon as possible was exactly what he was looking to do.

It didn't take long for the others to come back out of the information center. Daniel noticed Mirantil had started heading in their direction, but paused, then turned back to the wagon and directed Travers to come collect them.

Ugh. I need to finish this quest asap. I'm tempted to just log off now, but I want to try and at least finish this crap.

Tapping Alvira on the shoulder, he gestured back to the wagons and started making his way over as she bent down to scoop up a protesting Abby.

The trek to Gwenithe's house took a lot longer than Daniel expected it to. They got lost several times, having to pull off to the side and ask some people nearby for directions. At first, Estavold and Travers adamantly refused to stop and ask for help, loudly proclaiming it should be just up ahead, until several hours passed and night started to darken the sky. Alvira scolded the both of them for getting them all completely lost.

It was nearing time for Daniel to have to log out by the time they finally reached the Strike Maiden's estate.

There was a flurry of activity once their reason for being there was understood.

They were all escorted to a small parlor with plenty of seating options for them to relax as refreshments were brought and the acting head of the house was brought before them.

Unfortunately for them, it wasn't Gwenithe, but her primary aide that attended to them.

"I'm sorry to say that the Strike Maiden is not presently here in Aeryenous, but we do have a method to verify the legitimacy of this childs patronage."

The elven woman was prim and proper, with a stiff straight back as she sat on the edge of a cushioned chair and faced them all. Her name was Palimore and she directed the other elves about with an imperious tone.

"Go now, and bring the lady's heartstone gem."

The letter that Faellintis had sent them off with, lay open on the small table next to Palimore. Words alone would not be enough to justify a bloodline claim with the Elven Strike Maiden herself.

Abby looked mildly terrified as she watched everyone around her with big, bright eyes.

Behind his mask, Daniel felt a small smile spread across his face.

At least she will be safe here. That whole mess back in Dharesia really was my fault. I could have kept running or turned and fought them all off instead of trying to hide. Lessons learned I guess. Many lessons learned on this trip actually. Fuck, I'm depressed. I want to just log off already, give me the damn quest update please.

A stone, one much smaller than the jewel attached to the necklace in his inventory, was brought forth on a soft velvety cushion.

Reverently, Palimore removed the stone from the small pillow and held it in her hand, palm up. She beckoned for Abby to approach and instructed the small girl to put her own hand on the heartstone.

As soon as her little hand touched it, the thing lit up like a christmas tree. A prism of colors danced across all the walls as they were witness to a dazzling light show. Moments later the gem settled down to a soft glow as Abby held her hand to it.

"Well that confirms it. Miss Abbyzael, welcome to the Strike Maiden's estate. Welcome to your new home."

With a gentle pat on her head, Palimore returned the heartstone to the proffered cushion and the elf holding the pillow disappeared through the parlor doors once more, leaving all of them alone with Palimore.

Tears welled up in Abby's eyes as she quietly croaked out, "I'm home now?"

Pulling the little girl into a warm embrace, Palimore gently cooed to her and stroked her back as she was wracked with tiny sobs.

Wow. She must have been trying her best to be brave this whole time. The trip along the borders of the Aerfall must have been a terrifying ordeal for her. That whole dungeon mess didn't help any, either. I kind of forgot that she was just a little kid, she seemed so mature. Tragedy breeds maturity, I guess.

Palimore handed the tiny elfling off to another household servant who whisked the tired, sleepy girl out of the room.

"Now that that's settled, let me officially welcome you all to Gwenithe's estate. There are plenty of rooms for all of you to stay, and from what I understand, most of you are here to start new lives. Is that correct?"

Her questioning gaze passed over all of them, pausing a moment on Daniel then moving on to the rest.

"Yes, Lady Palimore, we are hoping to sell the merchandise we brought with us and work to establish ourselves here in Aeryenous."

Estavold spoke for the group with Palimore nodding her head to his words.

"Our household can definitely help with that, and you can ignore the paltry sums you would receive for that junk. We will cover all your expenses for the near future until you've acclimated to the city and are able to sustain yourselves. This house cannot truly express the gratitude we feel for all of you. You've brought home someone thought lost to us forever. Rooms are being made ready for you as we speak."

All of the elves bowed their heads and as one gave their thanks to Palimore.

As she smiled at all of them, her eyes landed once more on Daniel and her demeanor subtly changed. Daniel was aware of the shift, but he couldn't quite pin down what exactly was different.

"I suspect you are looking for something the others are not. Might I ask you to remove your mask so that I may know the faces of all those who've brought our lost one home?"

Reaching up, he pulled the mask off his face.

For a brief moment, Daniel noticed the slight widening of her eyes.

She's surprised? Is it because I'm not an elf?

"And how might the house of the Elven Strike Maiden reward you for your service, good sir?"

"Oh, I guess I haven't properly introduced myself. My name is Daniel. It's nice to meet you, uhh, Lady Palimore."

"Be welcome here, Mister Daniel. How might we serve you?"

"Ahh, well, I'm actually hoping to speak with.. Uhh.. Miss Gwenithe herself."

"*Lord Commander* Gwenithe is presently not in Aeryenous. She departed just hours before, but it is unlikely she will return for several months."

"Oh, sorry, I am not really sure how I should address people here. Wait, did you just say she will be gone for *months!?*"

Curiosity gleamed in her eyes as she looked him over.

"Yes, I'm afraid you just missed her. Why is it that you are looking to meet with her, if I may be so bold to ask?"

"Uhh, well, I have a quest. I'm looking to become a Sword Sage and she is the fir-"

"I'm sorry, did you say you wanted to become a Sword Sage?"

The look of curiosity had changed to something that looked like calculating intensity.

"Umm, yes."

"Are you just a beginner, or perchance, are you already highly ranked?"

"Ohh, I'm at the mastery level for all five combat forms."

"WHAT?!" Alvira blurted out.

"I knew it." Travers muttered.

A strangled gasp came from Estavold.

Daniel hesitantly glanced at Mirantil.

She was staring at the floor, with a sad smile on her face.

Maybe there's still a chance I could–

"Oh how wonderful! This is fortuitous indeed Mister Daniel! Come with me please, I would like to speak with you in private."

His thoughts of some way of reconciliation with Mirantil were interrupted as Palimore rose to her feet and beckoned him to follow her from the now open doorway.

"Right this way, please."

"Uh, yea, sure, coming."

He followed her down a few corridors and into a private study.

Only three chairs were in this room, with books lining the walls and the sound felt extremely muffled.

Pointing to one of the chairs, she addressed him once more, "please sit. The kingdom of Aeryenous is in dire peril and Lord Commander Gwenithe has been sent to her death."

Midterms And Monsters

The shock was evident on Daniel's face as he sank down slowly into his, rather comfortable, chair.

"Come again?"

Sitting down across from him, Palimore started up once more, "It's just as I said. Some political infighting has led to some disastrous results. It pains me to say, but our elven royalty can be as petty and self-serving as any of the other races found throughout the world. This time, Lady Gwenithe is the one made to suffer. I must ask that what I say to you now will remain in confidence."

Daniel had to lick his lips and force moisture into his dry mouth as he responded, "Yea, of course."

"Good. One of the royal princesses managed to get her hands on a *very* precious relic. The fool girl used it on her brother and effectively banished the boy to the deepest parts of the Aerfall. Lady Gwenithe, well, she is the strongest of all of us and the only person with the strength to reach the banished prince. She refused to allow any of her subordinates to join her since she knew it would likely be a fool's errand."

Palimore made a fist with her hand and struck the armrest on her chair.

"I begged her to take a regimen, anyone really. She forbade it. I don't know of any powerful adventuring guilds that we could leverage without dire consequence. Certainly, there are those who could come to our aid, but to embroil a large adventuring guild into the schemes and plights of the elven royal court would be blasphemous. Never shall we cross that line, may the grand stars above keep it so. But you. You are a lone adventurer, as I am told. You could brave the deep wilds of the Aerfall and survive. So now I beg a favor from you. Please find Lord Commander Gwenithe and help rescue our lost prince."

Quest Update:
The Hunt for Sword Sages
After discovering Abbyzael's family link to a Sword Sage, you have safely escorted her to the home of Gwenithe, her grandmother. The Sword Sage Gwenithe is in need of your help. Find her in the wilds of the Aerfall.
Reward: Sword Sage Training
Penalty for Failure: Loss of advancement potential

"Okay, sure. I'll do what I can to help. Ah, just.. One thing though."

"Hmm? What is it?" A look of trepidation skittered across her face, unsure of what Daniels' hesitation might be stemming from. As he explained, her face relaxed and she smiled at him.

"So, on the way here, we never actually ran into any monsters. Sure, there were some dangerous animals prowling around the outskirts of Dharesia, but I have to admit that I haven't even seen any monsters since we left. We ran across an overturned wagon once, with.. Well, we guessed it was a monster attack, but again, we never ran into a single thing on the way here. I was given the impression that the Aerfall is supposed to be full of dangerous things, is that really true?"

"Yes, yes it is. Your trip was likely uneventful due to the protections that most roads have built into them and your warded beast which is meant to protect you. That would be the work of your summoned Vulneur. A powerful one at that. They are not the most common form of conveyance, but many are used around the Aerfall. They have a passive effect that tends to repel the monsters roaming about the Aerfall. I am very happy it did its job so well. In fact, I was planning to dispose of it, but you've given me pause to do so. Do you have any other pressing concerns before we continue?"

"Uhmm, no, not really. Oh! I do, yea. I need some better gear, honestly. This stuff I'm wearing is cool looking for sure, but I'm way over leveled for it."

Her brow scrunched up as she looked closer at his gear.

"Your gear is.. WHAT! This is absolute trash! The others mentioned you fended off an entire adventuring party of over a dozen people, all highly ranked! You did that wearing this?!"

The look on her face was incredulous.

"Uh, yea..?"

She barked a laugh.

"You will be well outfitted before you depart, I assure you. This certainly assuages my fears. I must admit, I was a little worried you wouldn't be able to reach her, but that doesn't seem as likely to me anymore. Anything else?"

"Umm, no."

Daniel could feel a slight flush of embarrassment cover his cheeks. Despite his combat prowess that he recently discovered himself, it was a bit embarrassing when others spoke so openly about it.

"Good. I have in my possession a ring that is linked to the Lord Commander. You should be able to use it to track her position. One moment."

Rising out of the chair, she walked around to a side table and pulled open a drawer, taking a small box out.

She shuffled around the drawer a bit more until she found a gold token and set it down next to the small box.

Opening the box, she pulled out a blood red colored band. It seemed a bit large for a ring, but Daniel didn't voice his concern. Bringing the blood colored band and the golden token over she offered both of them to Daniel.

Carefully, he picked the ring up.

BONDED RING OF BLOOD
EFFECT: WHILE EQUIPPED, FOCUSING ON THIS RING WILL
LEAD THE WEARER TO THE PERSON WHOSE BLOOD HAS
BEEN BONDED

"If you wear this, it will lead you to her unerringly. And this is a token from her house. Present this to the outfitter of your choice and you can have your pick of the wares. If I may make a suggestions, Ovoue's Armors would be an excellent choice."

Taking the golden token and placing it in his inventory, he then put the overly large ring on, and it magically resized to fit his hand.

Oh, neat.

He now had rings on both fingers, the one on his right hand having come from his very first boss battle when he completed a dungeon with Alyssa.

Man, that happened such a long time ago, it was some kind of lich. My magic infused blade attacks really did a number on those undead.

"I must attend to the others. Would you like to stay here or.."

She left it unsaid, but he got the feeling she could read the emotional strain between him and the others.

"Ahh, no, I won't be staying, but can you give me directions to that armor place and the nearest bind stone?"

"Absolutely, right this way Mister Daniel."

As she led him back through the hallways of the estate, they were soon back outside, standing by the gate.

"Fortunately, Ovoue's Armors happens to be a block away from the soul obelisk in this city district. To get there, please just follow the avenue here until you hit the plaza with the large fountain. From there you should be able to find both."

"Got it, thanks!"

"Of course. Oh, and when you catch up with Lady Gwinethe, tell her Palimore sent you, and also please don't spoil the surprise of Lady Abbyzael's return. I pray the heavenly stars above guide your way and keep you safe, Mister Daniel."

"Ahh, yea, you bet. Thanks again Miss Palimore, ahh-er sorry, Lady Palimore."

Snickering at his fouling of the formalities, she smiled at him, "It's quite alright Mister Daniel. Safe travels."

With that, she turned and closed the gate, then disappeared back inside the extremely large manor.

Taking a deep breath, Daniel steadied himself, then started walking toward the plaza she mentioned.

Sure enough, just on the other side of the large fountain, the bind stone was glowing softly.

After binding himself to the stone, Daniel did a quick circle, trying to spot the armor merchant. It was fully dark now and lights could be seen flicking on along the many winding and twisting streets.

It took him a moment, but he finally spotted the place she recommended. Before he could take a single step, his parental alarm went off giving him his ten minute warning to log off.

Ahh, guess it'll have to wait till tomorrow.

Scanning the shops around the plaza once more, he spotted what looked to be an inn and headed over. The room was pricey, but he had enough to cover a single night, barely.

Once he'd logged out, he fell into his typical routine. Finding the house still empty, he checked his phone and had an unread text from his parents. They would be home soonish, but he wasn't in the talking mood so he texted them to drive safe and that he was going to bed early.

Crawling into bed, he curled up and just mutely lay there for a bit. Then, as if a dam burst, he cried. The heartache from the loss of the budding feelings he had for Mirantil had him grieving. In the end, he cried himself to sleep, completely worn out from all the emotional turmoil.

The next day wasn't an easy one.

He still struggled to focus while in class. His mind kept going over all the things he could have said to Mirantil to try and fix things, or fantasizing about what would have happened if he'd chosen her instead of Abby to save.

When he got home from school, he started back up his quest exercise routines. After his workout, he was grabbing a light snack and was about to head to his room and log back in when his mother called out to him from the couch. She had taken a sick day off from work after getting far too hammered the night before at the wine and art event.

"Hey sweetie, how was your day?"

"Eh, normal I guess."

"You look unwell, are you feeling alright?"

"Hmm? Yea, I'm fine."

"Mmm, well, since it's your midterm week, I don't want you playing that game until all your tests are over."

Taking a deep breath, he let it out slowly.

"Actually, yea, I think that's a good idea. I'm gonna go study for a bit."

"Okay sweetie, I'll let you know when dinners ready."

"Thanks mom."

Falling heavily onto his bed, he laid there without moving.

He got up from his bed when he heard his mom call for him to come to dinner.

After his routine small talk with his parents, he was back in his room, curling up on his bed once more.

A deep feeling of depression took him.

He felt zero motivation to do anything.

His alarm woke him up the next day.

He didn't even change his clothes as he grabbed his things and left for school.

All morning, he struggled to keep his head raised, most of the time losing the battle and resting his head on his desk.

He didn't even pack a lunch, so when he found himself in the library, he just leaned his head on the side of the chair and stared listlessly at the floor.

"Hey you!"

Startled, he looked up.

Alyssa was sitting across from him with a cheerful smile.

"Oh, hey."

"You seem down, is everything going alright?"

The concern was evident in her voice.

Daniel just shrugged it away, "Yea, I'm fine."

"Mmm, okay. You wanna come have lunch with us?"

A spike of panic lanced down his spine.

"No, that's ok. I'm good, I'm not hungry or anything."

"Are you sure? You don't have to eat anything, just come hang out with us."

"Oh. Well, I'm kind of tired so I'll just hang here."

"Okay. Feel free to come join us if you want. We miss our overpowered damage dealer, heh."

She got up and walked away, leaving Daniel feeling even worse than he had been, even though he knew that wasn't her intention.

I should have gone with her. I'm sorry Alyssa..

He continued to feel bad about his interactions with Alyssa for the rest of the day. Falling into his workout routine once he got home from school helped a little as the exercise worked its magic on his depression.

Tomorrow is the first midterm. I should actually study something tonight, just in case.

With what felt like a monumental amount of effort, he managed to pull open his textbooks and started to review his study guides for the test scheduled for tomorrow.

As Thursday finally arrived, he found himself sitting in class with a spike of anxiety and nerves pushing past his depression. The teacher was handing out their tests. It was a multiple choice answer sheet that would be graded right away. Looking over the first set of questions, his anxiety calmed down as the questions were things he was familiar with.

Before long, he was flipping his test back to the first page, having made it all the way through without running into any curveball questions. Around half of the other students had completed their exams and were waiting quietly for the rest to finish.

With a little trepidation, Daniel picked his test up and walked it over to the teacher. It was scanned and graded right before his eyes.

94%!! Yessss.

Sighing in relief, he went back to his seat.

The serotonin of doing well on his test had buoyed his flagging spirits.

Three more to go!

By the end of the day, he'd found his smile once more. He'd managed to ace all of his midterms. And what's more, his holiday break had finally started. He was off school on Friday and wouldn't be returning until after the new year. On his walk home from school, he pumped his fist in the air, calling out to nobody in particular.

"I did it! Now to become a Sword Sage! FBO here I come!"

Getting his workout quests done, he texted his parents the good news on his grades and plopped down on his bed. Feeling fired up for the first time since that horrible Monday.

Waking up in the same inn room he'd logged out from at the start of the week, Daniel stood with a start.

Oh shit. I only paid for one night. How many nights has it been since I've logged out? Shit, what was the conversion again? Two to one? So Monday, which I paid for, then two more nights on Tuesday, and two more on Wednesday, then what, one more for today while I was in class? Damn, that's five additional nights. This place was expensive as shit too. I don't have any platinum left. I totally should have robbed that dead guy..

Thinking he might be able to sneak away, he silently approached the room door and peeked out. Seeing nobody around, he slithered his way out of the room and down the stairs to the main floor of the inn.

Peeking as little of his face as he could around the corner, he saw a few staff members bustling about.

It should be early to late morning in game from Daniel's estimation, so he was hoping the place would be mostly empty.

There were a few patrons having what looked like a late breakfast. After an agonizing half minute, the coast was finally clear. Daniel was preparing himself to bolt across the floor to the entrance and make his escape when a voice called from the stairs above.

"Well if it isn't the sleeping corpse. We'd started a betting pool on how long you'd be out for."

Panicked, Daniel turned and watched the same lady who had checked him in the first night, descend the stairs and walk out to the main reception area.

"We nearly tossed you out for the guards to deal with the second night. Yer rather fortunate that Lady Palimore stopped by and asked after you. Once she found out you only paid for a single night and had already overstayed, she promised to cover your bill until you woke up."

"Ohh, thank goodness, cause I'm totally broke."

She gave him a very serious look.

"You count your blessed stars son, you would've found yourself in prison with quite the fine had it not been for her."

"Ahh, got it, thanks. I'll just be on my way then.."

Daniel hesitantly turned towards the door, looking back over his shoulder to see if anyone planned to try and stop him.

The woman just huffed and headed into a back room out of sight.

Escaping into the bright sun, Daniel quickly made his way over to the armor shop he'd been recommended to. He felt as if he'd made out like a bandit. Once he'd shown the proprietor his golden token, the man had snatched it out of his hands and led Daniel to a second floor that had all different kinds of what looked like extremely valuable armor. The token was good for a single full set, giving Daniel the pick of the place. The sets were all mostly the same, with some focusing on specific stats while others were more well rounded. Daniel wasn't looking to focus on anything specifically, so he went with a well rounded stat set of armor. Narrowing down his choices to anything fit for a level 70, all he was left with was a handful of outfits. There was gear for level 90s available, but Daniel was only sitting at level 73, not having leveled up any since his fight in Dharesia. The ambush on the road wasn't enough to level him, but he knew that he was close to 74. Even if he went outside and leveled up today, the armor choices would not have changed, since the sets went from 70, to 80 then to 90.

It was all down to aesthetics.

All of the combined pieces looked great and he had to admit that they made him look like the cover art models of most fantasy books.

He went with the dark blue leathers accented with dark gray artistically designed metal plating. The metal swooshed and swirled about his arms and legs, with an intricate design covering his chest and back. It came with a dark blue leather cloak with a hood and fit perfectly over his head and mask.

I look SO. Friggin. COOL!

Inspecting one of the pieces, he drooled once more over the scaling stats.

Ovoue's Finest Gloves
Armor Class: 1 * character level
All Stats: 5 * character level
Durability: 7500/7500
Effect: while equipped as a set, provides an additional (1 * character level) to all stats
Effect: Self Repair - Passively works to Repair itself over time

He had ten pieces in all, all of which had the same stats and effects. The hood of the cloak when drawn up could act as an eleventh piece, providing stat bonuses and all as a helmet slot. The set bonus was not affected by the hood, but

Daniel saw no reason to not have it up since it provided additional scaling stats and armor.

Too bad he took the golden token, I could have gone to a jewelry shop next. I'm still missing some earrings and my old ring could use an upgrade. Don't know if I'll ever get rid of the necklace I got from Henry. It has all the different types of mana stones in it, allowing me to imbue my blades with any kind of magic strike I might need. Plus it looks cool.

Making his way to the same gate he'd used to enter the city, Daniel felt supremely confident in his new digs. His mask design complimented his overall armor look as well. He hadn't yet tried his hand using the customize design function of the mask. He figured he wouldn't need to with his current armor set, since it matched so well.

Leaving the city was much less of a hassle than entering it had been. He didn't even have to slow his walk down as he breezed right through.

Pulling up his hand, he focused on the ring.

It was slight at first, but after focusing a little harder, he could almost see a translucent, glowing path leading off to his left.

Time to find me a sword sage!

The Deep Aerfall

Daniel carefully picked his way across the busy thoroughfare. Moving in between the line of people waiting to enter Aeryenous, he slid down a slight embankment and stepped into the forest of the Aerfall.

The elves had allowed the trees to grow right up next to their walls, which seemed a bit dumb to Daniel.

Couldn't someone just climb one of these trees and jump over the wall?

He let the thought slide away as he focused on the trail ahead.

I've only got about six or seven hours to find her or get to a safe place to log. I need to ask mom to turn off the parental restrictions while I'm out of school. I would be bored to death if I had to sit around the house all day and only got to play for a few hours during the weekdays. I did really good on my tests so hopefully they ease up on the controls.

Setting his mind to the task before him, he pushed himself forward and disappeared in the blink of an eye.

Woooaaahhh!

The new influx of stats had done a number on his mundane movement speed and flexibility. He was fast, *incredibly* fast, as he zipped along the forest floor. He was certain his current movement speed had to have been a match for his boosted speeds while burning his lightning aura in his old armor.

With an excited yip, he cranked up his lightning aura and the world around him melted away.

He was suddening moving so fast that he nearly ran straight into a tree. He was forced to boost his cognition speed to keep up with everything around him.

It took a bit of practice to get into a decent rhythm with his newly enhanced stats. Something felt off though.

It's like I'm having to push through the space around me. I think I'm feeling the air resistance hampering my body as a physical weight. I wonder what would happen if I channeled some wind blades to form the air in front of me, kinda like a streamlined airplane or something..

Equipping one of his swords, he pointed it in front of him and charged it with wind mana. It sort of worked, but it wasn't quite enough. Pulling out the other blade, he hunched down a little as he ran and channeled as wide a wind blade as he could in both blades.

The effect was immediate.

It was like he was in a kind of slip stream. If he flared his elbows too far he would feel the drag on them.

This is sooo freakin awesome. How fast am I even moving right now?

He pushed his aura a bit harder, watching as his health started to very slowly drain down. Easing up a bit, it remained steady at around 96%.

That's the sweet spot.

Burning a lightning step, he leapt twenty feet in a blink.

Off he went, blitzing his way through the Aerfall.

He finally saw his first monster.

It was only for a brief moment, and then he was long gone, moving so fast the creature hadn't even been aware of his presence. He kept up his pace for several hours. Passing countless monsters and what looked like battlefields where massive trees had been uprooted and the ground covered in huge divots. Often, large areas of what looked like bloodied ground could be seen where the ground was cut into.

The farther along he got, the more bloodied battle grounds he blazed past.

It was obvious to Daniel that this was all the work of Gwenithe.

Damn, she's been tearing it up out here.

With a bit of surprise, he saw what looked like fighting up ahead.

It's only been a few hours, there's no way I've caught up to her already.. Couldn't be..

Carefully coming up on a battle between a massive spider looking thing and a smaller glowing figure, Daniel paused to watch.

The glowing person was about one fifth the size of the spider monster. Daniel didn't envy that person. He hated spiders. If he ever saw one in his room, he would have to make sure to get rid of it, but if the unthinkable happened and it crawled away before he could get to it, he wouldn't be able to sleep in his room for days. He would go and sleep on the living room couch instead.

The battle was over in moments, but it looked like the person took a hit before landing the killing blow.

It was hard for him to parse just what it was he'd seen.

The spider had lashed out with two successive leg strikes, the first one somehow being parried, but the second one struck home. Then the person slashed their sword in the air and the spider simply fell to the ground, cut in two.

What was that? Some kind of magical blade strike like that orc used on me? What was his name.. Carve something.. Craven? Ahh whatever. Let me go check on them.

Making his way over to the figure slumped on the ground, Daniel paused when he suddenly felt two sword blades pressed against his throat. The kneeling figure had gone from the ground to moments away from decapitating him faster than he could register.

I should really keep my aura pumped up..

"Who are you?"

"Uhh, I uhh, Daniel ma'am. Are you.. Gwenithe?"

"Excuse me?" The authority in her voice was palpable as the blades pressed harder into his neck, likely to have already cut deep had it not been for his necklace.

"Ahh, uhh sorry ma'am. Lady Palimore sent me to find you, and uhh, looks like it is you since the ring is flashing."

Holding up his hand to show her the bonded blood ring, it was pulsing lightly, being so near its target.

The blades were withdrawn from his neck, but the Elven Strike Maiden still towered over him. His head didn't even crest her shoulders.

"Palimore, what's she on about? Why did she send you?"

"Ahh well, she asked me to help you, something about a prince needing rescue? And ahh, I uhh, have a quest to find you."

"What? Stop with all the ahhing and uhhing boy. It's annoying. Why would she send you to help me?"

Swallowing down his habitual sentence starters, he paused to collect himself before speaking.

"She believed I might be able to help you complete this rescue, due to my sword skills."

At that, she took a small step back and really gave him a once over.

"Palimore said you had the sword skills to help me?"

"Ah- Yes."

He wasn't able to keep his bad habit in check that time.

"Well? You said something about a quest."

"Yea, I .. I have a quest to find a sword sage, to advance to the sage rank myself."

Taking a steadying breath, she turned and started walking toward some kind of golden chest.

"Come, we can talk more as we move."

She stepped up to the golden box and tapped it on the top.

"Wake up, it's safe now, show me the way."

The golden box unfolded into a strange golden insect-like creature. It seemed to test the air once, then its legs clacked away as it darted into the trees.

Gwenithe was following closely behind it.

Daniel burned a quick lightning step to catch up and fell in beside the terrifying Elven Strike Maiden.

She intimidated him.

So much so, that he got a skill up from his Mental Fortitude skill while she was towering over him with her blades to his throat.

"So, you think you're ready to become a Sword Sage?"

"I .. I believe in myself, that uh-.. Yes I'm ready for the next step."

"Well, I'm a bit injured from all these pointless fights, following this stupid thing. Let me observe you a bit as we go. Take over fighting all the monsters that cross our path and we'll see just how ready you are."

"Yes, ma'am."

Daniel was afraid to look over at the woman.

The mental image in his head was of a fiery angel of death, all glowing and wreathed in divinely punishing light. If he hadn't been so terrified of her, he would have seen a very tired looking elf with a few graceful age lines creasing her face. Her eyes were a sharp blue with specs of gray floating about the iris. If a person looked hard enough, they would notice a strange luminescence about those gray specs. She was certainly taller than average, but her physical build was rather normal, if not accentuated by her powerful looking armor.

Onward they ran for ten or so minutes, until a roar echoed around the nearby trees.

The golden bug leading them instantly curled up into its box form and lay still.

Daniel readied his blades as he moved towards the direction the sound had come from.

He'd only managed a few steps before a huge six armed bear came barrelling at them from in between the massive tree trunks.

Flaring his aura, he slowed everything down until it appeared as if the bear monster was moving in slow motion. Then he used a lightning step to appear next to a tree above and behind the creature. Twisting acrobatically in the air, he braced his feet against the tree and pulled on his aura a little harder as he positioned both of his swords out in front of him after channeling some wind mana into the blades.

Pushing off the tree with all his strength, he blurred through the air, even with his massively enhanced cognition, and barely had the wherewithal to whip his arms open wide before his face planted into the ground. His legs scorpioned up behind him as his body smashed into the earth.

Struggling to regain his feet, he jerkily turned to face the bear creature once more.

He'd burrowed a Daniel sized hole right through its upper back. It had fallen to the ground having its initial momentum of the charge stymied by a missing upper spine. Millions of tiny pixels began floating in the air as the system lay claim to its corpse.

I really need to work on my super hero landings. Pretty sure I felt my foot kick the back of my head for a sec there. I might have broken my swords if I didn't pull back at the end. I really need to be careful with them since I don't know how much stress they can bear, isn't that right Bear?

Giving himself a small smile at his silly mental pun, he turned to see the Lord Commander of the elven kingdom frowning at him.

Letting his swords return to the ether, he slowly walked back over to the terrifying woman. He continued to have trouble looking directly at her, so instead he just looked down and to the side.

Once he'd got as close as he felt brave enough to, he came to a stop and quietly stood there.

Silence.

His face started to flush a light crimson behind his mask.

Finally, she spoke, questioningly at first, "Did you just recently go through some kind of stat growth?"

"Yes.. ma'am."

"I couldn't think of another reason why you would seem so.. Like a child stomping on its toys."

Ouch. Was I really that bad? I might have been trying too hard to impress her..

Hearing her long suffering sigh, he watched her from his peripheral vision as she tapped the golden bug and they started moving once more. Daniel turned and followed, keeping pace with them while running slightly behind the heavily armored sword sage in front of him.

It didn't take long before they heard more monster shrieks. This time it was a flock of people sized bat looking things. They seemed to be unleashing some kind of sound attack that blasted chunks of ground out of the earth as he dodged their initial swooping volley.

He'd decided to try fighting a bit more conservatively for this round, taking his time to gauge his enemies and only attack if they got too close.

"You're taking too long, hurry up."

Tck.

Daniel let out a slightly frustrated noise and blasted into the air, swords ablaze with lightning mana channeled through them. As he smashed into the first flying monster, his blades just paralyzed it in mid air, causing it to fall bonelessly to the ground below.

Meanwhile, Daniel had shoved off its falling body and was zipping through the air towards the next one, this time with one wind mana blade and a fire mana blade.

As he slashed and leapt from one flying creature to the next, cycling through all the mana types, the only ones that seemed to cause any real harm to their exceptionally tough leathery hides where his wind and fire mana strikes. The wind imbued blade would actually cut through whereas the fire seemed to catch on their tiny stubble fur and sweep over them, turning them into mini fireballs that were sent wailing to the ground or careening into nearby trees.

Switching up his tactics while flipping through the air, he focused on using wind mana strikes while he pulsed out his aura to zap them down to the ground as he flew past them.

There were about two dozen of the flying beasts that had swarmed them at the start. Now, only two remained airborne, the rest either stumbling about haphazardly on the ground after being immolated or twitching spasmodically from the lingering effects of his aura.

Only after focusing solely on his wind attacks, had he been able to land killing blow after killing blow, leaving a rain of falling bat monster corpses that were pixelating into nothingness as they fell to the forest floor below.

He'd had to use the nearby trees to assist his movements so high up in the air. The last two creatures had enough intelligence to try and put some distance between themselves and him by moving much higher into the canopy above.

Daniel bounced off two different trees and rocketed after them. Zipping past the first, he'd let his speed and momentum carry his left blade clean through its stubby and thick leathery neck. The last one tried to dive bomb him as he floated freely through open air beneath it.

Letting the beast charge him, he waited until its massive jaws were less than a foot away from his body, then pulsed his aura paralyzing it as they collided with each other.

Allowing himself to be spun about, he stuck his left blade into the side of the creature and rode it as they both plummeted towards the ground. Bracing for impact, they hit the forest floor with a loud thud.

Without wasting any time, Daniel quickly went around and dispatched the remaining monsters that were still alive. Many of which were slowly trying to flap their wings and escape the ground beneath them.

As he let his swords dissipate once more into nothingness, he heard a word spoken quietly from his new traveling companion.

"Better."

Following after the two of them as the golden bug stretched its legs and clambered forwards once more, Daniel opened his notifications.

Congratulations!
You are now level 74
Hit Points, Mana, and Endurance: +10

Nice! That last level took a long time. I guess it's true what they said on the online wiki. The higher you get, the longer it takes to level. I think the last I saw of the highest leveled player had him sitting at level 98 and he's been playing since the game launched.

Lost in his calculations of just how many monsters he would have to kill to break through into the eighties, he would have been monster food had it not been for his Attack Prediction skill triggering to save his life.

At first, he wasn't sure where the attack had come from, other than somewhere off to his right as that entire side of his body tingled violently from his skill going off.

Materializing both blades to deflect something large and brown, he'd lost track of it after being pushed backwards through the air.

Landing on his feet, he flared his aura, slowing everything down as much as possible while he took in his surroundings. His threat detection finally went off and he turned his head to look down to his left as he felt the pull of it coming from that direction.

Confusion blossomed in his mind as he looked towards the threat but saw absolutely nothing.

What? Is the skill broken? Nothings over-

With startling clarity his enemy became visible as a massive snake's mouth opened and tried to swallow him whole.

He would have been eaten without the aid of his lightning step. Jumping several feet off to the right, he spun to get a better gauge of the size of this monster.

To his horror, it was nowhere to be seen.

His threat detection was screaming at him that the monster should be right there in front of him, but it just looked like a normal forest floor, similar to everything else around him.

The damn thing is invisible!

Toggling on his magical vision effect from his mask, colors swam about the world around him. He typically kept the effect off since it made it hard to focus on anything as his brain tried to process all the new visual inputs.

Directing his gaze back towards the invisible snake, he now saw a shimmering, slithering outline making its way around to his left side.

It's trying to ambush me from the side again. To bad buddy, I can see you now.

Daniel charged his blades with lightning and lunged at the snake's head. It reared back as his strike ineffectually bounced off of what he assumed must have been its scales.

Shit!

Jumping back to avoid the snapping jaws, he started cycling through all his mana types as he slashed at the snake's body.

It curled its body around itself and rose up in a somewhat defensive position and forced Daniel to dance back out of range. None of his strikes had caused any damage, except for one. He had no idea why that type of mana strike did anything to this creature, but decided he would puzzle it out afterwards.

Channeling dimensional space magic into his blades, he launched into a flurry of attacks. Each of his strikes cutting deeply into the invisible creature and causing strange dark pixelating wounds to appear.

In a fit of rage, the snake lunged hard at him, but he easily danced to the side and brought both blades down, severing its head from the massive undulating body.

"Whew"

Turning to look back at the elf, he was surprised to not see her, nor was the golden bug thing anywhere to be seen.

Focusing on his ring, he felt it pull towards his right slightly, off in the direction of where he had first assumed the elf to be waiting while he'd fought the snake.

I guess they didn't stop?

Sprinting to catch back up, he found them a few moments later, pressing ever onward into the forest.

As he finally caught up, Gwenithe glanced his way.

"You survived."

"Ahh, yea."

Damnit! Now I'm extremely self conscious of my ahhs and uhhs.

"Did you kill it?"

"Yes. It was weird though, the only attack that worked against it was space type mana."

"It was a Phase Viper. Didn't you inspect it?"

"Er- No.."

Shit. I haven't been inspecting anything lately. It's like I forgot the ability even existed outside of equipment.

"Well, I recommend you get in the habit of actively inspecting monsters. You should look into purchasing an information skill as well. It can be very handy, knowing about a creature's weakness before you even engage with it. The Phase Vipers live in a sort of liminal space, a world slightly askew from our own. They can interact with us, but we, for the most part, cannot reach them. Unless of course you have dimensional space mana to use against them."

They lapsed into silence as Daniel processed her words.

There are purchasable skills? How did I not know this? Is this because of how I started off? Instead of going to those training centers, I went running off to Henry's. When I log off tonight I'm gonna check online to see what purchasable skills there are.

As the light from the day faded and the trees began to cast long shadows, Daniel started to get worried.

He'd encountered several more monsters, all of which posed little threat to him. He wasn't sure about where or how to log off though.

Will she stop for me? No, probably not. I should find a safe place to rest, really. Then catch up tomorrow. Where is there a safe place out here though? I'll probably die while I'm logged off, then I'll have to run all the way back. Ugh..

When his logout alarm went off, he hesitantly spoke up.

"I .. I need to rest."

"How long?"

"All night, and for a bit after sun rise. Maybe sixteen or so hours?"

"Can you shorten it?"

"Mm, maybe a little."

I mean, I could technically log back in at 1 am, but I really should get some sleep.

"I'll wait."

Reaching down she tapped the golden bug thing and it curled up into its box shape once more. Then she placed a bunch of stones with magic sigils on them in a wide circle around them. After that, she cleared some of the ground with her foot and sat down.

Daniel did the same, clearing some space inside the circle and laid down on his back to log out.

He had a bunch of questions he'd wanted to ask, wondering what those stones did and how long the bug thing would stay boxed up and would she sleep herself or stay awake to fight off any monster attacks.

Instead of asking anything, he just logged out.

She was far too scary.

Secrets Of The Soul

That evening before turning in for the night, Daniel was perusing the online forums for Final Bastion Online. He was reading a list of some of the most commonly known purchasable skills.

I am such an idiot. Most of the skills Alyssa and her group used were all purchasable, like that taunt ability and the ice attacks. Even the druid heals and Alyssa's monk abilities.

The list was massive, and it would take a long time to sort through it all. Using the search functions, he noted down some commonly available skills that he wanted to make sure he purchased when he found himself back in the elven city.

He'd managed to get permission from his parents to allow him unfettered access to play as much as he wanted over the holidays. This was mostly due to his decent grades from the mid term tests, of which he was still not sure how he'd done so well.

Surprising even himself, he was wide awake before the sun had risen. As stealthily as possible, he creaked open his fridge in the kitchen and made a very quick bowl of cereal, then took care of the necessities before slipping on his equipment and logging in.

"You're awake."

Before he'd even opened his eyes, Gwenithe had called out to him.

"Yea.." He trailed off as he finally got a good look around.

It was still early dawn in the game with the forest around them covered in deep shadows.

His threat detection skill was pinging like crazy, making him feel like they were completely surrounded by hundreds of monsters. Despite the skill warning him of danger, he didn't actually see anything, just the long, dark shadows all around them. Even more confusing to Daniel, Gwenithe just sat next to him in the same place and position he'd seen her take the night before.

She sat in a meditative pose, with her legs crossed in a lotus position and her hands resting palm up with her eyes closed.

She doesn't seem concerned, but she has to know that something's out there, right?

Slowly, getting to his feet, he toggled his different vision types from his mask. Once he turned on a mana sight and infrared combination, he saw them. Focusing on one of the dark clumps, he just stood there for a minute trying to observe it, wondering what it was.

Ohh duh, inspect..

Triggering his inspect skill, he figured out what they were.

NAME: UNKNOWN
RACE: SLUDGE
CLASS: (82) DECOMPOSER

A sludge? Like a slime monster? The class is kinda creepy..

Panning his vision in a circle all around them, there had to be hundreds of these things.

They were everywhere.

Everywhere except for where the marked stones were placed and in the center of the stones where they had stopped to rest.

"What is your assessment?"

Her sudden comment echoed out in the eerie silence.

My what?

Taking a minute to pause before answering, Daniel looked back over their situation with a more critical eye.

"There are many sludge monsters and they have us completely surrounded, but they don't seem to be attacking, probably something to do with the stones you placed on the ground. The sludges are also invisible unless I use my mana sight with infrared. They are mostly non-moving, just sitting there, but my threat detection skill is going off, giving me warnings that they want to attack us."

"You have mana sight and infrared?"

"Uhh, yea.."

Mentally facepalming himself, he was again super conscious of his bad habit of using 'Uhh' all the time.

"Your assessment was lacking. You failed to identify any potential weaknesses, even though you possess the capabilities to do so. Even with a basic inspection skill, learning of the enemies race along with the need to use enhanced vision types to see them and failing to consider their overall placements in the deepest parts of the darkness, it should have been easy to deduce that their primary mana type is shadow. Simply channeling some light mana could very likely drive them off. If not, it should be a simple matter to infuse your weapons with light mana using that necklace of yours with those weapons, since they contain null gems, thus giving you a bane weapon to use against them."

Daniel just stood there, not really sure what he should do or say, but everything she just mentioned made complete sense to him.

"Well? Go on then, get rid of them, we have much to discuss if you want to become a Sword Sage."

Her breathing was measured and her eyes had remained closed as she peacefully sat there meditating.

Mentally shrugging to himself, Daniel channeled some light mana into both swords after he materialized them in his hands and went to work.

They didn't run, but instead started trying to spit some kind of dark blob at him as he cut through them all like a hot knife through jello. It only took one swing of his sword to obliterate them, so it was just a matter of flaring his aura to dodge the flying goo and zip around to tag them all with his blades.

Overall, it took Daniel less than a minute to sweep their little campsite clean. As he stepped back into the circle of stones, he dismissed his weapons and watched them pixilate into nothingness.

"Good, now sit here, and imitate my posture."

She had indicated the space right in front of her.

Daniel plopped down where she wanted him to and did his best to match her position.

They sat there for a long time, her with closed eyes while taking deep breaths, him trying to match her inhale and exhales.

Daniel wasn't sure what, if anything, he was supposed to be doing, so he just quietly listened to the trees around them. As the sun slowly began to cast its light on the many trees, some of them began to creak. A loud snapping sound would occasionally echo out from somewhere deeper in the forest.

He felt a soft breeze against the back of his neck as he smelled the earthy and woodsy scents that filled their surroundings.

He found it peaceful and relaxing.

I should look into meditation a bit more, this is so refreshing.

Gwenithe's eyes snapped open and he felt a chill down his spine.

The intensity in her eyes was extremely intimidating and reminded Daniel of Henry. That spark of a memory filled Daniel with resolve and instead of shying away like he normally would have, he stared right back. After a moment, he realized she probably couldn't see past his mask, so his eyes could have been closed for all she knew. Something told him that she was looking past his mask somehow, so he continued to defiantly hold her gaze. A few moments more and the energy around them shifted. The intensity of her eyes softened and her head tilted slightly to the side as she seemed to ponder on something.

"You have a strong spirit and your skills are adequate, though lacking in refinement. I will try and teach you how to tap into the power of a sage. Not many can unlock the power of their soul, so do not get discouraged if it seems impossible, because it usually is."

The power of my soul? What does that mean?

She paused for a moment and shifted slightly. A small frown crept across her face.

"I know you have questions and normally, I find silence as a virtue, in this instance it will be important for you to ask your questions, despite how annoying I may find them."

It was as if a floodgate had been opened.

Daniel started asking rapid fire questions, not giving her any time to provide a single answer.

"What do you mean by the power of the soul? How does a soul make someone a Sword Sage? I thought souls were, like, metaphysical or something. Is there soul mana or magic? What parts of my skills need refinement? What should I be focusing on to get better? I totally understand how I can work on my observation skills, I've just been following my gut instincts mostly. Do you have any tips or unlisted skills I can try and learn-"

Taking a loud breath and pinching the bridge of her nose, she had to interject herself to stop his sudden tirade of questions.

"STOP! Let me just.. Let's start with what I know about souls."

Daniel sat attentively in front of Gwenithe, ready to soak in everything she was about to say.

"In all honesty, there isn't much known about soul mana or if it really even is soul mana that is unlocked by sages. The power of each person's soul is considered Divine. There are very old legends that speak of unlocking the soul as the first step to entering the Divine Realms as an equal to the Gods themselves. I don't know much about Gods and Divine Realms myself. I'm a warrior first and foremost, not a religious scholar. What I do know, is that empowering my sword skills with my soul is exceedingly difficult and unimaginably powerful. It's not something that I can personally maintain for long, but even for a few seconds, it can bring down *any* foe."

"How many times can you do it?"

"There isn't any known limit on how often one can unleash the power of their soul. It's just extremely difficult to channel in the first place. Your mind, body and spirit must all be in alignment. What I mean by that is also very difficult to explain. Everything needs to be vibrating together, the same way, with the same intent and energy."

She sat a moment and rubbed her right hand across her jaw as she contemplated on how best to describe complete alignment.

"Do you mean, like being in the 'zone'?"

That was the best comparison Daniel could surmise based on the vague description Gwenithe had provided.

"I'm not sure I know what that means? Can you better explain that?"

"Yea, so, being in the zone is like when you are just purely existing and reacting to everything but your reactions are basically perfect. Athletes talk about it a lot, when suddenly their bodies just perform at their absolute peak and every movement is perfect. Kinda like they become one with themselves and the world around them. They also say it is a fleeting feeling but when they channel it, they can become unstoppable."

"I see. Yes, that does sound very similar. I would think the only real difference between being in this 'zone' and using the power of your soul is intent. Entering a state of complete alignment is just the first step, and that sounds exactly like this zone concept. The next part is manifesting your intent upon the world. Just from my experience, the power of the soul is terrifyingly vast. A Sword Sage only manifests their intent upon their blades in very specific ways. I am a dual wielding specialist and focus my intent upon the movement of my body and weapons. There are others who focus on other aspects such as striking or defending. Those are not concepts that I have truly mastered yet."

Gwenithe suddenly rose to her feet.

She stretched and then collected all the stones on the ground, placing them in a small satchel resting on her lower back. She then tapped the golden box that unfolded into its insect form. It began crawling its way deeper into the Aerfall.

"Come, we have a long way yet to go. The next group of monsters we encounter, I will take on. Pay close attention when I fight. I'll be empowering myself with my soul."

Daniel hurriedly followed after them, eagerly awaiting the display of a Sword Sage's power.

He didn't have long to wait.

Less than ten minutes later, Daniel stood enthralled.

He watched as their guide curled up into a box and Gwenithe unsheathed two longswords. Both blades were covered in glowing runic script that continually oscillated between all visible colors.

She then released a presence and a pressure that Daniel felt pushing against him in some unidentifiable way.

Her body lit up from within, but the light seemed ethereal and it coated her entire being, swords included. It was a very unexplainable luminance that didn't seem to cast any sort of shadows. His brain was struggling to even comprehend what it was seeing, unable to make sense of a light that didn't seem to exist, but that somehow covered Gwenithe from the inside out and enveloped both of her blades as well.

The three aggressive, six legged, massive wolves didn't stand a chance.

Gwenithe seemed to melt and flow in and out of existence as she danced around them for a moment before they all fell dead.

It was over far too quickly and Daniel was left on the side lines, struggling to recreate everything he'd just witnessed in his mind so he could try and replay it over again.

As she tapped the guide to get it moving again, she nodded his way.

"The rest of the monsters we encounter today are yours. For now, just try to get into this zone state while fighting them. I will explain more about leveraging your intent and manifesting it once you are able to maintain complete alignment with some regularity."

Despite Daniel's best intentions, he was completely unable to enter any zone-like state. He was certainly getting a lot of experience from killing monsters nearly every quarter hour. They paused when he logged out to take a lunch break and then resumed their journey once he returned.

It took Daniel three more days in the real world, which amounted to twice that in the game until he'd even achieved alignment during one of his battles. He didn't try to latch on or force the feeling, as he'd read up on how other prominent figures often spoke about being in the zone and how to get there. The one thing that seemed common amongst all of them was that any time you tried to force it, it never worked.

He'd gotten confirmation from Gwenithe that he had indeed entered a state of alignment between mind, body and soul. She had been scrutinizing his constant skirmishes and often giving him tips and advice on how best to polish up his combat forms.

Daniel felt very fortunate that he had a little over two weeks off from school, so he felt that he would have plenty of time to become a Sword Sage. He'd briefly felt a bit depressed about not having anyone to brag to once he unlocked the Sage rank, since the closest people he had as friends were Alyssa and Mike, but they felt more and more like acquaintances with every passing day. He hadn't received any in-game messages from them and during the week of midterms, he never got the courage to chat with them or go hang out with them in the cafeteria. Especially after the whole ordeal with Mirantil and Abby, he was feeling especially awkward when he thought of bringing up what happened with the elves to his real life 'friends'.

Not having to worry over social anxiety, despite his desire to have some actual close friends, he instead focused intently on figuring out the secret of becoming a Sage. It wasn't until after his lunch break on Tuesday, four days in, that he finally got a quest update and a lecture from Gwenithe in manifesting his intent.

Quest Update:
The Hunt for Sword Sages

After discovering Abbyzael's family link to a Sword Sage, you have safely escorted her to the home of Gwenithe, her grandmother. The Sword Sage Gwenithe is in need of your help. You have found her deep in the Aerfall and she has agreed

TO TRAIN YOU, NOW THAT YOU HAVE ATTAINED
ALIGNMENT WITH YOUR MIND, BODY AND SPIRIT.
REWARD: SWORD SAGE TRAINING
PENALTY FOR FAILURE: LOSS OF ADVANCEMENT
POTENTIAL

"Well done. Although you still need to improve on how long it takes for you to enter alignment, we can at least begin focusing on your intent. The concept I focus on to manifest my intent is movement. For now, let's rest and meditate. You need to focus and think on your bodily movement while wielding your swords. I want you to visualize the dual wielding specialization stances and forms. What's most important here is that when you think on them, do not feel the swords as separate, but as one with the body. The entire form and movement needs to be one entity, not separate things."

For the rest of that afternoon, they sat and meditated.

Daniel asked a few clarifying questions now and again as he sat with his legs crossed and reviewed the dual wielding combat forms in his mind. He played them over and over again, while trying to focus on understanding the movements. He visualized himself going through the forms very slowly, trying his best to see the swords and his body as one whole thing. At first, he tried to envision himself as a monster with pointed arms. This initially helped define the concept in his mind that his body and swords were one. As he used this combined concept and focused on all the individual movements in the duel wield form, he felt his head get warm and his body started vibrating, something he could detect peripherally as he meditated.

When he was startled out of his thoughts by his log out alarm, he stood up and did a little stretch, then actually went through the forms he had been meditating on for hours.

It felt good to him, to be up and moving instead of sitting and just thinking of moving. He also felt a bit more fluid as he moved from stance to stance, strike to strike. Finishing up one of his old exercises that Henry had him do over and over again, he truly felt that he'd achieved a whole new level of skill and understanding. The meditation had done wonders for him.

The Light From Within

The following week left Daniel a bit disappointed in himself.

Try as he might, he couldn't manifest his intent. He couldn't bring his concept of movement from theoretical in his mind to physically manifesting and empowering his actual movements.

He practiced while not in combat and also while fighting off all the various creatures that inhabited the Aerfall. They had been lucky that only simple beasts and monsters had attacked them, and no raid bosses or overpowered monsters came their way. Even with a steady stream of simple encounters over the past several days, he still was unable to figure out how to mimic or replicate what Gwenithe was capable of.

She had provided many demonstrations over the last week, and each time he felt like he was right on the cusp of learning the secret to it all.

As the first week of his holiday came to an end, no closer was he to becoming a Sage as they were to finding the banished elven prince.

Daniel started to get a bit anxious about needing to take a few days off from the game, since today was Christmas Eve and once he logged off for lunch, he likely wouldn't be back online until the day after Christmas.

After the last unsuccessful attempt at unlocking his soul power, his frustrations gave him an opening to bring up his expected absence to the imposing Elven Strike Maiden.

"Lady Gwenithe, I will need to take an extended rest soon. I'll be gone for roughly four days time."

She paused for a moment to look at him, then at their surroundings.

The trees of the Aerfall had slowly gotten larger as the days went on. Daniel honestly felt like an ant compared to the skyscraper sized trees.

"Let's find a decent place to hole up for a bit. When do you need this extended rest?"

"As soon as it gets dark."

That should be around lunch time, I need to find out from mom what our plans are for tonight and tomorrow.

"So from tonight on, got it. Let me grab the tracker and we'll find a spot."

They spent the next hour or so looking for a defensible or secluded refuge. All they could find was a small, dirty cave that didn't go very far. It was deep enough to keep them out of the elements, but it wasn't tall enough for Gwenithe to stand up in. Daniel's head came close to brushing the ceiling while Gwenithe had to crouch over as they pushed up against the back of the small cave.

Gwenithe had placed the warding stones, as she called them, around the mouth of the cave to keep any monsters out. Then she went about making the space a bit more comfortable after putting the golden bug that she called a tracker down next to her, along with some blankets and other trinkets.

As the light from the day started to fade into night, Daniel made himself comfy and before logging out, gave Gwenithe an awkward, "See you in a few!"

Finding his mother in his parents bedroom, she was sitting at a mirrored desk, putting earrings on.

"Hey mom."

He always felt a little sheepish when entering his parent's bedroom. He didn't like to think about what went on in there, it was just a place that existed and one he didn't like to exist *in* at the same time. Something about the room tended to dampen the sound, so he also felt compelled to keep his voice down when in there.

"Oh, good, I didn't have to pull you from that game. You should start getting ready, we'll be leaving here in a bit. Try to wear something festive. I do like your winter sweaters, they make you look handsome."

As she spoke, she continued to try on several different sets of earrings.

"Yup, can do. Buuuut, where are we going again?"

"Honey, this is the fifth time I've told you, we are going to your father's corporate holiday party. They've rented out an entire museum! Now shoo, I need to hurry up, and so should you!"

Quickly making his way back to his room, he scrounged around for some christmas themed sweaters and found a decent looking dark blue one with white snowflakes scattered across it. Pulling on some dark gray slacks, he then found his nice pair of shoes and tried them on.

It's really depressing that all of this still fits me. This is what I wore through middle school, even these dumb shoes.

As he stood in front of his mirrored closet, he gave himself a once over.

My hair is sporting some crazy bedhead, but damn, I do look good in this.

After putting far too much gel in his hair and making it look like he just got out of a shower, he finally managed to style it, sort of.

Making his way to the kitchen to grab a snack, he found both of his parents already there, drinking what suspiciously looked like wine out of some small, clear, stemless glasses.

Once his mother noticed him, she put her glass down and rushed over.

"Oh honey, no no no. What have you *done* to your hair?! Come with me, now."

She grabbed him by his wrist and practically dragged him into his parent's master bathroom. She then had him put his head in the sink and washed nearly all of the gel out, then dried his hair and had him sit down on their toilet with the lid closed. Pulling some of his fathers styling gel out, she began styling his hair with just a touch of the actual gel.

Ohh, yea, I definitely used waaay too much gel, she only put like the smallest amount on her palm.

After the impromptu styling session with his mom and all the accompanying advice that came with it, they loaded up into the family SUV. The next thirty minutes passed by with bits of laughter and conversation between his parents while Daniel just sat in the back as he blankly stared out the window.

He enjoyed the break from struggling to unlock a sage rank, not having to spend time trying to get in alignment or think on manifesting anything. Nothing was pressing and his eyes took on a slight glazed sheen as he watched the traffic pass by with hardly a single thought in his head.

When they got to the museum that his father's company had rented for the evening, his mother kept fussing with his hair and straightened his father's collar while trying to remove the invisible lint at the same time. She didn't let up until they got to the entrance and his father pulled out his work badge.

He meekly followed his parents as they were led through the main entry lobby and into a large foyer that was filled with people. The murmur of hundreds of voices all talking at once, reverberated throughout the room.

Daniel spotted a very long table along the wall to his left that was covered in different kinds of foods. A bunch of standing tables were interspersed throughout the foyer every five feet or so. Several of them were empty while others had clusters of people with food and drinks standing around them, chatting away.

A band was setting up some equipment on a raised platform at the other end of the foyer. Museum staff could be seen moving about, answering questions or idling by doorways.

"Hey dad!" Daniel called out to his father as he tugged on his arm.

"Yea? What's up?"

His father hadn't stopped walking but looked over his shoulder.

"Is the whole museum open? Or just this area?"

"Ohh, umm, I don't know, let's ask!"

They were halfway across the foyer by then and his father called out in a loud voice while waving an arm in the air, "Morgan! Hey! Come here a sec!"

A stout man in what looked like a red velvet suit came over with a drink in his hand and a smile on his bearded face.

"Tyler!"

They shook hands as his father introduced his family.

"Hey Morgan, good to see you."

"You too man!"

"This is my wife, Meghan, and my son Daniel."

Shaking hands with his mother, the man was very polite as Daniel noticed his demeanor shifted slightly.

"Nice to meet you, Meghan."

"Same to you Morgan. But please, just call me Amy, it's my middle name and what everyone calls me. Tyler likes to annoy me by introducing me as Meghan, even though he knows better."

His mom shot his father a pointed glance and both men shared a laugh.

Morgan shifted his attention and looked down at Daniel. He extended his large hand that Daniel was just now noticing for the first time.

Dude, your hands are huge! I bet you could palm a basketball no problem!

"Hello there, Daniel."

"Hiya."

"And what grade are you in?"

"High School, 9th grade."

Morgan couldn't hide his shock, even letting out a questioning, "Really?" while looking at Daniel's parents.

To which both of them just nodded their heads.

"Ahh, well, I'm sure you'll get a growth spurt soon, probably be taller than your father before you graduate."

He let out a bit of an awkward chuckle as he turned back to face Daniel's father.

Unless I take after my mom.

Daniel's parents were a height mixed couple, with his father being six feet and his mother just over five feet tall. As it stood, Daniel was still smaller than his mother.

His father deftly changed the topic of conversation, "So, you wouldn't happen to know if the entire museum is open to us or just this inner area?"

"Oh! They rented this whole place out. You can go anywhere dude! Even the aquarium is open. You guys should really go check it out while you can, not sure how long till they close everything up."

"How wonderful! I heard they have penguins here, do you know where they are?"

His mother had a bit of an obsession with penguins, reminding Daniel of the several porcelain penguins that decorated their home. He'd broken one once, bringing his mother to near tears over the glass shards of the shattered thing. Daniel tried his best to never touch them after that.

He zoned out of the conversation as he looked around at all the people milling about. Scoping out the food tables, he spotted several things he wanted to try. Noticing that more people were headed their way, what looked to Daniel to be a rather large group, he decided to try and make a hasty escape as the thought of introducing himself to so many people spiked his social anxiety.

"I'm gonna go hit the food table."

Without pausing their conversation, the three adults just briefly glanced his way and his father gave a slight nod.

Taking the nod as approval, Daniel bolted towards the food. Narrowly escaping from the horde that descended upon his poor father and mother.

Wow, lots of people are eager to chat with dad, guess he's a big shot or something.

After stuffing his face with mini hotdog things and some delicious sushi rolls, he grabbed a bottled water and started walking around. As he made his way to the exit of the foyer, he saw the door was open and a museum employee was standing by the opening. The staffer just nodded at Daniel as he traipsed passed and Daniel couldn't help the smile that formed on his face as he turned to his right and went to explore the mostly empty museum.

This is pretty cool. Getting to play around in a museum without all the normally annoying people everywhere. That dude mentioned the Aquarium, where the heck is that at?

Making his way through a large area labeled as the 'African Hall', he found the penguins. They were all just sitting still, mostly sleeping and weren't all that interesting to him so he quickly moved on.

Lazily making his way past a bunch of interactive exhibits, he found a stairwell leading down. Above it read a sign indicating that it led to the aforementioned Aquarium.

As he descended the stairs, the overhead lights went away and a world of blue washed over him.

Wow.

Daniel found himself transfixed in front of a gigantic glass wall. On the other side swam tons of different kinds of fish. Lots of artistically added coral were placed about the massive tank and the many fish were gracefully swimming through the loops and currents.

He wasn't sure how long he stood there, but it was more than twenty minutes and probably less than an hour.

A presence was suddenly next to him.

Turning his head to the right, he looked to see who was standing so close to him.

After a quick glance, he turned back to the world of water before him. It took a good thirty seconds for his brain to process what he'd seen. A woman in a muted red dress, with flowing red hair was holding a small purse in both hands as she looked into the tank in front of them.

I know her, she was that girl who offered me a fry. The one at Alyssa's lunch table. Wow, she's pretty as hell. Why is she standing so close to me? Am I just in a good viewing spot?

The sudden implications of a girl he would never have expected to run into, standing nearly shoulder to shoulder with him as they gazed into the massive fish tank, had his adrenaline flood his system.

He started fidgeting a little, not sure if he should move away, or stay perfectly still.

Feeling a bead of sweat trickle down his back, he'd finally made the decision to walk away. The thought of trying to strike up a conversation made him practically nauseous from the overwhelming anxiety. Running into a classmate here had completely thrown him for a loop, much less someone he wanted to turn and stare at for an uncomfortable amount of time.

Turning to the left, he managed to take a few steps, but then stopped himself.

He didn't know why he stopped, but he did.

Standing there with his back to her, he could feel her watching him. He knew she was looking at him, and he wanted to run away, but his feet were rooted in place.

Finally, breaking the strange stalemate, she called out.

"Hey."

Tension was released, like a bowstring set free and Daniel nearly fell to the ground.

That was so weird..

Turning around, he walked back over to her, "hey."

It would be really rude to just walk away now. At least my voice didn't crack when I said 'hey'!

"Been playing much FBO over the break?"

"Yea, I'm actually stuck on a quest. Can't figure out how to move forward."

"What's got you stuck?"

"I'm trying to unlock a skill, but I need to do some kind of visualization thing to make it work. I just can't seem to make what I see in my head come through."

"You're doing visualization training to learn a skill?"

"Yea."

"What kind of visualization?"

"Movement. Like I see myself moving and I'm trying to empower my physical movement, but it doesn't seem to be working."

"Are you just seeing yourself walking? Or what?"

"Ahh no, I'm doing the sword combat forms, which I can do without any problems, it's just the enhanced movement that I visualize isn't there."

"Who told you to do this kind of training to unlock a skill?"

"The quest giver. She seems to be a pretty important NPC and knows what she's doing, so I trust her."

"Ohh. Well, are you visualizing what she told you to do or your interpretation of the skill?"

"I'm just doing exactly as she told me."

"Then that's likely your problem. Visualization training only really works, at least for me, when it's based on my own personal interpretation and feelings, not what someone else told me to do or feel. You should try using your own feelings to guide you, not what somebody else tells you to feel."

They stood there, quietly once more, as Daniel tried to absorb what she was telling him. Watching the fish swim through the water and trying to understand what he interpreted as movement was difficult to do.

This entire encounter had left Daniel feeling heady and strange. Her perfume was making his mind fuzzy and he wasn't sure what was happening, just that he really liked standing there next to her.

"Whelp, see ya, and good luck with your skill!"

"Yea, thanks."

Daniel watched as she disappeared around a corner.

What's her name! I don't remember hearing anyone mention it, and she wasn't from my middle school. Could I ask Alyssa? Nah.. too embarrassing.

It took a while for Daniel's legs to start working again.

He started walking around the rest of the Aquarium, secretly hoping and praying to any God that would listen that he might run into her once more while also being completely terrified of running into her once more.

Unfortunately, that would be the last time he saw her that night. Even after making his way upstairs and finding his parents in the crowded foyer, he quietly scrutinized every person he saw, but couldn't find her anywhere.

Where the hell did she go?

Djinn

Daniel's Christmas Eve ended with his parents partially stumbling through their front door after drinking far too much from the open bar.

Christmas morning, he was the first one up and so he went downstairs and plopped down on the couch after pulling out his phone. Using his nanite connection, he held his phone up as he searched for all things related to Final Bastion Online just by thinking of it. He was rather adept at performing multiple searches at once, tabbing through different screens on his phone with a slight mental command.

Nothing interesting, not even a holiday in-game event or anything. Seems they want to keep the world lore separate from the real world.

His parent's finally made their way downstairs, both of whom were hung over. The rest of his Christmas day was relatively relaxed as he hung out with them. They opened some presents, with Daniel getting some new clothes and a few books to read.

His father kept trying to get Daniel interested in the same material he was. It was mostly how to be successful in life and business type books. Daniel's father had recently found an author that he kept raving about and wanted Daniel to read all of their published works.

Daniel had zero interest in them and would just put these new books on his dust covered bookshelf, intending to never actually read any of them.

The rest of the day they just watched some Christmas movies and enjoyed a few meals together.

When he finally logged back in the next day, he was startled to find himself alone. Gwenithe and the tracker were both gone.

I wonder where she is?

Taking a few tentative steps outside, he saw nothing unusual or out of place. Surrounding the small cave were several monolithic trees. Looking around, he didn't see any obvious signs or tracks to follow, so he decided to just hang out and practice his sword forms.

What does movement mean to me?

Daniel contemplated on his idea of movements and how he could better visualize this concept in his mind.

As he stepped through his forms, he felt a bit of inspiration flowing through him. His understanding was at the edge of his finger tips. It was nearly there, and he just knew that soon he would unlock his soul power.

Before he could truly manifest anything, his form practice was interrupted as Gwenithe came jogging over with a worried look on her face.

"Daniel, your back. I need to get you caught up, come."

She slipped into the small cave and took a seat near the back wall. Daniel followed in after her and sat down next to her, both of them facing slightly towards each other.

Lightly pressing his back to the wall, Daniel looked over at the powerful Elven Strike Maiden. Her look of concern was obvious, giving Daniel a small spike of anxiety about what might be the problem.

"How much do you know about my quest out here in the Aerfall? What all has Palimore told you?"

Daniel rubbed his chin as he tried to remember everything Lady Palimore had said about Gwenithe's mission.

"Mmm, If I recall correctly, it has to do with one of the elven princesses using some relic to get a prince banished and you are out here to rescue the prince? Something like that?"

Shock was evident on her face.

"I must admit, I am very surprised that Palimore gave you so much detail, especially with it being so sensitive and dealing with the elven royal court. You must have truly earned her trust in such a short amount of time."

Daniel just quietly nodded his head, also remembering Lady Palimore's wish to be the one to reveal Abby's return. He didn't want to accidentally ruin the surprise so he just kept silent.

"Well, let me give you a bit more context, seeing as you already know more than any outsider should, I trust that what I say will remain between the two of us. The battle for succession has been raging for many years and has been a constant point of strife within the royal court. One of the more devious princesses managed to get ahold of a relic she shouldn't have even known about. An elven king of old managed to secure a Djinn's cup. A Djinn will only reward such a thing for a life debt, and for good reason. The cup only has a limited number of uses. To activate the cup, a small ritual is needed, then a wish is given and the Djinn are bound to try and uphold the spoken wish, in good faith."

Pausing to take a breath, Gwenithe's fury was visible.

"The cursed girl made a wish that Prince Felcore be, 'sent to the deepest and most dangerous place in the Aerfall and keep anyone from bringing him back'."

Gwenithe took a moment to calm down, then continued.

"So, of course, the Djinn were honor bound by the life debt to uphold this wish. We then had to burn another use of the cup to ask for that tracker, so it could lead us to Prince Felcore. And before you ask, no, a second wish cannot undo a previous one. The best we could negotiate for was that stupid tracker. Yesterday, I found the place where the prince is being held. The tracker melted upon arrival and was absorbed into the door. It was both a compass and key, so now we can open the door and attempt our rescue. What worries me is what the door itself is made of. Not only the door, but the whole of the cave itself. The door is underground and seems to be right in the center of a massive chunk of Adamantian Muramite. That stuff is impossible to cut or mine, unless you use the power of a sage. The entire damn door is carved from it with many artistic flourishes. I would have already gone in myself, but the door and the stone surrounding it is really troubling. It is very likely that the Djinn themselves will fight to keep the prince."

She took a moment to gather herself.

"Honestly, I'm a bit relieved to know that Palimore has put her faith in you. I might not have revealed as much and that may have led to my death and that of Prince Felcore. The Djinn are unimaginably powerful. I will not hold it against you if you do not wish to enter their lair. But I must ask, will you join me and try to save a banished prince from a fearsome enemy?"

The look on her face was not one of desperation or hope, it was a visage of conviction. She would step into a place that she feared would be her end and she would do so without trepidation.

Daniel found his respect for Gwenithe blossom as the thought of marching into an army of monsters at her side filled him with excitement.

Heck yea! I would follow you anywhere, lady.

In a much more restrained voice as compared to the trumpeting in his head, he responded, "Of course."

It was a simple response, but it garnered a small smile from the Lord Commander of the elves.

"Good. Detailed strategic planning is useless here, with just the two of us going into an unknown environment. I will attempt to distract or defeat the greatest threats, while you handle the minor ones and focus on finding Prince Felcore and extricating him. Got it?"

"Yes, ma'am."

Getting up, she then led him through the forest at a very fast pace. He was easily able to match her pace, but it did require the use of his lightning aura, though not enough to start draining his health. Had it not been for his new set of armor, he would have been pushed past his limit and unable to keep up.

Man this is awesome. Every level I gain just makes me a bit more stronger with this scaling equipment. I'm only level 76 though, even after this last week and a half of grinding monsters, all of them high level too! I can see why so very few people are above level 90, even after five years since the game's release. I wonder what kind of gear those guys have, bet it's insane.

They flew past a few groups of monsters, none of which decided to try and go after them. Forty minutes later, Gwenithe slowed down and slipped into a nearly invisible root covered entrance to a tunnel that seemed to disappear underneath one of the gargantuan trees.

Daniel was hot on her heels and raced into the tunnel, switching his mask to an infrared vision mode.

The tunnel was, oddly, a straight shot downward.

They reached a rather large twelve foot set of double doors.

The walls around the doors looked like a rough, slate, striated stone with hard edges. Some sections were a pure white, while other bits were a dark colorless black.

It was obvious that the doors were made out of the same material as the walls. The only real difference was a golden circle with a hand imprint in the center of it which was positioned roughly where a door handle would have been.

Guess that was the tracker? She did say it melted and became a key or something like that.

Turning around, Daniel could see a small pinhole of light showing the entrance to the tunnel they'd just descended.

Gwenithe loosened her blades from their scabbards and placed her hand on his shoulder, giving it a little tap.

"Are you ready?"

"Yea, let's do this."

Putting her right palm into the visible imprint, both doors flashed a crimson color then without a sound, they opened inwardly revealing a very large cavern, roughly the size of a small stadium.

There were a few stalagmites hanging from the ceiling and the entire cavern was made of the same stone as the doors. The ground was extremely uneven with random protrusions of the hard edged stone marking the floor.

What arrested Daniel's attention were the three floating monsters watching them from the center of the cavern. They all looked the same, except for their skin tones. The one on the left was a deep russet red, while the one in the middle had a dark green tint and the one on the right was a light blue color. They all wore a multi-colored sash about their waists, and below that was just a strange misty vapor. Their upper torso's were bare and they had four arms, all of which were crossed, with bald human-like heads. The musculature gave Daniel the impression that they were all incredibly strong, since their forearms were as wide around as his waist.

NAME: UNKNOWN
RACE: DJINN
CLASS: (146) WISH CASTER

Level 146?!

"Dude."

"Yes, they appear quite formidable. Look, back to the left, I see the prince."

Roving his eyes over to where she had indicated, Daniel spotted a crystal shaped object embedded in the back wall. Using his zoom ability on his mask he was able to identify an elven male inside the crystal.

It doesn't look like he's moving.. Is he alive?

"I see him, but he isn't moving around."

"It's a stasis summon, which means unfortunately we will need to defeat the caster to release the prince and dispel the summoned crystal."

"Ahh, I bet the caster is one of those three."

"Indeed."

Neither of them had taken a step inside the large chamber. Both of them having made their observations from the open door way.

Not seeing anything else of note, Daniel returned his attention to the floating Djinn. Out of his peripheral vision, he noticed Gwenithe stepping into the room. He walked in as well, just a half-step behind her.

No sooner had they crossed the threshold that a resounding crash boomed out behind them.

Startled, Daniel spun around, only to see the doors slammed shut.

Damn, that scared me.

"Looks like there is no turning back."

"That's correct, Elven Strike Maiden." A booming voice echoed from the otherside of the cavern.

The green tinted Djinn had uncrossed its arms and was floating over. The other two slowly drifted in its wake, following the first.

Daniel could feel Gwenithe steel herself. To him, she felt like a predator ready to strike. A spring coiled tight, tension about to burst.

The tension had his adrenaline pumping.

Ohhh man, I am soo ready for this!

A quest update pinged and threw him off for a moment.

QUEST UPDATE:
THE HUNT FOR SWORD SAGES

AFTER DISCOVERING ABBYZAEL'S FAMILY LINK TO A SWORD SAGE, YOU HAVE SAFELY ESCORTED HER TO THE HOME OF GWENITHE, HER GRANDMOTHER. THE SWORD SAGE GWENITHE IS IN NEED OF YOUR HELP. YOU HAVE FOUND HER DEEP IN THE AERFALL AND SHE HAS AGREED TO TRAIN YOU, NOW THAT YOU HAVE ATTAINED ALIGNMENT WITH YOUR MIND, BODY AND SPIRIT. YOU HAVE AGREED TO HELP RESCUE A BANISHED PRINCE AND MUST DEFEAT THE DJINN GUARDS HOLDING HIM PRISONER.

CONDITIONS: AUTOMATIC QUEST FAILURE IF GWENITHE DIES

REWARD: SWORD SAGE TRAINING

PENALTY FOR FAILURE: LOSS OF ADVANCEMENT POTENTIAL

Shiiiit. It's game over if she bites it.

The excitement of the upcoming battle suddenly shifted to an anxious dread. Daniel wasn't all that confident in his odds, but had just assumed that Gwenithe would be the unstoppable game character that would ensure victory. Now, she was the precious cargo that must be protected at all costs.

"Welcome, Lady Gwenithe. I must apologize, this is rather unfortunate. Due to the nature of the wish, we cannot allow you to leave and must eliminate you to uphold the will of the wisher."

The Djinn's words may have claimed to be apologetic, but the tone and demeanor was apathetic at best.

"I suspected as much. Would you be willing to face me one at a time?"

Gwenithe had taken out both of her blades and was edging forward a bit, giving herself some room to maneuver.

"No. To do so would be in violation of the will of the wisher. We must try our very best to eliminate you and your compan-"

Before it could finish, she leapt forward striking out with both long swords.

The Djinn was prepared, despite its casual demeanor.

All four arms were a blur of steel as four massive scimitars were suddenly being wielded in a terrifying way. The clash and clang of steel on steel rang out through the cavern. Daniel could feel the subtle reverberations of the powerful blows wash over him. Gwenithe had unleashed her sage abilities right from the get go.

She isn't holding back, but she isn't overwhelming it either.

The other two Djinn that had been lazily making their way over, suddenly burst into action. Both of them had equipped their own massive scimitars and were racing towards the clashing fighters.

Unbeknownst to Daniel, he did the first thing he could think of and enacted a tried and true method of dealing with more enemies then you intended.

He started kiting the other two Djinn.

Flaring his aura in the extreme, he took a leaping charge, positioning himself in front of the two incoming Djinn. With another burst of movement, he rocketed through the air in between the two of them, scoring a glancing blow on both and doing enough damage to get their attention.

Looking over his shoulder to make sure they were pursuing him, Daniel started dancing about the other side of the cavern, dodging magical blast attacks and sweeping in to strike when one of them turned to disengage and moved to support the fight against the Sword Sage.

He could practically feel the frustration coming off the blue and red Djinn. They kept trying to work together to pin him in, or hold him down with all sorts of magical snares. Daniel just burned them away with his aura or slipped around them with ease.

Any time he had to engage directly with them to keep them from running off, he was quickly overcome by their melee attacks and had to sometimes burn a lightning step to get away. Every time he managed to flee from them, they grew more aggressive and tenacious the next time he came in range. After trying to use his aura surge to damage the Djinn, he realized that they were somehow able to completely negate it and force him into melee range to keep their attention.

He honestly felt like he was doing quite well, until a scream cried out from the otherside of the cavern.

In alarm, Daniel gained some distance from the Djinn he was kiting and focused on Gwenithe's situation.

It wasn't looking good.

She was tightly holding the left side of her body while on one knee, with only one sword held in a defensive position in her right hand.

Fortunately, the Djinn appeared to be injured itself as it was not floating as high off the ground and seemed to only have three arms left, two of which were pressing down on open wounds with only the one arm on its left side still holding a weapon.

Fuck!

As Daniel watched the wounded Djinn lift its blade to end the Elven Strike Maiden, several things happened at once.

His attack prediction skill triggered in two places, first around his legs, then along his right shoulder and back. He felt the cool down for his lightning step end just as the red Djinn surrounded his feet in magical vines. The blue Djinn had caught up to him and was slicing into his shoulder and back as he burned his lightning step, putting himself directly in front of the green Djinn's attack that was meant for Gwenithe.

He felt the flare of pain register along his back and shoulder as he used both blades to parry the massive scimitar.

Flooding his body with his lightning aura, his health began to drop precipitously as he gave everything he had to finish off the wounded Djinn in front of him.

It somehow wasn't enough.

Despite its many wounds, the Djinn was able to fend him off with a single weapon.

In a slight panic, Daniel shifted his aura to accelerate his mind and slow everything down as much as he could.

As the world came to a crawl, a massive headache started to build so he let up on his aura a bit. He could only maintain this level of mind acceleration for a handful of seconds at best, as it would drastically consume his health. He was willing to risk it since he needed time to think.

So, she's basically going to die, unless I stop them, but I can't even beat the wounded one that only has a single sword. I'm going to fail this quest.

As soon as the thought of failure entered his mind, he felt himself grow stiff. His body started to turtle up as old habits of losing and being bullied intermixed. Just as he was about to completely surrender to his inevitable defeat, another errant thought skittered across his mind.

"You should try using your own feelings to guide you, not what somebody else tells you to feel."

A sudden confluence of watching fish moving through water, seeing the Djinn around him moving very slowly as if also underwater and the words from his classmate the other day all merged into a concept of movement.

It suddenly just made perfect sense to him.

Movement is just my entire being flowing through different mediums, like a fish through water, or a worm through dirt or a Djinn through constrained time and space.

Inner light that cast no shadow covered his body and both of his swords. Empowering his movement with his soul, amplified his speed in conjunction with his lightning aura.

With contemptible ease, he deflected the next incoming sword strike from the green Djinn and decapitated it with his next swing.

It burst into a million tiny pixels as his attack had caused fatal damage.

Turning to face the other two Djinn, his inner light flickered and died.

Ah, fuck.

He took off toward the other side of the cavern once more, both Djinn in hot pursuit.

This is such a weird feeling. I know I can turn that on again, but it will only last like a few seconds. But I'm not sure if I can use it a third time, for some reason it feels like this soul power will become unreachable, so I only have one more burst of soul juice.

Racing around the cavern, an idea started to form in Daniel's mind as he got a better look at his surroundings.

That spot over there to the left looks like a good place to try. The hanging chunk of rock should crush them if I time this right.

Gambling on the chance that his soul power could cut through the stone, he enacted his reckless plan.

Drawing the enraged Djinn over to a natural depression in the cavern floor, he burned what little health he had left to push his aura as hard as he could. All he was trying to do was not get skewered by the massive swirling scimitars while trying to get the two Djinn into the perfect position.

That's it! Now jump!

Just as Daniel squatted down to leap to the ceiling, an errant blade came slicing through his left leg, removing it cleanly.

"Ahh!"

Burning a lightning step, he suddenly appeared high up, between two massive stalagmites. Unleashing his soul power, he sliced through both pieces of stone and turned and watched as all three things fell back down towards the Djinn, himself included.

They were spinning around trying to locate him as he fervently prayed they stayed still as he fell back down to the cavern floor.

With a resounding boom, both stalagmites crushed their intended Djinn, turning them both into pixelated nothingness.

Yessss!

"*Heurk-*"

Daniel had temporarily forgotten that he was missing his left leg and landed rather harshly, nearly getting pinned under one of the huge pieces of stone before limping desperately away from them.

Checking his health, he had a bleed effect and was dropping a few percent every couple of seconds. He was sitting at under 14% health and wouldn't last for more than half a minute.

At least she'll live, gonna have to respawn and run back here.

Limping over on one leg to check on Gwenithe's health, he was surprised to see her up and about, looking very much uninjured as she walked over to him.

"Impressively done, Daniel. You don't look so good though, here take this, I only have a few of them but it's an imperial grade health potion."

Handing over a red vial that was giving off a strong vibrancy, Daniel didn't hesitate as he gulped it down. He was under 5% and only had a few seconds left before the magic of the potion kicked in.

His entire body gave off a faint red glow as his left leg rematerialized with his boots and pants still equipped like nothing had happened. His health refilled in the blink of an eye and was completely full.

"Wow, thanks, I would've died a second ago if not for that."

"Glad you're feeling better, now let's go see to the prince."

Gingerly testing his newly reformed leg, he followed Gwenithe over to the prone form of the elven prince. After the green Djinn had perished, the crystal holding the elf had dissipated and sent Prince Felcore smashing face first into the ground while still unconscious.

More Escort Quests

Daniel stood off to the side as Gwenithe administered some healing potions to the elven prince.

It didn't take long for them to rouse him from his unconscious state.

"What. I don't. Where am I? Auntie Gwen, is that you? What's happening?"

In a soothing and motherly tone, Gwenithe spoke to the wild eyed young elf that Daniel surmised as being a young teen, much like himself.

"There there, little Felly. Yes, it's me, Aunt Gwen. Don't worry now, I'm here to get you home. Look at me. Now tell me, how are you feeling?"

Turning to face her, his eyes seemed to lose the panicked edge in them and he calmed down.

"I.. I'm feeling okay."

"Nothing hurts? No strange pains anywhere?"

"Uhhmm, no, nothing like that."

"Good. Are you fit to walk? We need to get moving."

"Uhh, yes Auntie Gwen, I can walk."

Standing up from her kneeling position, she turned and grabbed his hand, escorting the young prince towards the now open double doors.

"Let's get a move on then. Prince Felcore, that is Daniel. Through considerable risk to his own safety, he slew the Djinn that had imprisoned you. Without him, I would have surely perished. I estimate that he is about the same age as you. You would do well to imitate and learn from him while you can."

"Ohh, wow. He's my age? And he defeated the Djinn?!"

Daniel silently followed along behind them, watching as a gawking princeling stared open mouthed at him as he was yanked along towards the exit of the cavern.

No quest update yet, are we still in danger?

Stepping back out into the fading light of the sun, his quest notification finally went off.

Ahh, there it is.

Quest Update:
The Hunt for Sword Sages

After discovering Abbyzael's family link to a Sword Sage, you have safely escorted her to the home of Gwenithe, her grandmother. The Sword Sage Gwenithe is in need of your help. You have found her deep in the Aerfall and she has agreed to train you, now that you have attained alignment with your mind, body and spirit. You have rescued the banished prince and defeated the Djinn guards holding him prisoner. Now you

MUST ESCORT HIM SAFELY HOME TO THE ELVEN CITY OF
AERYENOUS.

CONDITIONS: AUTOMATIC QUEST FAILURE IF FELCORE
DIES

REWARD: SWORD SAGE TRAINING

PENALTY FOR FAILURE: LOSS OF ADVANCEMENT
POTENTIAL

Ugh, another escort quest. And I'll fail if the prince dies, geez.

After exiting the tunnel, they began the long trek back to Aeryenous.

Unfortunately, the prince was very slow.

Their pace was atrocious. It was even slower than when they were forced to follow the tracker.

Luckily for Daniel, the prince wasn't much of a talker, and just quietly watched as himself or Gwenithe dispatched any monsters dumb enough to assault them.

Daniel tried to experiment with his new found soul power, but it seemed like it was locked away for some reason. He also noticed a new gauge underneath his health meter and a stat for soul essence showed up in his character tab. In the character tab, it just showed the soul essence as a percentage that kept changing from 1% to 9999% and anywhere in between. The gauge that was now under his health bar showed it as full and was a shimmering gray color. He wasn't sure if there was an issue with the game or if he had broken something with his character. He thought about filing another help ticket, but in the end decided against it.

If it keeps flickering and acting weird by the time we get back to the city, I'll do something about it then.

As night began to descend upon them, Daniel realized he would need to log off for a bit to get some lunch and do his fitness quests.

"Hey, I'm gonna need to take a break soon."

Stopping to give him an assessing look, Gwenithe nodded and then instructed the prince to climb up onto her back and hold on.

"Let's head to the spot we left this morning, it should suffice for a defensible resting place."

Finally moving at a decent speed, they arrived back at the cave his avatar had spent the Christmas holiday sleeping in. Gwenithe didn't waste any time setting up the warding stones. Daniel found the indentations in the ground from the last time he was there and laid down into them, logging himself off.

Finding the house empty, he figured his parent's must have gone out since they both took vacation days through the new year. Heating up some leftovers, he sat down and did some internet sleuthing, looking up anything he could find on Sage's and this new soul essence stat. His efforts were in vain, since the running theory on every info site around Sage's was that they didn't actually exist.

Finishing up his fitness quests, he took a quick rinse and loaded back into the world of Final Bastion Online.

The prince was fast asleep and Gwenithe was sitting in her meditative pose.

Whispering quietly, so as not to wake the boy, Daniel called out to Gwenithe, "hey."

She opened her eyes and looked over at him.

Taking that as a sign she was listening, Daniel voiced his suggestion, "you think we could alternate carrying him and just run back to the city? Otherwise it will take weeks."

She gave a half smile and snorted softly, "In a hurry?"

"Well, no, but, yea, I don't have much free time left before I have to start taking extended breaks."

"I see, in that case, I think we can speed things up a bit. I wanted to give him a bit of a break, but we are still in very dangerous territory."

Reaching over she started violently shaking the sleeping elf.

"Hey! Wake up! It's time to move! Hustle up!"

With a half smile on her face, she hunched her way out of the cave, grabbing the ward stones as she left.

The frazzled prince took a moment to gather himself, then crawled out of the cave and dusted himself off.

Daniel slipped out of the cave and bid it a fond farewell as Gwenithe forced the prince onto her back. They took off in a blink and blazed a trail back to Aeryenous.

After mindlessly following behind the two of them, Daniel was much more satisfied with their pace and rather glad that he didn't have to try and remember the way since he was completely turned around. Without Gwenithe, he would never have found his way back.

It didn't take them more than a few hours at their new pace to arrive at the eastern side of the massive city wall. As they started their trek along the wall towards the main entry gates, Daniel once more wondered at why they didn't just climb one of the massive trees and jump over the wall. His curiosity finally got the better of him and he voiced his question to Gwenithe.

"Hey Gwen, can't we just scale a tree and jump over the wall?"

Turning over her shoulder to look at him, she responded a bit confused, "What? No, of course not. There's an aerial barrier that covers the city as well as a subterranean one. All major cities have such protection. It prevents tunneling invasions and aerial bombardments. Only small outposts and villages are lacking such essential defenses. Also, please use either Lady Gwenithe or Lord Commander Gwenithe when you address me. Short names are reserved for familial relations only."

"Oh. Sorry. Makes sense."

Guess that answers my question to see if there was any shortcut to get back inside. She didn't seem mad at me for not using her name properly. Gotta remember the formalities.

As they approached the gate from the side, one of the guards noticed their approach and called a halt to all activity. He then summoned an escort group and hurriedly surrounded the three of them in a protective barrier.

"Lord Commander Gwenithe, how might I serve?"

Without breaking stride, she set the prince down and began issuing orders. Several guards took off at a run to deliver messages while the remaining men formed up tighter around the prince and essentially boxed Daniel out, not that he minded all that much.

With Gwenithe in the lead, they marched into the city and straight towards the royal compound.

Occasionally, one of the messengers she'd previously sent out reported back to her. Some had messages of their own to deliver elsewhere while most were just sent back to their posts.

Arriving at the fortified gate that blocked off entry into the royal estates, a contingent of guards wearing much fancier armor took over the protection detail around the prince and the other group were dismissed.

The prince was whisked away and Daniel was left standing at the gate with Gwenithe as she spoke with some of the remaining royal guards. He hadn't been paying much attention, but he focused back on the conversation when he heard his name.

"-is Daniel. Allow him entrance to the gateway gardens. An attendant will come for him shortly."

"Yes, Lord Commander."

"I must report directly to the king, see that my orders are carried out."

"Yes, Lord Commander."

Turning on her heel, she marched towards one of the royal estates in the same direction the prince had gone.

The gate guards returned to their posts, stoic and silent. Only a few of them glanced his way before they settled into position or ventured off to do as they'd been instructed.

I was hoping to get a quest update by now, but nothing yet.

He started looking at his character sheet once more, getting ready to file another support ticket to fix his flickering soul essence stat when it suddenly grayed out. Instead of a moving percentage, it just showed two dashes and the label was italicized and in a very light font color. The visual gauge was still there and hadn't changed, but the character tab made it seem like it was something that was currently unavailable to him.

Well, I guess it's better than flickering percentages.

"Excuse me, Sir Daniel?"

A smartly dressed elf with weirdly pointy shoes stood before him, with his hands clasped behind his back and his body bent forward at a slight angle.

"Hey, yea, that's me."

"Wonderful, if you would please follow me?"

"Sure."

The elf escorted Daniel through the gate and down the main, paved path. In front of him, he was able to see a massive structure poking up above a huge set of hedges that lined the paved road. His guide then veered off to the left down a small walking path leading into the immaculately kept hedges.

"Just this way sir, and the gateway garden tour will begin."

"The what?"

"I was instructed to provide you with a tour of the gateway garden and then send you on your way."

"Oh. Send me on my way to where?"

He spun about and had a look of utter disdain on his face as he asked, "how am I to know what you filthy humans do in your spare time? After the tour you are to leave these grounds, what you do beyond that is of little to no consequence, to me or anyone else i'd imagine."

Turning back around, he stiffly made his way through the hedges.

Woah, what a jerk.

Daniel followed along and listened to the elf stop and give random bits of commentary on a bench here, or a fountain there, or a particular bush along the path.

This is the most boring thing ever. And this guy totally sucks as a tour guide, or maybe he's really good at it and just hates me cause I'm not an elf. Who knows, but I'm totally over this.

They came to a statue of a mighty warrior elf slaying a two headed snake monster.

Daniel had completely tuned the guy out and was just waiting for this silly tour to end when something odd happened.

The elf was facing him, pointing up at the statue.

That in itself wasn't odd, what happened next was.

He was pointing at the statue, but in the space between his index finger and the actual statue was another building off in the distance. Daniel would have completely missed the tiny person who was scaling the side of the building, right where the elf's finger was pointing, if the attendant hadn't been so aggressively rude.

"Excuse me Sir! I must demand that you at least pay attention to this last bit. Look. Here. Please! This is one of our greatest Heroes and I will not have Lord Palimar disrespected by one such as you!"

"Okay, yea, I see it."

As Daniel tried to placate the elf, he used his zoom ability to focus in on the tiny person who was quickly making their way towards one of the large open balconies as they climbed the side of the building off in the distance.

Is.. is that a ninja?

Getting a better view, the person was covered in all black cloth. Their head was covered in something very similar to a ninja's hood that made Daniel instantly suspicious and somewhat mirthful.

"And with that, the tour is over. I hope you enjoyed your time here among the elven royal elite. Please make your way to the gate once you are done here in the gardens."

The elf turned and strode away, leaving Daniel by himself.

Just like that? I'm free to wander wherever? Weird.. I kinda wanna see what that ninja is up too.

Banking on his good credit after saving a royal prince, Daniel decided to be a bit nosy as his curiosity peaked.

He hung out by the statue for a bit longer as he watched the climber slowly scale the outside of the building and clamber over the protruding balcony on one of the upper floors. When the person disappeared inside, Daniel made his move.

Flaring his aura, he darted across the vast empty space between the garden he was in and the building that he assumed was the personal quarters of the royals, since both the Prince and Gwenithe had gone towards it after arriving.

Pushing enough aura strength into his legs to cause his health to dip a bit, he created a small divot in the ground as he catapulted up and over the balcony where the masked ninja had been.

Once more, he flared his aura's power, slowing everything down to give him time to process what he'd found.

Seeing a person wearing what was definitely a ninja outfit rifling through some drawers, Daniel used his inspect ability.

NAME: PROFESSOR PLUCK
RACE: HUMAN
CLASS: (87) SWASHBUCKLER

Professor Pluck? .. is that Emilio?!

"Emmy?"

The ninja that was hurriedly looking through a desk drawer jumped and whirled around startled.

"Wha- what? Who.. Do I know you?"

Looking back down at the drawer, the ninja garbed man seemed to have found what he was looking for, as he snatched up a palm sized metal object and shoved it into a sack around his waist.

"Are you Emilio Fairchant?"

Daniel was certain it was his first and only childhood friend, Emilio after hearing his voice and seeing his avatar's name.

"Wha- yea, who are.. Wait.. like *Daniel* Daniel?"

Giving a half wave, Daniel couldn't help but smile behind his mask.

"Hey, yea it's me man."

Emilio spread his hands out as she nearly shouted, "Dude! NO. WAY. How the hell are you man! Shit, I haven't seen you since we moved away, like just before middle school started."

Daniel scratched the back of his head as he reminisced a little, thinking back on how he and his best friend Emmy had been neighbors for a long time. They used to spend nearly every waking moment hanging out with each other, having both their parents tease them and call them brothers.

When Daniel's parents had relocated him, it was a very traumatic experience. They lived so far apart now that getting together wasn't a realistic expectation.

"Yea, it has been a while man. How have you been?"

Emilio just scoffed at him and ran over, giving Daniel a bear hug and lifting him straight off the ground.

Geez, he got tall, what the hell man..

"Hahhah! Danny! You're like the same size! Not eating your vegetables still?"

"Wha- hey, put me down! Of course I eat my veggies, well.. the ones that aren't gross."

Laughing together, Daniel punched his oldest friend lightly in the ribs as Emilio squeezed his right neck and clavicle.

They play wrestled for a minute until loud noises could be heard rushing towards the room they were in from beyond the closed door.

"Oh shit, I gotta bail. You good if I bounce or you need my help to get away?"

Daniel waved his friend off.

"Nah, I'm probably good, but you better get outta here, lookin sus in that outfit."

"Pah, for real, bro meet up with me at the Foreign Fang, its a bar on the west side of the city. See ya in a few!"

His friend tapped the ninja head covering and a cloud of black smoke filled the room. It only took a few moments for the smoke to clear, leaving him completely alone in the room.

That was pretty damn cool, some kind of escape ability?

The door burst open and a handful of elven royal guards burst through into the room, all shouting and yelling at him to not move.

Daniel just raised his hands in the air and allowed the guards to escort him out.

They took him down to an outer courtyard with spears and swords pointed at him, some of them even attempting to shallowly pierce his armor.

As they were escorting him across the grounds, they had caused quite a bit of a disturbance.

They are taking me away from the gate.. Is there a prison or something here? Oh shit, am I being locked up?

"Halt!"

A loud, commanding voice echoed across the royal estate grounds. It was a voice that Daniel recognized.

Gwenithe!

In less than a blink, she was standing tall in front of all of them, a deep frown on her face as she glared at all of them, Daniel included.

"Explain."

The Arch Demon Seal

That one word had a palpable effect on every person present.

Daniel felt a shiver go down his spine, while the guards all sheathed their weapons and snapped into a formal salute.

"Lord Commander. Moments ago, we spotted someone running across the estate lawns and jumping into the King's private study. As we ran to investigate, we discovered this miscreant and what appeared to be several drawers open and objects scattered about. We are now taking him to be interrogated to determine his vile purpose and what he was searching for, as it's likely he didn't find it, or else he would have fled before we arrived to detain him."

"Daniel."

All she had to do was call his name and his posture unconsciously shifted to mirror the guards surrounding him.

Hearing the ordered command from her tone, he held nothing back.

"So, I was given a tour of the gateway gardens, then told to leave, when I saw someone climbing the side of that building and entering a room from a balcony. I followed them to see what was happening. When I got to the room, I saw this person take something from one of the drawers and then vanished in a cloud of smoke. That's when the guards arrived."

"What was taken?"

"What? Uhh, I don't.. know."

"What did it look like?"

"Oh, it was a circular, golden piece of metal that had a swirly pattern with some kind of magic runes on it."

"How big was it?"

"Mmm, about the size of my palm, I think?"

Turning her commanding eyes over the guards surrounding Daniel, she called out, "It appears you've failed to identify the true culprit and your lax vigilance has allowed something very precious to be taken. You will all face disciplinary actions for this failure. You are all dismissed. Return to your posts. Daniel, if you would accompany me please."

"Yes, Lord Commander!" The entire group of guards spoke in unison, saluted and marched stiffly away from them.

Daniel followed a bit meekly behind Gwenithe as she led him into the very building he was just escorted out of. Together, they went back into the King's study.

After watching Gwenithe search through the open drawer that held the thing Emilio had taken, he heard a long sigh escape her.

"It's as I feared. This is very troublesome, Daniel. All of Aeryenous is now in grave danger."

With a tired look on her face, she turned to face him, clasping both hands behind her back.

As the silence stretched, Daniel felt compelled to speak up.

"Is.. is there anything I can do to help?"

The far away look she'd had a moment before, focused once more upon him.

"I hesitate to ask this, especially after everything you've already done for us, but it seems I have no choice but to rely on you again. Will you lend your strength to the Elves of Aeryenous and help recover the Arch Demon Seal that has been stolen?"

The Arch Demon Seal? That sounds.. Freaking Awesome!

"Yes! I would be happy to help!"

New Quest (Epic Unique):
The Arch Demon Seal
Find and return the arch demon seal to Gwenithe.
Reward: Special event title
Penalty for Failure: Unknown
Accept Quest: [Y / N]

Whaaaat?! An epic unique quest! How do I keep getting so lucky with these quests?! I gotta meet up with Emmy and see what he knows about this demon seal thing.

Accepting the quest, he returned his attention to Gwenithe as she pulled over two chairs and gestured Daniel to take a seat. Getting comfy in the chair, he listened to the Lord Commander's tale.

"I must tell you a story of the founding of Aeryenous. Not many know if this, as it's been generally kept a secret from all but the royal family. So please, do not share this, ahh, I fear I continue putting undue burdens upon you, asking you to keep so many secrets of the Aeryenous's royal family. But this story is one you must hear, if the worst should happen. Going back to the very founding of this city, our people were in dire straits. Many wars had been fought and our previous home was left in ruin. Fearful of being completely destroyed, my great great great grandfather, Lord Palimar, led what was left of the Elven Empire deep into the Aerfall."

Daniel was listening intently to her story. As she mentioned the name Palimar, his memory flashed to that annoying attendant pointing at the statue in the garden.

So she's related to the statue guy?

"I suspect you are wondering about my lineage. Lord Palimar became the first King of Aeryenous, and I am a distant relative of his, making me a great Aunt of the current King."

Daniel made an 'Oh' motion with his mouth, but that was likely lost on the royal that sat before him, as it was hidden behind his mask.

"Back to my story. The Aerfall was significantly more dangerous in Lord Palimar's day. In order to found a large city, much like all of the current race capitals found throughout the world, a significant source of pure magic is required. Again, I am not much of a scholar, but suffice to say, there are places where pure magic accumulates and is focused, creating a sort of high density magic region. The city of Aeryenous was founded upon such a spot. When my ancestor discovered a place with enough pure magic to establish a new home, he led his people deep into the Aerfall."

Sighing to herself, Gwenithe crossed her legs and arms as she continued.

"They were met with harsh resistance. It was a brutal and bloody battle, just to get here. Once they'd arrived, despite a sense of relief, they were filled with terror. A demon lord had somehow forced its way into this realm and built a castle at the very center of the high mana density region. An Arch Demon, which is one of the most powerful denizens of their infernal realm. They are the rulers of demon kind, and to find one here, my .. Lord Palimar nearly gave in to despair. A very clever and crafty elven sorcerer devised a plan to defeat the demon lord. Lady Palimore's ancestor, the hero sorcerer Danithor, had truly worked miracles."

Wait, Lady Palimore as in your secretary lady that ran your estate? Huh..

Daniel kept his comments to himself and he continued to be enthralled by Gwenithe's storytelling.

"Danithor found a way to lure the Arch Demon out of its castle, and into a very carefully prepared artificial dungeon. Using types of magic and sorcery that only exist in legends now, Lord Palimar and Danithor sealed the Arch Demon into a phantom realm. That seal you witnessed being taken from here is the key to this artificial phantom realm where the Arch Demon is held prisoner, even to this day."

As she paused for a minute, Daniel took this time to ask some questions he had.

"So, why didn't anyone destroy this key? Wouldn't that have kept this demon sealed away forever?"

"Unfortunately, if the key was destroyed, it would shatter the prison, freeing the demon to return to its infernal realm where it would surely spend its days seeking the complete annihilation of Aeryenous and its people. So, the key was kept, passed down from one royal to the next, hidden in plain sight as an innocuous object. How anyone or anything even discovered its existence is beyond me."

"Ahh, makes sense, I guess. Is it fragile? This seal, that is."

"Fragile? Oh no, it is exceptionally sturdy. I'm not really sure *how* anyone could destroy it. But it would very likely be used to open the cage and release this monstrous foe upon us. I do not hold much faith in our ability to overcome a fully manifested Arch Demon. A small portion of their aura's are often enough to topple most cities, much less one in the flesh."

I can see why this is an epic quest. Sounds like this Arch Demon is one of the highest tier raid bosses. I should look online and see what's on the wikis about them.

"Okay, got it. So, return the seal to you, or if it gets released, then.. ?"

"Then gather as many adventurers as you can to banish it from this realm, or all of Aeryenous will be destroyed."

The gravity of her words hit Daniel harder than he'd expected. It was as if they carried a physical kind of weight.

MENTAL FORTITUDE - LEVEL (17)

Hey! Did she use a skill or something just then? What the heck.

Feeling the heaviness of the words wash away, Daniel returned his attention to Gwenithe.

"I will do my best to get it back."

"I trust you will. Come, I'll escort you out."

With that, she rose from her seat and led Daniel back through the building, which was almost entirely empty. He'd been hoping to catch a glimpse of a royal family member or something, but the hallways were deserted.

He followed her in silence as they approached the gate that protected entry into the royal estate.

"Thank you, and know that you have my full support if you run into any trouble. Farewell, Daniel."

"Thank you, Lady Gwenithe."

Leaving Daniel alone once more at the gate, many of the guards were giving him the side eye. Feeling self conscious, he turned and started heading westward.

Time to find this Foreign Fang place.

Less than half an hour later, Daniel found himself inside a bustling tavern. At first, he didn't see his old friend anywhere, but a voice called out and snagged his attention.

"Hey, Daniel! Over here!"

As Daniel approached the man who had called out to him, he was shocked. It was obvious that this was his old friend, but he had grown quite a bit. He even had a few sparse hairs on his chin, showing the beginnings of a beard.

His outfit was completely different as well. On his head was a black bandana wrapped around his hair. He had very flashy jewelry on his ears, hands and neck. His shirt looked like scraps of cloth used as rags that were covered in a brownish leather vest that was left unbuttoned, not that there were any buttons Daniel could see. He had a deep blue cloth sash around his waist that held a curved sword that wasn't in a sheath and a dagger was strapped to his back and others around his thigh. His pants and boots looked like they belonged to some kind of pirate.

Are these his normal clothes?

"Dude! Took you long enough! Hah, did they throw you in a brig or something? Sorry about that, also, accept my friend request already you ass!"

"Oh shit, one sec."

Bringing up his social windows, he found the pending friend request from Professor Pluck and accepted it.

"Friend request accepted, Mister Pluck."

"Oh fuck off, don't call me that. I'm so embarrassed by my name. I made this character when I was in middle school and I've put waaay too much time into it to start over."

Taking the seat next to his old friend, Daniel enjoyed a small laugh as he remembered Emilio and himself playing superheroes in their backyard. Emilio had come up with his hero persona as Professor Pluck. A wise and intelligent hero that was full of courage and pluck as he used his wit and intelligent creations to slay their imaginary enemies. Daniel had just called himself Super Daniel, as they both wore towels as capes and ran around their houses, getting scolded for climbing onto each other's roof tops and getting into all sorts of trouble.

"So man, for real, did you get in any trouble back there? I'd feel like shit if you did."

Daniel waved away his friend's concern.

"Nah, I'm on good terms with the elves, so I was able to get out of it, ended up getting an epic unique quest out of it as well."

"Oh nice! An epic unique quest? That's redic bro."

"Yea, so I'm gonna need you to hand over that seal, or else.. no christmas presents for you this year."

Laughing together, Emilio pulled out the seal and tossed it over to Daniel.

"Well shit, Christmas was last week, so here's my present to you bro. What's up with this thing anyway? My quest just said to retrieve this thing and it was just some faction quest with a few coins as a reward. Also, what's up with the mask?"

"Oh, sorry, I'll take it off, it's just got really nice stats. You said a faction quest? Which faction? Cause apparently this thing is a pretty big deal. It's some kind of demon seal."

Daniel felt a slight spike of anxiety for accidentally revealing some of the secrets of the elves, but dismissed it right away. Pulling his mask off, he put it into his inventory.

This is Emmy. It doesn't feel right keeping things from him, this is just a game after all.

Feeling a bit more justified about his actions, he was a bit alarmed to see the strange distant look on his friend's face.

"What? What is it Emmy?"

"I .. my quest just updated. Dude, it's now a secret epic unique quest. What the hell?"

"Wow, really?"

"Yea, I've never had one of those before, and the rewards have changed! I get some kind of title."

"Oh neat, mine just offers a title too, but I need to take this thing back to the elves."

Thinking about his friend and all the unique quests he's had already, he really wanted to share the fun with his oldest and best friend.

I should give this back. Sounds like this will create a raid event for the demon. We can just have one of the huge guilds come to kill it.

"Here."

Daniel handed his friend back the seal.

"Merry Christmas Emmy. I really missed you man."

"Danny, dude, are you sure, sounds like we both get some kind of title for this, and damn, I've missed you too bro."

"Yea, it's all good, I've had my share of special quests, your turn!"

Daniel couldn't help the smile that was plastered across his face.

Putting the seal back into his inventory, Emilio then put his arm around his old friend and smiled right back.

Daniel felt the irresistible urge to make fun of his friend's struggling facial hair. "So, why did you draw lines on your face to pretend at having a beard?"

"Hey!"

"You could've just given your avatar facial hair."

"At least I have some facial hair, have you even gone through puberty yet you shrimp."

"Bro, uncool. I didn't make fun of your lanky spider arms so lay off my height."

"At least my lankiness extends to my dick, I bet yours is just a nub."

"Ow, harsh. I thought we were friends, man?"

Laughing with each other, Emilio slid a drink over in front of Daniel and together they cheered their reunion.

"Hey, you wanna go with me when I turn this quest in?"

"Dude, of course, you better not leave without me."

"Hah, you got it. Says I need to go to some rando place out in the woods on new years eve. You free then?"

"Sure! My parents will probably be out doing their own thing."

"Cool, so I guess we got a few days to mess around until then. You in any guilds or anything?"

"Nah, just playing solo mostly."

"Ahh, no wonder your bitchass is under level 80. We should try and level you up some. I don't mind babysitting your weak ass."

"Pfft, I bet I could wipe the floor with you."

"Dude, your gear might be all matching but that's just faction vendor city shit right?"

"Uhh, yea? I think?"

"Well see, that's the difference between you and me, all my gear is extremely rare. Each piece has awesome stats and effects. I've got raid gear man. My bandana is what turned me into that ninja and had that escape ability. And that's just one piece. How long have you been playing?"

"Ohh, mmm, I started back in August, the first day of high school."

"Damn, you're actually higher level and better equipped than I thought, for how long you've been playing. What's your adventure society rank?"

"Ohh, uhh, let me think.. E?"

"Huh? Just pull out your token."

"Oh yeah!" Daniel materialized his adventure society token and inspected it.

ADVENTURE SOCIETY TOKEN
REGISTERED TO: DANIEL
RANK: E

"Looks like rank E, what's yours at?"

"I'm A rank obviously, my guild raids the elite missions."

"Cool. I should probably raise my rank a bit to match my actual level. Seems like it's worth it for gear like yours."

"Oh man, it's totally worth the effort. A single piece of my gear would out strip your entire set. Even if it's one of those super expensive stat scaling sets, which I doubt that's what you have on."

"Mmm, this is a stat scaling set."

"What? Bullshit, show me."

Daniel pulled off one of his gloves and handed it to his friend.

"Bro, get the fuck out, how do you have these? I mean, they're garbage for a raider, but still these are stupid expensive. Did you find some kind of platinum exploit or something?"

Handing the glove back, Daniel was both happy at being able to get such expensive gear and disappointed that it was apparently nothing compared to the raid gear his friend wore.

"I got it while doing a quest, hey let me see one of your pieces if they're so great."

"Oh, damn getting some quest love then. I can't show you my stuff, it's all soulbound. You can only see the stats when they drop. Makes it really difficult for high end PvPers to keep track of other player's capabilities and gear since you have to be there when the stuff is created by the system. Some of it is straight up mission rewards and no one else even sees the stats but you. I can only imagine what other people have scored. You should definitely join a raiding guild, maybe even mine, unless you suck. Can't have you hurting my rep and all."

Slapping Daniel on the back, they spent the next few hours just chatting about the old days and all the things that they had gotten in trouble over.

Promising to meet up tomorrow to work on Daniel's adventure society rank, they both went and found a player inn to log out in.

Daniel was in an exceptionally good mood as he sat down with his parents for dinner that evening. Even they noticed and asked what was up. Upon finding out that he'd managed to reconnect with his old neighbor, both his parents were very happy, seeming to think that finally all his days of being bullied were over as they encouraged and supported his friendship with Emilio.

Palling Around

Over the next several days, Daniel and Emilio continued to reestablish their old friendship and worked to get Daniel's adventure society rank up.

Daniel's soul essence stat continued to show a grayed out value and despite his best efforts, he was unable to call upon the power of his soul. It was as if an invisible wall was separating him from a part of himself. Ignoring the strangeness of it all, he was having a blast running around and doing rather normal quests for the adventure society to unlock the higher ranks.

Before he could test for another rank, he was required to do a series of different types of quests. Some of them dungeon clearing, others were escorting or guarding and quite a few very simple fetch and return quests. Emilio was by his side through all of them as they messed around and made quick work of the low level quests and dungeons. It was as if no time at all had passed between the two of them and they were back in their own little world, having fun. Daniel's mask had remained in his inventory the entire time, never feeling the need to put it back on.

By the time New Year's Eve rolled around, Daniel had made it to the B rank. Adventure Society ranks roughly covered the span of twenty levels each until they got to the B rank. As Daniel was still under level 80, he had effectively caught up in ranks, with B rank being the 70 to 80 level range. Rank A, in which Emilio was in, covered the level 80 to 90 range, and the fabled S rank was for those above level 90.

Despite all of his rank ups and quest completions, the only rewards Daniel saw were to his digital wallet. He hadn't gotten any level ups and as he thought about it, he realized that the last time he'd gotten any levels was before the fight with the Djinn.

Them being in the 145+ level range, I should have gotten hella experience for basically soloing them. What's going on with my expee?

Daniel figured that since most of the quests he'd done were lower level, it might just have been that they weren't worth enough to push him higher. He figured that the Djinn were like a special encounter and didn't really count since he'd unlocked a new stat type from it. Deciding to not worry much about it until after the quest with Emilio, he put the thoughts of missed experience from the Djinn out of his mind.

They spent the morning going over the quest and making sure they knew which way to go to find the meeting spot for Emilio and his quest contact. They had to consult with some local cartographer's to make sure they had the right place. Emilio bought Daniel one of the best available player maps as a gift, since he already had the same version, and together they marked the quest location and prepared to leave Aeryenous.

Deciding to start out after their respective lunch breaks, it didn't seem that it would take very long to reach their destination. Daniel had convinced Emilio to start doing the fitness quests as well. Getting him a fitness quest token that was available for purchase from the adventure society, it was Emilio's turn to work on leveling his fitness quest ranks.

Finding his parents getting all dressed up, Daniel popped into their room to ask where they would be going before grabbing a quick lunch. They were off to another work event being hosted by his fathers company and they wouldn't be back until tomorrow afternoon, since they'd be staying in a hotel where the New Year's party was being held.

Rinsing off and logging back in to Final Bastion Online, Daniel was buzzing with excitement. The last few days, both he and Emilio speculated on what rewards he'd get from his quest. Emilio was convinced that this was going to trigger a new epic raid dungeon and was ecstatic at being the one to open it. Daniel wasn't really sure, since he'd never actually gone on a big raid and was just having a blast hanging out with his old friend.

Finding Emilio waiting for him down in the lobby of the inn they'd booked rooms from, Daniel snuck up behind him and put him in a headlock.

"*Argh!* You wiry little shit. Huah!"

Throwing Daniel over his shoulder, they both laughed as Daniel bumped into a table and rolled to his feet.

A grumpy old elven staffer was bustling about as he saw their shenanigans and yelled at them to cut it out.

"Hey! Quit wrastlin around in here! I'll have ye both fined if anythin gets broken!"

"Ahh, sorry, we were just leaving."

Daniel, ever the apologist, was the first to try and placate the old elf. Emilio just laughed and dragged Daniel out the door.

"Come on! We got some questing to do!"

It took them a few hours to find the meetup spot that was marked on their maps. They had gotten lost a few times, having to backtrack, both of them arguing with each other over who had led them astray.

"I think this is it, I just got a quest update saying to wait here until my contact shows."

"Oh, cool. How long will it take, you think?"

Shrugging, Emilio just looked around at the crumpled remains of some old building that was nothing but rubble now.

"Beats me, there isn't a timer or anything on the quest."

Taking a seat on the ground, opposite from one another, they tossed a small rock, that was once a piece of wall, back and forth while they waited.

"So your guild, they raid all the time?"

"Hmm? Oh yea, we usually get together twice a week and once on the weekends to raid stuff. Every Tuesday, Thursday and Saturday. They take the holidays off all the time though, a bunch of people tend to spend a lot of time with their families when the holidays hit. We won't start raiding until the second week of feb. So it's basically free time to do whatever."

"Nice. That isn't too bad, twice a week and on the weekends seems very doable. Are you penalized for missing any?"

"Yea, but it's just in DKP."

"What's DKP?"

"Oh, uhh, it's called, like, Dragon Kill Points or something like that. Every raid that you show up to, you earn DKP. The guild officers keep track of everyone's DKP and you have to maintain a certain attendance percentage to be able to use your DKP on the loot that drops. They use a kind of auction system, letting people bid on stuff, using their points earned from raiding to get the raid loot. This system works for us. Some guilds out there use a loot council, where the leaders decide who gets what. Others allow people to buy the gear with money. Those are known as plat raids, and the profit at the end is split with all those who showed up."

"Oh wow, I didn't even think about how large guilds handled the loot. Do you like the DKP thing?"

"Heck yea, I get to spend my hard earned points on things that make my play style better and better. The bidding wars are awesome to watch as well. People get heated, man, it's hilarious."

"Hah, I can't even imag-"

"Why are there two of you?"

A creepy voice drifted through the rubble all around them.

Both Emilio and Daniel stood up and were looking around wildly, trying to identify where the voice came from.

"Answer me!" It croaked.

"I have the seal, this is just my friend. Can't two people turn in the quest?"

"It's no matter, show it to me."

As Emilio pulled out the Arch Demon seal, a man in a blood red hooded robe materialized next to them and reached for the seal.

Was that some kind of invisibility?

The robed man snatched the seal from his friend and carefully scrutinized it for several minutes. He cast several quick spells on it, all of them seeming to fizzle out as they encountered the seal.

"Wonderful, just *wonderful*. Come with me for your reward."

Turning around, the man took a few steps and bent down, touching the ground. The air around him shimmered as a stairwell became visible at his feet. He disappeared into the darkness, leaving both friends standing still, quite a bit on edge.

They shared a look, both nodding at each other. Emilio led the way down with Daniel right behind him.

When they used to play as kids, the one that led was always the one that birthed the idea. So if Daniel had wanted them to climb over fences, it was him that would be in front. When Emilio had wanted to climb onto the roofs, he was the one that climbed up first, with Daniel right behind him. Without needing to say a word, they fell into their old patterns as naturally as breathing.

The way was dark at first, until they came to a solid stone wall that was giving off a faint purple light.

After touching the glowing wall, Emilio nodded back at Daniel and said a single word.

"Dungeon."

A moment later he poofed.

Daniel stepped up and touched the wall, following his friend into a place called **Cranzor's Cradle**. There wasn't any kind of level indicator, just that it was a dungeon.

The first thing he noticed was the smell.

It was rancid.

Emilio had already clamped a hand on his nose as he started picking up random bits of things scattered around on the tables.

There were no chairs, just large tables all along the walls, with a balcony railing. They stood on the elevated floor that overlooked a larger room that was barren, except for the obviously evil looking red magic circles and scripts on the floor.

The hooded man had taken the seal to the lower area and placed it right in the center of all the magic sigils, giving Daniel a very bad feeling about what was going to happen next.

Backing up to stand just outside the lines on the floor, the man beckoned the two of them over.

"Come, it is time for your rewards. My Master shall grant you such wondrous recompense for setting him free."

Ohh shit. Yeah, he's totally unlocking the Arch Demon. Also, it's his master? Wonder how that happened..

Both himself and Emilio watched as the man cast some kind of spell and the entire room became awash in a dark purple color with tinges of red everywhere. A powerful heat wave came crashing down on all of them, causing the robed man to jump back and cackle hysterically.

A presence was suddenly before them.

It felt as if the world was muted.

Daniel's lungs were being crushed by the air and he struggled to catch his breath. He felt Emilio grasp onto his left shoulder, to steady himself.

An aura began pressing down on them and made it very hard to stand.

Both of them seemed to wobble as if their legs were about to give out.

As sound came rushing back, the aura dimmed slightly and Daniel was finally able to let his brain catch up to what his eyes were seeing.

Yup, that's a demon alright.

It stood at least ten feet tall, with a powerful body.

From the waist up, its skin or scales were red, with a purple detailing, almost like a wicked looking tattoo, scrawled across its chest and arms. From the forearms down to its hands, the scales, Daniel had definitely confirmed it to be scales, were pitch black. The legs were huge and it had cloven hooves with a tail that lashed around violently.

The face was oddly very human-like, with deep purple eyes set against a light red skin tone. Two six inch long, black horns, with purple detailing, were protruding from its forehead, in between its long black, shaggy hair.

"Master! Look! I've brought a delightful snack for you to feast on. You must be so very famished from your long imprisonment. How may I ser-"

The demon had raised its hands and a suction sound could be heard as the robed man was suddenly pixelated into millions of tiny pink pixels and those tiny particles were then sucked into the demon's outstretched hand.

It happened in mere seconds.

Emilio's hand squeezed down harder on Daniels left shoulder as he breathed, "bro, we are so fucked, inspect it before it eats us."

Daniel, firing off an inspect, was dumbstruck.

NAME: UNKNOWN
RACE: ARCH DEMON
CLASS: (175) DEMON LORD

Uhhh.. what the fu-

PING!

QUEST UPDATE:
THE ARCH DEMON SEAL

YOU HAVE FAILED TO FIND AND RETURN THE ARCH DEMON SEAL TO GWENITHE. THE DEMON IS NOW FREE AND WILL DESTROY AERYENOUS UNLESS IT CAN BE STOPPED.

TIME REMAINING: 5 MIN. 28 SEC.
REWARD: SPECIAL EVENT TITLE
PENALTY FOR FAILURE: THE COMPLETE DESTRUCTION OF THE ELVEN CAPITAL AERYENOUS

PING!

WORLD EVENT:
THE ARCH DEMON OF AERYENOUS

ATTENTION ALL PLAYERS. THE ELVEN CAPITAL OF AERYENOUS IS IN GRAVE DANGER! DUE TO THE ILL ADVISED ACTIONS OF THE FOLLOWING PLAYERS: **PROFESSOR PLUCK** AND **DANIEL** AN ARCH DEMON LORD HAS BEEN UNLEASHED UPON THE MORTAL REALM. AS THE DESTRUCTION OF AERYENOUS DRAWS NEAR, PREPARE YOUR ARMIES. THIS IS A CATACLYSMIC EVENT. IF THE ARCH DEMON LORD IS NOT STOPPED, IT WILL DESTROY ANOTHER CAPITAL CITY EVERY **48 HOURS** UNTIL NOTHING IS LEFT. YOU ARE THE FINAL BASTION. SAVE THE WORLD OR PERISH WITH IT.

TIME REMAINING (FOR AERYENOUS): 5 MIN. 26 SEC.
REWARD: SPECIAL EVENT TITLE
PENALTY FOR FAILURE: UTTER ANNIHILATION
SPECIAL WARNING: ANY PLAYERS DEFEATED BY THE ARCH DEMON LORD WILL HAVE THEIR CHARACTER ERASED. THIS IS A PERMA-DEATH EVENT.

"Emmy."

"Yea, I saw."

"Perma death."

"Yup, at least I can get a new player name."

"You're infamous now, Professor Pluck."

"Fuck me, but so are you."

"Nah, my names pretty common."

"Not as a player name, you idiot."

"Ohh, yeah.. maybe."

"Should we make a run for it?"

YOU ARE NOT ALLOWED TO LEAVE.

Both Daniel and Emilio grabbed at their heads. The unexpected telepathic shout was ringing in their minds.

"Ow, shit."

MENTAL FORTITUDE - LEVEL (18)

"Yea, no kidding, I just got a skill up from that."

"For real? What skill?"

"Mental fortitude."

"Huh, ohh, is that like the fear resistance thing?"

"Hmm, maybe, I got it when some monster took control of my body and had me running around."

"Yea, that's the fear resist skill. I haven't unlocked it myself, not like it matters much now."

"Less than four minutes left."

"It doesn't seem to be attacking us. It's just standing there, not even really looking at us. What do you think we should do?"

"Fuck it, lets try to kill it. I know you're a hoarder, so use all your expendable shit, don't hold anything back."

"Aww dude, you know I hate using my precious items."

"That's why I'm telling you to burn them all, it's perma-death so all that super raid gear is gonna get deleted *along* with all the crap in your inventory."

Daniel heard a very deep sigh escape his friend. He couldn't help but laugh out loud.

"Shut up! Here, use this, it's a temporary combat booster, fuck it cost me so much DKP."

Daniel grabbed the proffered bottle of glowing green liquid and drank it down. He felt a bit of a vibrancy, but didn't pay much attention to the benefits it provided. Instead he pulled out his mask and put it on, trying to give him as much of a stat edge as possible.

With under three minutes left they did a fist bump and summoned their weapons.

Emilio had two glowing pistols, one in each hand.

The Arch Demon seemed to finally look at them, as they both prepared to engage.

Daniel flared his aura as hard as possible and burned a lightning step to appear behind the demon.

Emilio was the first to strike, firing off both pistols as they dissolved in his hands, holding only one charged shot each.

The demon waved its left hand as the two shots landed, making a light scuff mark on its chest, but also sending Emilio slamming into the wall with some kind of telekinetic attack.

Daniel slashed down at the demon's back, as his friend slumped down the far wall to hit the floor with a muffled thud.

Losing Friends

To the surprise of both the Arch Demon and Daniel, his two blades cut deep.

As an opening salvo, he had imbued one with life mana and the other with space mana. Remembering his battle with the dimensional viper, he wanted to see if this demon from a different realm was susceptible to such attacks. The life mana was just an assumption that demons were weak to such a thing based purely on mythology.

The space mana did the greatest harm, and Daniel imbued both blades with it as he maneuvered around the demon to strike once more.

The demon was having none of that.

It began to take Daniel a bit more seriously.

Its left hand swiped out at him, sending a dark wave of energy towards Daniel.

He hopped backwards and to the right, evading the attack.

As the wave of darkness splashed up against the back wall, it started dissolving the stone and made sploshing and hissing noises.

Definitely need to avoid that..

The demon sent out a few more waves of darkness in Daniel's direction, but he easily avoided them.

A vial of purplish energy smashed into the demon's left shoulder, causing a mini black hole to appear. The effect was immediate and the black hole disappeared in an instant, taking with it a huge chunk of the demons back and shoulder. Its left arm was dangling precariously by a very small stretch of sinew as the demon shrieked in pain and rage.

"Nice! Got any more of those?" Daniel shouted.

Emilio was up and running around the other side of the chamber, pulling out more vials with multi-colored glowing energy inside.

"Nope! But I got some other things, like this!"

He hurled a blue vial at the demon's side, and it struck, releasing a mini thunder cloud with millions of tiny lightning bolts striking out at the creature.

The after effect was sadly disappointing, as it only left a small burn pattern on the demon's waist.

As the demon swirled and rushed towards his friend, Daniel didn't waste a second and pierced through the creature's back with both blades.

What followed was a furious back and forth where Daniel would strike, then flee out of melee range and Emilio would toss another vial at the demon, getting its attention and further enraging the wounded monster.

The damage from all the attacks seemed to be piling up as its reaction time started to slow and the dark energy waves it randomly tossed out were becoming much easier to dodge. A faint hope started to blossom in Daniel's chest.

We might actually do this!

"Emmy, keep it up! It's slowing down!"

"Hell yea, bro!"

Their constant barrage of random elemental attacks and sword strikes had really done a number on the demon. Its left arm was still completely unusable and its body was covered in countless elemental scars. Daniel had managed to slightly hamstring it as well with a lucky sword strike when it was distracted while trying to hit Emilio with a wave of darkness.

The two of them kept up their coordinated assault until Emilio ran out of expendable items.

"Shit! I don't have anything else to throw at it!"

"What about a range weapon? Can you shoot it with anything?"

"Nah dude, I'm a melee fighter, no range gear equipped!"

"What about that pistol strapped to your chest?"

"Huh? Oh, that's just part of my outfit."

Daniel had been on the defensive, now that the demon's attention was focused primarily on him.

Frustrated with the demon's tenacity for life, despite its overwhelming injuries, Daniel felt a twinge of panic as the combat booster he'd taken before they started the fight began to wear off.

In a sudden flurry, Daniel pushed forward, angling himself to ensure Emilio was behind him and let off a series of attacks, followed by a point blank release of his aura surge.

The room was lit up in blinding light as Daniel's aura drained his health rapidly while it washed the demon in a barrage of lightning.

With only a quarter of his life left, Daniel jumped back to stand near his friend as they both surveyed the damage.

"Dude, that was sick, too bad it wasn't enough.."

"Yea, shit, this thing just won't go down."

Limping forward, its entire body a charred mess, the demon moved with surprising speed as it closed in on them once more.

Without saying a word, they nodded at each other and circled the wounded creature. Together, they began to inflict more and more damage as they worked in tandem. Emilio's blades weren't able to do much to the demon, despite its horrid state, but Daniel's strikes continued to bleed the creature.

It was hardly any effort for Daniel to avoid its attacks, but Emilio started to take considerable damage from errant blows he wasn't able to evade.

An unlucky swath of darkness hit Emilio square in the chest, causing his health to rapidly decline.

"Shit, Emmy! Be Careful!"

"Yea, yea, I'm fine."

Pulling out another vial, Emilio tossed it onto the ground and a good portion of the floor was suddenly glowing green.

Both Daniel and Emilio's health began to regenerate to full while they were in the healing field he'd just used.

"Nice!" Daniel called out in elation.

We've totally got this!

With renewed vigor, the two of them continued to whittle down what was left of the demon, both of them smiling at each other as victory was tantalizingly close.

The healing field faded, leaving both of them in perfect health.

After finally disabling the demon's right arm, Daniel geared up for a finishing blow.

Summoning all his strength and with a powerful aura burst, he gave everything he had in an attempt to decapitate the Arch Demon.

Feeling both his blades sink deep into its neck, Daniel was consumed with adrenaline and excitement.

PATHETIC

The voice of the Arch Demon was like a mental attack.

It forced Emilio onto the ground and had Daniel cradling his head.

MENTAL FORTITUDE - LEVEL (19)

Feeling the world return to normal, they both got their bearings quickly, but what they saw swiftly stole away their sense of impending victory.

Both of Daniel's blades were still embedded in the demon's neck, but it was rapidly regenerating from all the wounds they had inflicted.

As both of its arms were restored and all of the elemental scarring disappeared, the demon flexed its neck and sent the two blades scattering across the floor, its neck sealing back up.

What followed was a desperate scramble to regain his weapons and not get decimated from all the blades of darkness that were flung about the room.

Emilio had burned another expendable item that seemed to cover him in a protective bubble, making him appear invulnerable for the time being. This freed up Daniel to focus on his own survival.

The room was bathed in thousands of swaths of darkness as Daniel was blasted about with telekinetic attacks.

It seemed almost unfair.

As soon as Daniel would get back to his feet after being blasted against a wall, he had to nearly instantly dodge the blades of darkness, only to be blasted off his feet once more.

He wasn't even able to swing a sword.

The onslaught finally slowed down for a brief moment, only for Daniel to realize in horror that the demon was turning its attention back to Emilio. His protection bubble was fading.

Daniel had been pushed to the far side of the room, but he drew heavily on his lightning aura to give him as much speed as possible and he pushed himself to get at the demon before it had a chance to claim his friend's life.

He wasn't fast enough.

The protection bubble popped and the demon flung Emilio against a wall then hit him with a blade of darkness.

Emilio's health dropped to just a sliver of life from that one attack.

As the demon raised its clawed hand to finish off his friend, Daniel slammed into the side of it with all his might.

It was as if he'd crashed into the side of a mountain.

The Arch Demon didn't even flinch from the impact.

Faster than thought, it grabbed Daniel by his neck and whipped him around to its front side, then impaled him with its other claw.

As Daniel's chest was shredded by the demon's claws, he was then sent smashing into the wall on the other side of the room by a telekinetic blast.

Ahh fuck, that got me.

Daniel watched as his body started to pixelate.

Everything was happening in slow motion.

The demon stretched out its clawed hand and started slurping up Daniel's pixels.

Emilio jumped in front of the demon's claw and threw something at Daniel as he called out, "I gotchu brother!"

As the glowing crystalline teardrop shattered upon Daniel's chest, he was instantly restored.

"Wha- How many of those do you have left?" He called out in a panic.

The entire fight had been completely one sided after the demon recovered itself. He was pushed to his limit and his mind was scrambling to keep up.

With a dumb smile on his face, Emilio stood with his back to the demon.

"Just the one."

A claw burst through his chest.

Daniel watched as his best friend was then tossed to the side. What looked like blood was oozing from the demon's fingers, and it contemptuously wiped its hand down its side, as if his friend's blood was disgusting.

Emilio began to pixelate.

The demon, with a distasteful frown, turned its clawed hand to his friend and started consuming his pixels.

Tears welled up in Daniel's eyes.

Not now. I don't want to lose him again. We just started hanging out. I.. I don't want this. Why? Why does this always happen to me?

Closing his eyes hard, Daniel focused on that invisible wall that blocked off his soul power.

With an outpouring of rage, anger, hurt, sadness and despair, he pushed. Intertwined with all those emotions were feelings of unadulterated happiness.

All the fun times he'd had as a kid and just recently, as they'd reconnected, those emotions of joy bound together all his negative feelings. His desire to save his friend solidified into an indomitable force of will. He was unaware of it at the time, but the game administration had forcefully attempted to block his soul essence. The wall they had built to sever him from his soul essence was torn asunder as Daniel's Intent solidified in his mind, body and soul.

A feeling of peace washed over him as he embraced the power of his soul.

His body began to glow with an inner light that had no shadow.

In less than a fraction of a second, he was standing before the Arch Demon, both swords coated in that eerie light.

The battle that took place was beyond the speed of human cognition. Their movements were stressing the entire global game engine that ran Final Bastion Online.

Every player logged in at that moment experienced a strange sensation of lag as the two of them clashed.

A vast amount of processing power was redirected towards the Arch Demon by the games administration as thousands of eyes watched the remarkable battle taking place in the tiny artificial dungeon.

More and more resources were allocated to support the Arch Demon as it struggled desperately against a fourteen year old boy.

Many voices called out at once, warning a collective mind that several failsafes had been breached and that no more power could be diverted or else millions of lives would be lost.

So the Arch Demon reached its limit.

Daniel kept going, faster and stronger.

His battle never ending, his resolve unwavering.

The Arch Demon could not escape Daniel's blades.

It was cut into ribbons, then what was left burst apart.

A shower of multicolored light washed over the artificial dungeon, completely obliterating it, walls and all.

Daniel was left floating in a null space, surrounded in nothing but a dull endless gray in all directions.

Worriedly searching for Emilio, he felt his alignment dissipate as his inner light faded.

Unsure of what else to do while he floated in this null space, he sent out a private message to his friend.

<u>Daniel to Professor Pluck:</u> Hey, you okay?

As he waited, a gnawing uncertainty ate at his gut.

Should I try logging off? What happened to the dungeon I was in? Maybe I should submit a help ticket or som-

The world around him shifted violently.

Daniel found himself back above ground.

He was standing where they had been sitting earlier, waiting for the hooded man.

Making a beeline for the city, hoping desperately to find his friend at the bind stone, he was startled by a quest update.

WORLD EVENT:
THE ARCH DEMON OF AERYENOUS

ATTENTION ALL PLAYERS. THE ELVEN CAPITAL OF AERYENOUS HAS BEEN SAVED! IN A HEROIC CLASH THE FOLLOWING PLAYERS: **PROFESSOR PLUCK** AND **DANIEL** HAVE TRIUMPHED OVER AN ARCH DEMON LORD, SAVING AERYENOUS FROM CERTAIN DOOM.

REWARD: ALL PLAYERS WHO WERE ONLINE DURING THIS EVENT WILL BE AWARDED A SPECIAL EVENT TITLE: SURVIVOR OF THE FIRST CATACLYSM. SPECIAL EVENT TITLES WILL BE AWARDED TO THOSE WHO PARTICIPATED IN THE BATTLE FOR AERYENOUS.

PENALTY FOR FAILURE: UTTER ANNIHILATION

SPECIAL WARNING: ANY PLAYERS DEFEATED BY THE ARCH DEMON LORD WILL HAVE THEIR CHARACTER ERASED. THIS IS A PERMA-DEATH EVENT.

Oh, thank goodness. I was sure that our fight had gone past the event timer. I'm glad the elf city is safe. The quest message seems to show that both of us defeated the demon, I hope that means Emmy just died normally, and not in that perma-death way. Ughh, I should have gotten his cell phone number so I could just log out and call him.

As Daniel neared the city, he felt a huge wave of relief wash through him.

He'd gotten a message from Emilio.

Professor Pluck: Dude, we survived that shit? How the hell.
Daniel to Professor Pluck: Where are you? The dungeon we were in sort of got destroyed.
Professor Pluck: Hot damn. I'm in Aeryenous, at the bind stone.
Daniel to Professor Pluck: On my way!

Professor Pluck: I have terrible news.
Daniel to Professor Pluck: What?
Daniel to Professor Pluck: Hello?
Professor Pluck: ...
Daniel to Professor Pluck: Dude! What is it? What news?
Professor Pluck: All my super good consumables are gone! ;_;
Daniel to Professor Pluck: I hate you sometimes..
Professor Pluck: What are we going to do! It took me years to get all that stuff! That dragon tear was worth sooo much money! This special title better be worth it.

Daniel made his way to the first bind stone that was just inside the gates of Aeryenous.

Standing there going over his inventory was a distressed looking Emilio. His fingers were scrolling and hovering over an invisible screen that only he could see.

Daniel didn't slow down as he tackled his friend, laughing the entire time.

"Ouch, shit. You got here fast, what the hell."

"Hey! You just elbowed me in the face!"

"Well yea, you attacked me like a wild animal, it's the least you deserve. Now fork over all your plat to pay for that dragon's tear!"

A wrestling match ensued that caused a bit of alarm to some of the people watching the two. Only their laughter kept anyone from interfering.

Some guards came over and told them to settle down.

Sitting with their backs to the bind stone, they checked over their quests.

QUEST UPDATE:
THE ARCH DEMON SEAL
YOU HAVE SAVED AERYENOUS FROM CERTAIN DOOM.
RETURN TO GWENITHE FOR YOUR REWARD.
REWARD: SPECIAL EVENT TITLE
PENALTY FOR FAILURE: THE COMPLETE DESTRUCTION OF
THE ELVEN CAPITAL AERYENOUS

"Looks like I just have to return to Lady Gwenithe to get my quest reward. How about you?"

"Ahh yea, I have a note on that world event quest that says to go to someone named Lord Commander Gwenithe, the Elven Strike Maiden in Aeryenous to receive my reward. Also, got a quest update from that original quest after doing the turn in to that asshole that tried to feed us to the demon."

"Fuck that guy."

"Yea. Fuck that guy."

"What do you have to do next?"

"Oh, I have to find that guy's boss, some faction leader over in Vandean."

"Vandean? And you never told me what faction that quest was even for."

"Oh snap, it was for the Desert Orcs faction. You've never heard of Vandean? Dude, it's like the vegas of FBO! They have *everything* there. Most of the adults who aren't real gamers, log in just to go there. I heard you can have crazy orgies and build your own harems. There's tons of gambling and a huge arena crowd out there. It's a real bloodsport, they make the fighters turn off the pain blockers so they fight for real. I turned them off once as a joke, got punched in the stomach and nearly puked my guts out. Never gain, man, never again."

"I have the pain blockers off. You get a skill that makes it easier to deal with after a while. I hardly notice it anymore, honestly."

"Wait. WHAT?!"

"Uhhhh. I never told you that?"

Emilio had turned to look at Daniel, his face a mask of incredulity.

"You have them like, *off* off? Or just set above fifty percent?"

"I turned them off completely, that's how I'm so fast while using my aura. If you turn the pain blockers off you can develop a much stronger aura power."

"Dude. I thought you just had some kind of movement skill. You've been using some kind of aura power this whole time?"

"Yea."

Turning back around, Emilio crossed his arms.

"You know, I can't quite understand how you solo'd that demon. Like seriously, that should have been impossible. I basically did nothing to it and just hopped around, trying to survive as long as I could. But you. Somehow, you defeated it. What's up with that man?"

Daniel sat there a moment and let the silence linger as he tried to figure out how to explain what happened. He wasn't entirely sure himself.

"I .. it's kind of a long story."

"We've got time. The road to Vandean is a bit long."

Both Daniel and Emilio could feel the eyes of the crowd that surrounded them staring down at them both. Most of them made it obvious that they were players. Many of which were whispering to each other after identifying them as the world event players in the broadcast message.

Daniel cleared his throat, feeling a bit anxious at all the sudden attention. Turning to his friend he spoke softly, "we should get going, I know where Gwenithe is."

Nodding back, Emilio got to his feet and helped Daniel up.

"Lead the way."

Together they stepped into the crowd, with people parting before them.

This is weird.

"Dude, we're like celebrities, this is awesome."

"What? No. This is embarrassing."

"Oh stop whining, enjoy the fame Danny. You might get lucky and score a girlfriend. .. Do you have a girlfriend?"

"Emmy. Of course not .. you?"

Daniel felt his face flush pink under his mask at the thought of girls.

"Hah, not yet, but after today it's just a matter of time before women throw themselves at the feet of the mighty Professor Pluck!"

Daniel rolled his eyes so hard they almost fell out of his head.

"Yea. Sure. Keep telling yourself that, you nerd."

"What did you call me?"

"A nerd."

"I will have you know that I failed several midterms this year. Nerd I am not. Warrior of epic repute, I am."

Emilio started flexing his rather skinny arms as he flashed Daniel his cheesiest smile.

The further along they got, the less noticed they became, until soon, they were just another set of anonymous heads bobbing along a busy roadway.

Titles

Winding their way through the city, Daniel led them unerringly to the gates of the royal estate.

One of the guards pointed their way and another was sent off at a run before they'd even arrived at the gate.

"Hail, Daniel and company. The Lord Commander has been notified of your arrival. Please wait here a moment until she can attend to you."

"Of course, thank you."

Daniel barely got the words out before he spotted Gwenithe walking up towards the gate from the other side. A smile wider than he'd ever seen graced her elegant features. She looked genuinely pleased to see him.

"Daniel! You have eased a worry that has nettled me for countless decades. Come, a reception is being held in your honor. Who is this that you have brought with you?"

Waving in an overly relaxed manner, Emilio called out, "Hey, I'm company, nice to meet you!"

With the slightest burst of his aura, Daniel spun and punched his best friend in the shoulder, then turned back. Most people would have missed this interaction, but Gwenithe caught it and an amused twinkle sparkled in her eyes.

"Company you say? What an interesting name."

"Sorry Lady Gwenithe, this is Emilio, my goofball friend."

"Ahh, well, it is a pleasure to meet a friend of Daniels. I am Lord Commander Gwenithe, welcome to the elven royal estates of Aeryenous, Mister Emilio."

Blushing slightly, his friend just clamped his lips in a tight line and nodded back at the elven woman that towered over both of them.

Daniel laughed to himself as he felt Gwenithe assert her aura over his friend.

She really is an intimidating lady.

"If you would both follow me please, we are headed to the royal palace."

Turning toward the gateway gardens, she followed the direct path that led right through the middle of them, straight to the massive structure on the other side. As they got some distance from the gate guards, she turned her head over her shoulder and spoke to the both of them.

"Now, I understand that the two of you likely have very little notion on how to conduct yourselves while in the presence of nobility. I must press upon you to please be respectful and mind your manners."

Daniel couldn't help but notice the especially pointed stare at his friend as she said this.

Hopefully I don't trip on anything. If Emilio acts a fool, well, that's on him. He was always trying to be a class clown, but whatever, it's reward time!

Smiling brightly behind his mask, he followed Gwenithe past some very large and elaborately carved golden doors.

Making their way through an ornately decorated hallway, Daniel's gaze danced across many statues and huge paintings that adorned the walls and alcoves on either side. Their foot falls echoed loudly down the hallway making all the attending palace staff notice them right away. The guards seemed to try and stand a little straighter while the other attendants tried to remain completely invisible as they passed, bursting into motion after they were a certain distance away from them.

Gwenithe led them to another intricately carved set of double doors, both of which were closed. Two guards in very fancy shiny gold and silver armor stood proudly before the doors.

An attendant with a horn shaped object in his hand, stood in between both guards.

"Please state your names for introduction."

"Lord Commander Gwenithe, the Elven Strike Maiden, accompanied by Daniel and his friend Emilio, better known as Professor Pluck."

"Very well."

Daniel saw the look of concern cross his friends face as he raised his hand to object.

Before he could utter a single syllable, the double doors burst open and the man with the horn bellowed out towards a massive crowd through the magical megaphone.

"Attention! Now introducing Lord Commander Gwenithe, the Elven Strike Maiden, accompanied by Daniel and his friend Emilio, better known as Professor Pluck."

As hundreds of pairs of eyes turned their way. Daniel elbowed his temporarily frozen friend and followed after Gwenithe as she swept into the room with a regal air.

Meanwhile, Daniel and Emilio looked flat out awkward in comparison as they stiffly and somewhat meekly followed the intimidating and graceful figure in front of them.

"Bro, they're all staring."

Emilio's desperate whisper was tinged with panic.

Daniel responded with his own hushed whisper, "I can see that, captain obvious. Just play it cool man."

"That's easy for you to say, hiding behind that mask of yours. You don't even know how crazy this whole thing is. No player ever has met with a race capital city ruler. The nobility are untouchable. I'm pretty sure this is a game first."

"What? Seriously? I thought FBO has been out for like five years. How could we be the first?"

"Dude, I'm telling you, this has never happened before. I've never heard of a world event either. People would brag like crazy if they got a meet and greet with a city noble, much less the actual kings and queens."

They settled into silence as they approached an imposing set of thrones. Two large thrones were positioned on a slightly elevated platform and several smaller chairs were set just below them and to either side. The chair to the King's right was empty. The left was occupied by what looked to be the queen, and the row of chairs to her left were similarly occupied by elves in extremely intricate clothing.

Daniel recognized Prince Felcore in the farthest chair to his right, the youngest of the direct line to the King and Queen.

Pausing at a certain distance from the two huge thrones where the King and Queen sat, Gwenithe gave a respectful salute and bowed her head.

With pleasant smiles, both the King and Queen gave respectful nods in return.

"Aunt Gwenithe, I see you return with the heroes of the hour. Would you please introduce them to us?"

"Certainly, my King."

Turning to the boys, she caught both of their eyes, and pointed at the ground in front of her in two separate places, indicating where they should shift their standing position too. Many of the gathered elves behind them let out amused murmurs at their apparent lack of noble custom and culture.

Daniel saw the briefest flash of irritation wash across Gwenithe's face before it was gone, as if it had never been.

Moving to stand slightly behind Daniel and on his right, she gently laid her left hand on his shoulder. Another murmur rippled across the assemblage, this one full of surprise and shock. On Daniel's left, he could feel the nervousness oozing off his friend.

Ohh man. This is so much worse than being called on in class. Please let this end quickly. I can feel all their eyes staring into the back of my head.

"I am very proud to introduce someone quite special to you. This is Daniel. As you may already know, the world has echoed out his name for vanquishing our eternal foe, the Arch Demon Lord Cranzor. That alone is extremely impressive. To think that these two have managed to slay such a fearsome enemy by themselves, it astounds us all. To

Daniel's left is his friend, Emilio. His name, called out by the world, is Professor Pluck."

"Welcome to my hall, Daniel."

The King and Queen both gave *very* slight nods to him.

"Welcome to my hall, Emilio."

Again, the King and Queen both gave *very* slight nods.

"Now tell me, Emilio, are you the one that stole the very seal of the Arch Demon that inspired the events of today?"

Hearing his friend audibly gulp, Daniel felt a bead of sweat trickle down his own neck in sympathy.

"Ye.. Yes. Good King."

Good King? I mean, what do I call him if he asks me a question? He never gave us his name and Gwenithe called him 'my king' and I'm totally not calling him that!

Feeling a dooming sense of dread churn his guts to mush, Daniel panicked inwardly on how he should address the King.

"Hum, well. As the events have led to a fortuitous end, I will hereby pardon you of this crime against the royal house of Aeryenous. Furthermore, I hereby grant you this title, **Instigator of the first Cataclysm**. May you bear it with the knowledge that all decisions have consequences, many that are unintended and some that can be truly devastating."

Turning his attention to Daniel, the neutral expression he'd shown to Emilio slowly transitioned into a slight smile.

"Daniel. It has been made known to us, by the echoes of the world, that you are mainly responsible for the defeat of such a monstrous creature. For your incredible bravery and heroic deeds this day, I hereby grant you this title, **Hero of the first Cataclysm**. Know that the good will of all the people of Aeryenous travel with you, young man."

QUEST COMPLETE:
THE ARCH DEMON SEAL
YOU HAVE SAVED AERYENOUS FROM CERTAIN DOOM AND
RETURNED TO GWENITHE FOR YOUR REWARD.
REWARD: TITLE: HERO OF THE FIRST CATACLYSM
PENALTY FOR FAILURE: THE COMPLETE DESTRUCTION OF
THE ELVEN CAPITAL AERYENOUS

Nice, quest complete. Hopefully we can leave now.

"There is more, my King."

"Oh? Tell me Aunt Gwenithe, what more is there?"

"Daniel was pivotal in the rescue of Prince Felcore."

Raising his eyes questioningly, the King turned to look at his youngest son in the farthest chair to his left. Prince Felcore had a huge smile and nodded his head at his father.

"Tell me."

"Yes, my King. Daniel found me while deep in the Aerfall. He offered his services in exchange for the chance to become a Sage. This is known only to a few, but with your permission, may I reveal the events of the Aerfall, my King?"

Huh? So does he already know what happened? Then why did he look over at his son? Is this some kind of show for all the people behind me?

One of the elven women sitting near Prince Felcore had suddenly shifted her face to the floor as the color seemed to drain from her face.

That must be the princess that banished Felcore.

"I give my permission, Aunt Gwenithe."

"Thank you, my King."

Raising her voice slightly, the entire hall was silent in anticipation at learning a new tidbit of gossip.

"I was sent into the Aerfall after Prince Felcore. A Djinn relic had been used to make a wish to banish him to the deepest parts of the Aerfall. To uphold the wish in good faith, the Djinn themselves took up arms to keep Prince Felcore prisoner. Using another wish to find the Prince's location, I began the journey deep into the Aerfall, only to have Daniel come to my aid when I was wounded from having to protect the key to the Prince's cage. With Daniel's help, I was able to fully recover and we ventured together into the heart of the Aerfall. After observing his battle prowess and officially acknowledging him as ready to attempt the steps into Sagehood, I began his teaching while we escorted the very fragile key through some of the most dangerous territory in all of Aerfall. We arrived at the door of the Djinn and attempted to negotiate with them. Three Djinn were guarding Prince Felcore and refused to give him up. They sealed the doors and did their utmost to slay the both of us."

Pausing to take a breath, she let the crowd stew a moment before she continued.

"In what can only be described as a selfless act of heroism, Daniel drew the attention of *two* of the Djinn to give me the opportunity to face one of them in single combat. Despite my most valiant efforts, I was soundly defeated by just one of them. As the moment of my death drew near, Daniel appeared before me, deflecting the blade that was meant to end my life. In awe, I watched as a new Sword Sage was born. He overcame an incredible trial and was able to defeat *all three* of the Djinn on his own. Together, we carried the prince to safety. Along with rescuing our banished prince, he also performed another miraculous deed. He returned my long lost grandchild Abbyzael to my estate after valiantly protecting the lives of our exiled kin from monstrous invaders, who butchered my daughter along with many others. He has returned a lost piece of my soul after so many years spent in grief. I am proud to present my latest student, the Sword Sage Daniel, to the elven royal court of Aeryenous."

The silence was deafening.

Apparently, Gwenithe hadn't told the King everything, as genuine surprise seemed to radiate from him.

"A Sword Sage. Truly? And your granddaughter, Abbyzael, has been found?"

"Yes, my King."

"Astounding!"

Smiling, Gwenithe tapped his right shoulder once more, then made her way over to the empty seat to the King's right and sat down.

"Astounding, indeed, my King. I request you allow me to provide his rewards for saving our banished Prince and my granddaughter."

"Of course Aunt Gwenithe. Anything I were to give would only pale in comparison to your gifts."

"Daniel, might I ask that you remove your mask for a moment?"

Without pausing to think, he reached up and snatched the mask from his face, shoving it into his inventory as he called out, "Of course, Lady Gwenithe."

His words caused an agitated buzz throughout the assembly. This time, he even caught a few snippets of conversation amongst the nobles.

"Can you believe he shows such blatant disrespect to the Lord Commander!"

"Calling her 'Lady Gwenithe' as if he were an equal!"

"Well, he is a Sage, so maybe he is an equal?"

"Pffah, she is a direct descendant-"

"Enough!"

The King's simple command silenced everyone.

He then turned to look at Gwenithe, and nodded for her to continue. The crown atop his head seemed to give off an oppressive presence that caused the gathered nobles to collectively catch their breath. The pressure eased as Gwenithe took a deep breath herself.

"Two gifts I offer you, Daniel. One is information. The other is a title that can only be given by another Sage. The information I offer you is where you can go to find two more Sages. They are a married couple. Alistar has specialized in defense and his wife Rose is the opposite. She specialized in offensive soul essence and heavy strikes. They can be found in Vandean. Please take this letter of introduction and give them my regards."

Lady Palimore was suddenly standing to his right, holding out a wax sealed letter.

Surprised by her appearance, it took Daniel an uncomfortable amount of time to receive the letter and put it away. Lady Palimore gave him a deep bow and moved off to the side once more.

"This next gift is a very special one. I am so very glad to be the one who grants this title to you."

Closing her eyes, she seemed to cause all the air to momentarily remain still as a heaviness descended upon them all. In a voice that reverberated with tremors of power and with the inner glow of light that cast no shadow, she opened her eyes and looked deeply into his.

"With my authority as a Movement Specialist Sage, I recognize thee as a peer. Welcome to Sagehood Daniel. Let the world echo this triumphant occasion, and welcome to the first step of the Divine Path. May your light shine upon the world."

Quest Update:
The Hunt for Sword Sages

You have taken the first step on the path of sagehood. You have successfully unlocked the Sage Rank in the specialization combat form skill. Seek out the defensive and offensive Sages to advance further. Alistar and Rose can be found in Vandean.

Reward: Sword Sage Training
Penalty for Failure: Loss of advancement potential

New Title Acquired:
Title: Sword Sage

Title Effect: Empower body with soul essence
Note: Unlock Sage rank for other combat forms to increase soul potency

World Event:
The First Sage is Born

Attention all players! Congratulate your fellow player: **Daniel** for being the very first person to achieve **Sage** rank in any skill. There are many paths to Divinity. May this **Sword Sage's** light shine upon you all!

Daniel was overwhelmed by the influx of system messages.

Another world event? And a new title? What is this stuff about divinity? Can I become like a God in this game?

DING!

Congratulations!

You have gained multiple levels
You have leveled from 76 to 83
Hit Points, Mana and Endurance: +70

My levels! What the heck is that all about?

Feeling completely out of his depth, Daniel just numbly stood there. He wasn't sure what he should feel, but currently at the top of his list was queasiness from being the center of attention for so long. He didn't even want to think about the world event messages. Shoving everything to the back of his mind, he emotionally began to turtle up, falling into his old habits when the world just became too much to deal with.

He vaguely recalled being dismissed by the king and getting a small wave goodbye from Gwenithe. Lady Palimore came to his and Emilio's rescue, guiding the two of them out of the royal palace.

Once they were finally out past the gate entrance, Emilio seemed to come back to himself.

"Dude! That was SO. FUCKIN. EPIC!"

He was shadow boxing the air as they walked away from the royal palace, heading deeper into the city.

"Yea. I'm tired. I need to take a break."

Hearing the distance and strain in his friend's voice, Emilio's good cheer was instantly replaced with concern.

"For sure man, let's go find an inn, it's super late anyways. Bro, my guild mates are blowing me up. Let me answer all these damn messages."

They walked in silence for a bit until they found the same inn they had been staying at all week. Emilio's face had been rather animated as he conversed with his guild. Making their way upstairs, Emilio called out to Daniel just before they went into their separate rooms.

"Hey, see you tomorrow, right?"

"What? Yea, of course. I'll talk to you later."

"Wait! Give me your net number."

In a zombie like fashion, Daniel nodded and sent a private message to Emilio with his neural net number that was assigned to him last year when he'd been given his hand held phone display. Despite the ability to use the internal neural net to make phone calls and speak to one another with just their minds, most people still preferred to use a physical phone that was registered to their neural net phone number. Scam calls were still a big problem and it was much easier to forward everything through a physical device that you could ignore than have your neural net get pinged all the time by incoming messages.

As Daniel logged out, he just shoved all his game equipment to the side of the bed so he wouldn't damage it and curled up into the fetal position as he slipped into a dreamless sleep.

What It Means To Be A Friend

Waking up to a text message on his phone, Daniel rolled over in a confused state of being half awake and half asleep as he stared blankly at the phone screen.

What? Why am I getting a text message?

It was from an unknown number, but after reading the message, it finally clicked that this was from his friend Emilio. He was letting Daniel know that he'd be late logging on today, but would be on sometime after lunch.

Daniel responded, letting his friend know that he'd log on around the same time.

Taking the much needed break, he decided to veg out and watch some television. Being inundated with options, he actually spent most of his morning just clicking through all the different shows he could watch, without actually selecting anything.

His mind drifted over the events with the demon and the fight, followed by the meeting with the elves afterwards and the game wide messages.

Parts of him were ecstatic at being given such recognition, but a large part of him was terribly anxious about how all his classmates would react to the news. The fight with Jessica's guild was mostly just a small thing in comparison to all the events going on in the massive world of Final Bastion Online.

Getting bored from not actually deciding on anything to watch, he quickly started using his neural net to bring up some web displays and did some searches for news on the game. What he found was a bit startling.

An update was released this morning.

The info packet with all the changes and new enhancements from the update were listed. Many of them were small, inconsequential fixes to items or effects. The big update was the release of the Sage ranks. All it had was a small blurb about making sage's available for those who have mastered certain skills and they should all have quests to help them in their search for these new trainers.

Guess I won't be the only sage for long.

Closing out of his web searches from his neural net, he got up and made a quick lunch.

I wonder where my parents are. I haven't seen them at all today.. Oh is it a work day for them? No, wait.. It's New Year's Day. Did they stay at a hotel or something last night?

Daniel was glad at the thought that his parents were out enjoying each other's company when he was suddenly hit with a pang of loneliness. His thoughts centered around Mirantil and he wondered what she had been up to.

Stop worrying about her, she isn't even real.

Logging back into FBO, Daniel focused on some things he'd been meaning to do for a while now for his character.

As he stood up, he lightly pulled on his outfit to straighten it, even though he didn't need to. Some habits were impossible to break.

"Time to get a better inspect skill."

Not sure why I said that out loud.

Pulling out his map, he found a nearby store marked as a general knowledge hub for adventurers. He figured he'd find out from there how to go about acquiring some much needed skills.

It didn't take him long to get there and he was surprised to find that they actually sold a bunch of generalized skills, one of which was an enhanced version of inspect.

Following the advice he'd gotten from Gwenithe a long time ago, he finally purchased the highest rank inspection skill they had, which should include most general knowledge around nearly all cataloged creatures.

As he held the skill crystal in his hand, a prompt asked if he wanted to upgrade his current skill, and he affirmed the upgrade. He didn't feel any differently but he assumed the skill upgrade worked, despite the skill name not changing at all.

Spending a few minutes more browsing, he didn't see anything that he felt he really wanted, except the stealth skill, which he bought and activated right away.

Looking down at himself, he appeared a bit transparent, but that was it. The clerk in front of him didn't seem to have any trouble seeing him either, so Daniel deactivated the skill.

Soon after, he got a message from Emilio saying to meet him at the main gate of Aeryenous and he made his way there.

"Bro! I didn't even leave my inn room before I got a quest update from that Desert Orc faction! I need to go back to that lab or whatever, where we fought that demon. Supposed to find something there and bring it to a faction leader in Vandean."

"For sure man, let's go. But, that place was totally destroyed, like the game deleted the dungeon or something and spat me back out above ground. Not sure what all is left of that place."

"Nah, I'm sure a new dungeon is there, come on!"

Daniel and Emilio zipped their way through the woods of the Aerfall and found the ruins that led to the demon summoning dungeon. Sure enough, a new dungeon was available, but it was for Emilio only.

Daniel could only sit and wait outside.

Emilio returned and showed Daniel a massive chunk of crystal. Giving his new inspection skill a try, he was disappointed that it only showed the same kind of detail for items.

CRYSTALIZED ARCH DEMON ESSENCE
NOTE: REMAINS OF AN ARCH DEMON

"Crystalized Arch Demon Essence? What are you supposed to do with that?"

"I found a bunch of notes that said the guy who was summoning the demon was supposed to kill it and collect its essence, then turn that essence over to one of the faction leaders of the Desert Orcs. Some guy named Teal O'Gluich. So now my quest updated saying I should take this to that

Teal dude. It says he should be near Vandean. So, same destination as your other sage trainers."

"For sure, so should we head to Vandean.. Or?"

"Yea! Lets jet, it'll take us a few irl days to get there, no fast travel yet and the mount speeds kinda suck in FBO."

"Irl?"

"Oh, uhh, it means in real life, so like multiple real world days. Sometimes I forget you're a total newbie."

Daniel let out a half laugh and scratched the back of his head in embarrassment.

Putting the large crystal back in his inventory, Emilio then pulled out a small, magical flying carpet and hopped onto it.

"Well, mount up so we can go."

"Ohh, I don't have a mount, but I can probably keep up.. I think.."

"Dude, you think you can keep pace with this baby?"

He affectionately patted his undulating carpet.

"Maybe? How fast is it?"

"This is one of the ultra rare desert storm sand god carpets. It's probably the fastest mount in the game. Drops from a *super* hard to beat raid boss over in the western provinces. I don't have any spare mounts and all the stuff you can buy in town is garbage, so for now you lead and I'll float along behind."

Daniel scratched the side of his leg, not because he had an itch, but because he was slightly embarrassed again.

"I.. I don't actually know the way."

Face palming, Emilio pulled out his map and showed the city of Vandean to Daniel. Easily finding it on his own map, he was able to trace a decent line straight south through the Aerfall and into the desert lands beyond.

"Ahh, okay. Ready?"

Emilio leaned back on his carpet and imperiously waved his hand forward.

"After you, my friend."

Daniel turned in the general direction of Vandean and started lightly sprinting with his aura pushed hard enough to drain a little bit of health. He then burned a lightning step and allowed his health to tick back up while easing off of his aura before pushing hard again.

Before he could really get a decent rhythm going, a private message dinged his game interface.

Professor Pluck: Slow the fuck down man.

Letting his aura fade, he slowed down and looked over his shoulder.

Emilio was nowhere to be seen.

It took a few seconds for Daniel to spot him as he finally caught up.

"Geez, okay. Maybe you are faster than my mount."

They both started laughing and then it was Daniel's turn to wave imperiously at his friend.

"After you, good sir."

"Oh shut it, that aura thing is a damn cheat."

Emilio led the way and they made good time.

The carpet was much faster than the mounts Alyssa and her group used. It was also faster than those hell hounds Jessica chased him down on. But with his new gear and levels, Daniel's continuous aura speed was unmatched.

Daniel kept pace easily and the two ended up spending most of the time chatting about their lives and things they had been up to. Emilio talked alot about all the different people he went to school with and all the friend groups he was able to squeeze into. He'd already been to a bunch of high school parties and had lots of stories about all the antics of his classmates.

On the second day, Emilio had finally pried open one of Daniel's secrets. He told his friend all about Jessica and the big three. Their bullying all throughout his middle school years and the events that took place over the last six months.

Emilio was quiet at first, then furious as he heard more about what Jessica and her entourage had done to him. He laughed and joined in with Daniel's satisfaction at decimating her guild. He'd even heard of The Nameless and was happy they had been given some karmic payback for all their horrid in-game behaviors. Despite Daniel's insistence that he was fine with how things were, Emilio wasn't having it.

"Nah man. This isn't over. You said it yourself, she basically walked away in the end, not having had to really pay for her actions. You might be fine, but I'm not. That bitch has a reckoning coming and I plan to be there to see it through."

Daniel was at a loss for words.

He felt a strange warmth in his chest, and he had to admit to himself that it was a really good feeling when someone became extremely upset over his mistreatment for all those years.

As he was lost in his thoughts, Emilio brought him back with a question.

"So what happened after that? You left that elf village and went to Aeryenous? Why?"

Daniel pursed his lips as a slight blush crept over his face. He really wished he'd put his mask back on, but he'd left it off since their appearance at the royal court.

Emilio noticed his friend's embarrassment immediately and started pestering him relentlessly.

"Tell me! Bro! You have too, what *happened*?!"

"Fine! Ugh. It's not a big deal."

"Sure, sure, then tell me."

"So, I got an escort quest to bring some elves to Aeryenous. So I protected them and got them there."

".. Okay? If that's all, why are you all weird about it?"

Taking a deep breath in, Daniel let it out in a loud sigh.

"Well, that isnt it. One of the elves sort of had a thing for me and we kinda got together but then things ended just as we got to the city."

".. Dude .. What?"

"Huh? What?"

"Okay, so, first of all, was the elf you escorted a person or an npc?"

"Oh, an npc."

"Yea. You need to be a bit more specific when you say, 'you kinda got together' cause last I checked, we were minors and this game has *extremely* strict rules in place for anyone under eighteen."

"Well, like.. We kissed and stuff."

Emilio tossed both of his hands in the air and fell off the back of his flying carpet.

Daniel stopped and watched as his friend seemed to be yelling at the air incoherently while he waved his hands and walked in a small circle.

"You can't! .. Total Bullshit! .. How does he .. What kinda two faced.."

Emilio suddenly rounded on his friend and grabbed him by his shoulders.

"You have to tell me everything, how did you get to kiss an npc?"

The look in his eyes was intense.

"Wha- What do you mean?"

"Danny. Danny, danny .. danny. You need to understand something. If anyone under the age of eighteen even *attempts* to approach an npc with the thought of kissing them, much less even *hugging* them they get an instant warning, followed by a week long suspension. What you are saying is strictly impossible for us. But *SOMEHOW* you found a way to get past the ban hammer and actually get to first base with, I'm assuming, some smokin hot elf chick npc?! How? Daniel, HOW?!"

Emilio was practically shaking him back and forth in his earnest desire to uncover the secret of npc romancing.

With nervous laughter, Daniel tried to placate his friend.

"Look, I don't really know how it happened, we were just hanging out, we went for a walk and held hands, then later she tackled me and we made out for a minute. And yea, she was insanely pretty."

"But HOW? Was there a quest or something?"

"No, no quest. She led all of our talks and stuff."

"Wha- nah, bro you have *got* to be full of shit. Some smoke show elf was tryin to snatch your v card? Cause you're totally a virgin and you *have* to be lying about all this."

"Dude, I'm not lying, it happened."

Daniel started to get a bit defensive.

"Hah. *Suurrreee* it did."

While aggressively rolling his eyes, Emilio got back onto his carpet and took off.

Feeling a bit sullen at not being believed, Daniel followed behind his friend, calling out softly, "it *did* happen."

"Oh shit, check it out!"

Emilio pointed over the horizon as a small speck was now visible across the hard packed dirt. They had made it out of the Aerfall earlier that morning and were closing in on Vandean.

"Is that it?"

"Yea, that should be Vandean, I think."

Emilio pulled out his map for a minute to confirm.

"Yup, definitely Vandean."

It took them another couple hours to finally reach the city as it had been much farther away than it looked.

Before they arrived, Emilio finally got his answer out of Daniel on how he solo'd the raid boss. Daniel's sword sage skill along with his insane aura powers gave him a distinct advantage over other players. They debated the different methods to unlock a sage rank for one of Emilio's combat skills, but they ran into a wall when he flatly refused to turn off the pain blockers. Daniel firmly believed it was a requirement for unlocking a sage rank skill and a frustrated Emilio gave up on the idea of becoming a swashbuckling god of death and destruction.

As Daniel finally got a good look at the city, the building designs were all strange. Lots of deep blues and light purples and swirls everywhere. There was also a dark cloud cover that seemed to extend around the entire city and a good way out into the surrounding area. The dark clouds seemed to churn a bit, but never moved away from where they sat in the sky, casting a perpetual darkness over the city of Vandean.

There were guards around the walls of the city and by the gate they approached, but the guards didn't seem to be stopping anyone and simply allowed the flow of foot traffic without any sort of intervention.

Passing through the gates and into the outskirts of the city, Daniel got his first glimpse of the vampire races and dragonkin.

"Hey, is that a vampire with tiny wings?"

Daniel poked his friend's arm as he whispered, while nodding toward a group of pale skinned women with deep red eyes and stark white hair. All of them had tiny wings coming out of their backs through a light colored shirt.

"Them? Nah, those are succubus. Looks like a group of npcs. Hey, if you want me to believe your story, walk over there and try to grab one of their butts. Just be careful of their tails, people say they are super sharp."

"What. No way! They have tails? I don't see.. Ohh I see them."

Looking closer, Daniel could see a jet black, thin tail snaking around each of their waists.

"Look man, you won't get more than five feet away before you get hit with a warning then a ban if you don't stop, so either man up and grab some digital tush or you will forever be branded a liar."

Emilio had stopped and turned around to face Daniel, crossing both of his arms while pointing the sternest look he could muster at his old friend.

"Ugh, fine, move."

Daniel pushed his friend out of his way and started marching over to the group of succubi non-player characters.

He started to panic, and pulled out his mask and equipped it, instantly feeling a bit more bold in his actions.

As he got closer, he felt adrenaline flow through his body and his right arm started to shake.

What am I doing? Will I get in huge trouble? Why did I let him talk me into this. This is so stupid.

Step after step, Daniel got closer, until a few of the succubi stopped their conversation and turned to look at him.

He nearly lost his will right then and there.

Hearing a snort from his friend pushed him to take another step forward.

WARNING:

STOP! YOUR CURRENT ACTIONS VIOLATE FINAL BASTION ONLINES GAME PLAY POLICIES FOR MINORS. IF YOU DO NOT DESIST IN THIS ACTION YOUR ACCOUNT WILL BE GIVEN A TEMPORARY BAN!

The warning message popped up, completely obscuring his vision, causing Daniel to immediately take a step backwards.

Oh. Well, I guess Emmy was right, but then how did Mira..

Turning back towards his friend, Daniel was at a loss for how to explain his experiences with the elf and was only rewarded with a self satisfied smirk on his friends face.

"Well? How'd it go, Prince Charming?"

"Oh shut up, I got a warning message."

"Yea, see, you're full of shit, mate. Come on, I know a cheap inn where we can rent some rooms for a month at a time."

New Year, More Training

After finding the inn that Emilio had mentioned, they split up to work on their individual quests. Emilio went to find his Desert Orc contact while Daniel went in search of the two sages.

When they dropped the group they had formed back in Aeryenous, Daniel felt a pang of sadness. He knew he had his friends' contact info and could message him anytime he wanted, but they were essentially parting ways again to follow their own separate pursuits.

After stuffing his mild depression into a box and shoving it aside, he started wandering around aimlessly as he wracked his brain on how to actually find the sages. He ended up asking around at several adventurer information centers as well as the adventure society found in Vandean and finally scored a hint as to the whereabouts of Alistar, the defensive specialist.

Making his way over to a massive guard barracks, he hesitated while standing in front of the large doors that were closed.

I'm pretty sure this was the building that one guard pointed out. If he's not inside, then maybe someone will know where I can find him.

Gathering his courage, Daniel stepped forward to pull open the large door, only to have it open in his face, nearly knocking him to the ground.

"Ack-"

"Whups, sorry there mister."

A town guard wearing the symbol of Vandean on his chest plate brushed past Daniel and headed off down the street.

Before the door could close all the way, Daniel pried it back open and slipped inside.

Gross. It stinks in here.

The smell that assaulted Daniel was one that was reminiscent of a not very clean locker room. It made Daniel want to hurry and get out of there as the smell started to make his eyes water.

The room he was standing in looked to be a mix of an assembly area and a break room with several benches and chairs along the far wall. Off to his left, he saw a set of stairs leading up and just past them was another set of doors.

No guards were present in the large room, so he made his way over to the other doors and slipped past them.

He was greeted with a massive dusty courtyard that was walled in by the surrounding building.

Loud clangs and grunts could be heard from hundreds of people. Some of them were training and doing set exercises while others were sparring with each other.

Several men wearing thick, red, leather were walking around and shouting at everyone they passed by. Criticisms and praise alike were given nonstop.

One of the men wearing red leather spotted Daniel and walked over.

"Well, you're new. Here to get some training in?"

"N-No, sir. I'm here looking for .. Alistar?"

His soft smile was instantly replaced with a frown.

"Why are you searching for Lord Alistar?"

Swallowing the sudden influx of saliva in his throat, Daniel was intentionally careful with his answer.

"It's a private matter. Can I find him here?"

After a very long pause, the man just grunted and turned his head over his shoulder, calling out, "General Alistar, Sir! You have a guest!"

A hundred pairs of eyes looked over, scrutinizing Daniel.

He felt a chill pushed its way through his body as he squirmed uncomfortably under so much attention.

Several people exercising stopped what they were doing and made a path for a large bearded human to trot through the middle. His regalia was worn and was a match for any of the other exhausted men in the dusty courtyard. The only thing that made him stand out as anything special was the way everyone showed great deference to him and the pressure he gave off as he towered over Daniel.

"Yes? What is it?"

Finding himself standing before another imposing figure, it took a second for Daniel to collect himself.

He pulled out the wax sealed letter he'd received from Palimore and handed it over to Alistar.

The General paused as he examined the wax seal, then opened the letter, examined the contents, folded it closed once more and put it underneath his worn leather training jerkin.

Folding his hands behind his back, Alistar turned to the man in the red leather and dismissed him.

"Come with me, Daniel."

Alistar walked over to the mostly empty left side of the courtyard. He walked up to what Daniel guessed was a massive ballista and turned towards Daniel after placing his large meaty hand on the huge siege weapon.

"So, you're the newest Sage. Gwenithe spoke very highly of you. This here is an Arc Bolt Ballista. A single bolt from one of these can punch a hole through the scales of a child of Demy. The only thing I've ever seen stop one of these is a soul essence enhanced defensive measure. You see this cord over here? Just give it a good yank and it will fire off an Arc Bolt."

He then moved over to stand directly in front of the giant siege weapon. Using his foot, he carved a line in the dirt behind him.

"Go on, pull the cord and fire it off."

Obediently, Daniel gave the rope a solid yank, and a loud snap echoed out as a massive bolt was shot from the ballista straight into Alistar's chest.

There was a resounding boom as a metric ton of dust was scattered everywhere. Once it finally settled, Daniel looked over with concern at the man he'd just launched a ballista bolt at.

Ohh, phew, he's fine.

The General was dusting off his jerkin and combing out his beard.

He hadn't moved a single step.

"Your turn."

Alistar walked over to a nearby rack that was covered with more bolts and loaded another bolt onto the ballista then grabbed the release rope.

Daniel just stood there a bit dumbly.

"Well? Go on. Stand in front of the line. If you can keep from being pushed back past it, I will pass you as a Sage rank in defensive measures."

"But.. I haven't bound myself yet.. That will kill me."

"I thought you were a sword sage? Just release your soul essence and use it to shield you from the bolt. You'll be fine.. Probably."

Feeling a bit bewildered, Daniel stood to the side of the massive weapon.

Okay, focus, just activate my soul essence, then block the bolt. Damn, I really should have bound myself here first. If I die, It's gonna be a long walk back.

After using his soul essence a few times, Daniel had gotten better at feeling where the power sat inside his body. It tended to move around, but he could always sense a denseness in a certain area and it was almost like he just had to squeeze that denseness to have the soul essence pour out.

Feeling the denseness hovering near his left shoulder, Daniel put pressure on it and felt his soul power flood his body. Equipping both of his swords, he stepped up in front of the ballista and braced himself.

TWANG!

All of the air in his lungs were ripped out as he was sent careening across the dusty courtyard. He bounced twice before smashing into the far wall, where he rolled into a fetal position.

Uhhhnnng. What the fu-

"Oye! Hey! You alright, boy?!"

Daniel felt the presence of several shadows hovering over him as he clutched his stomach. Someone laid a hand on him and he felt healing magic flow into him, bringing his health back to full from under 5%. The Arc Bolt had nearly killed him and would have punched a hole through his chest if his swords hadn't partially deflected it.

"Medic! We need a Medic! Officer Luant was stabbed clean through by a flying sword! Quick! He's dying!"

Still struggling to catch his breath, Daniel could hear a bunch of movement as several people were rushing about nearby.

Did he say someone was dying?!

Blinking rapidly as he struggled to his feet, Daniel looked around the courtyard to see what had happened.

A few men wearing dark green arm sleeves were huddled around a group of people, all seemingly focused on someone laying on the ground. Off to his left, a bit high up on the wall, one of his swords was embedded in the wall, to the hilt.

He spotted his other sword just past the group of men tending the wounded soldier and limped over to grab it while surreptitiously checking in on the poor guy.

He seems to be doing okay. His health is going back up at a decent rate.

Daniel put his sword away and walked over to stand underneath the one sticking out of the wall.

Feeling a powerful hand on his shoulder, he turned to see Alistar standing there, giving him a bit of a rueful smile.

"Prolly should have warned the boys. I was just so excited to see what you could do. Glad you survived, but you have a lot of work to do before you're ready to try another Arc Bolt. Get that sword out of my wall and follow me over to the archery range."

With that, he turned and walked off toward the doors leading back into the building.

Daniel hurriedly surged his aura and leapt up to grab his sword and pull it from the wall. Landing lightly on his feet, he put the weapon away and quickly caught up to the General.

In a somewhat subdued manner, Daniel followed behind Alistar like a little duckling. He was still feeling a little rough from the ballista bolt.

The General led him out of the barracks building and down a few streets to another large structure. After passing through the inside, he was led out to the back where hundreds of guards were shooting arrows, throwing axes or chucking spears down a wide range.

Alistar called for one of the instructors and he let him know of his training plan for Daniel, one in which Daniel felt he was ill prepared for.

"You want me to get shot at by everyone here?!"

"Well, yes. We are marking a safe zone for you to rest in, but this will be excellent practice for our men, as well as you. Here, let me show you something."

Alistar stood in front of Daniel and crossed his forearms.

A pressure settled on Daniel's shoulders as he watched the man's soul essence pool into a circle that floated in front of his arms. The shadowless light was unmistakable, but Daniel was at a loss for how he projected his soul power outside of his own body.

"How are you doing that?"

"Same way you do it, I just focus it out in front of me. Now you try."

Daniel spent several minutes with just his arms crossed while keeping his swords in his inventory. He squeezed that floating denseness hovering around his right leg this time and flooded his body with soul power, but try as he might, he just couldn't get it to manifest outside of his physical self. He had to stop and rest as it seemed to take a good deal of mental strength to apply pressure to the moving ball of denseness. It was like he was flexing a muscle he never knew he had, and it was extremely taxing to do so.

"Well, the battlefield is the best place to forge new strengths, so just get out there and keep trying. I'm sure you'll get it. Come find me when you're ready to give the Arc Bolt another try. Good Luck!"

Alistar spent some time chatting with some of the other people around the facility before he departed, leaving Daniel to watch as a foot high barrier was erected on the far left of the main archery range.

That looks like my 'safe zone'. There isn't much room, hope the archers don't cheat and try to hit me when they shouldn't. I should probably go bind myself soon, just in case I take a stray arrow through the eye. Ouch, just thinking about that makes this whole thing suck.

The rest of the day went by in a blink as he was intensely focused on this new training regimen. He'd gotten a message from Emilio saying his quest was taking him out of Vandean for a bit, but he would message if he ran into any issues. Daniel updated him on his own quest and they promised to meet back up soon.

Every day until the start of classes Daniel was getting shot at by arrows, spears and axes. He started making miniscule progress once he used his swords to deflect the projectiles while trying to infuse the air just beyond his weapons with his soul power. His gains were small, but a definite change was taking place with his control over his soul essence.

School was back in session and his winter break was now over. Checking his class schedule, Daniel mentally mapped out a route to all of his new classrooms.

Fortunately, his first few classes went by without anyone paying him any attention, just the way he preferred it.

He was ambushed while on his way to the library during his lunch break by Alyssa and Jasmine.

"Daniel! How was your time off?" As Jasmine asked her question, the two girls surrounded him and essentially forced him to walk between them towards the cafeteria.

"It was good, how about yours?"

Daniel was a bit flustered as they essentially ignored his question and Alyssa started up, "hey, so that guild, The Nameless. After the video of you went semi-viral, a bunch of high end raid guilds banded together and spent nearly all December spawn camping all of their members. It. Was. Glorious. Even we got to join in."

They stopped at a vending machine so Alyssa could buy a few snacks, as both Daniel and Jasmine had brought their own lunches.

Jasmine spoke up as Alyssa was digging around for some cash, "yea, it was intense. There was this hugely coordinated effort to track as many of their members as possible and lock down their bind stones. Then it was essentially open season on all of them. I even scored a few kills myself!"

"Oh nice! I've read online that it can be really hard to play offensively when you're a healer."

"I do have a few damaging abilities, but I mostly just kept our team alive while we maintained an around the clock camp rotation. It was epic."

Grabbing her snack-lunch from the machine, Alyssa led them over to their same customary table and they all sat down, with Daniel in between them.

Alyssa leaned over and grabbed his arm as she excitedly shared the next bit of news with him.

"Apparently most of their guild members didn't even like each other and the constant spawn camping made several of them rage quit. The entire guild ended up disbanding and all of their most notorious jerks are essentially blacklisted from being able to join any of the other top raiding guilds. I heard that a few of the guild officers even went as far as deleting their characters to start over as nobodies!"

"Woah."

Daniel was floored.

"Yea, the community really came together to put the kabosh on all that player griefing. What Felly really wants to know about is your sage rank though, she's been pestering us about it all week."

The table was now full and Daniel was suddenly noticing he was completely surrounded by real life girls.

As Alyssa laughed at Jasmine's comment, Daniel felt his face turning red now that half the table had paused their own conversations and were focusing entirely on him.

"I .. uh."

Daniel's mind blanked out as he made eye contact with the redheaded girl across the table from him. She was the one who had offered him a french fry the last time he sat at this table. The last time he'd seen her was at the aquarium. Her advice had been a vital piece of the puzzle that was preventing him from unlocking his soul essence.

Alyssa elbowed him teasingly, "aw, come on! Tell us how you unlocked a sage rank. All I have is some vague quest that basically says 'git gud'. What are the prerequisites? Are there certain class trainers that will unlock it for you? We need the deets! Spill it!"

Daniel laughed a little at her silly commentary and did his best to not look at any of the smiling faces around the table. Instead, he focused on his paper lunch sack as he fiddled with the edge.

"So, I got the first quest from my starter trainer that only said to go find more information on sages, then that town I saved from The Nameless ended up having a relative of a sage there. I got the quest to escort her to her grandmother, and then met up with her, the grandmother that is, who turned out to be a sage. Went on a quest with her and I was able to unlock the sage rank. It seemed broken at first, with my interface being all weird, but it looks like it's fine now. When I got my quest reward, that was when the global announcement went out."

Alyssa scrunched up her face as she asked, "you got the initial quest from your first trainer then stumbled across a family member of a sage?"

Before Daniel could answer, the redheaded girl asked her own question, "who is the sage?"

"I .. uhh, it was the Elven Strike Maiden, Gwenithe. She is in Aeryenous."

"But isn't she elven royalty?" Jasmine added.

Daniel nodded as he responded, "Yea, apparently she's the king's aunt. She sat on a throne just to the left or uhh on the king's right, that is."

Alyssa breathed in a sudden gasp. "Wait, are you telling me you were in the Aeryenous throne room?"

"No way!"

"But nobodies ever spoken with any FBO royalty before!"

"I doubt anyone important was there, it was probably just a quest instance."

Daniel wasn't sure if he should let them know that he met with the entire elven royal court. He figured they wouldn't even believe him, so he tried to just keep quiet as the girls at the table gossiped about everything they've heard involving in game royalty.

As the conversations around the table devolved into several side topics that no longer seemed related to the game, Daniel started to actually eat his lunch.

Alyssa poked him in the shoulder and asked, "So what was up with that crazy world event, something about a demon?"

Hastily trying to swallow his bite, Daniel ended up lightly choking on his food.

"Hah, you okay?"

After taking a few struggling breaths, he nodded back.

"Ye- Yea. Sorry."

"Need some water?" Alyssa offered him a sip from her water bottle that he accepted nervously.

"Thanks."

Oh my gawd, is this an indirect kiss? Does she like me, or is she just being friendly?

"Who was that Professor guy that was named in the quest with you?"

Turning to answer Jasmine, Daniel cleared his throat as he returned the bottle of water to Alyssa.

"He is an old friend of mine. We used to be neighbors. It was his quest that actually caused the demon to show up. I could have stopped him and taken back the seal he stole, preventing the demon from even showing up, but I decided to help him out instead and had to basically fight the demon by myself."

"Oh.."

Why did I say it like that? I sounded so arrogant and full of myself!

Daniel had unconsciously tried to make himself sound impressive while in front of the girls. Their reactions were immediate as Jasmine and Alyssa both had slight frowns and their body language set alarm bells ringing in Daniel's head. He knew he'd messed up and tried to correct his statements.

"Well, I mean, it was pretty crazy how it became a perma death encounter and my friend used a bunch of costly one time use items to really wound the demon. I would have died if it wasn't for one of those items. The quest timer showed three or so minutes before we even attacked it, but I could swear the fight lasted much longer than that."

Alyssa nodded along, "Yea, the timer stopped at like two minutes and forty something seconds. A bunch of people were panicking and trying to leave Aeryenous while the coalition of raid guilds that had been hunting The Nameless got back together. They were trying to get everyone to the city for the event while the timer was paused, but then the event ended."

As Alyssa just shrugged her shoulders, Jasmine turned to look at him and tilted her head, "Did you say perma death?"

Alyssa's eyebrows rose as well, "Yea, seriously, what was up with that? I saw that as a special note on the event message."

"What? It said that in the event message? I guess I was all caught up in trying to get to Aeryenous and didn't even read that part!"

Daniel had a far away look in his eyes as he remembered the Arch Demon trying to steal away his friend's death pixels as he responded to the girls.

"Yea, it was scary, that's for sure. It nearly got both of us. It would stick out its hand and sort of vacuum up the pixels as you died. Emmy used a revive item on me and I was somehow able to keep it from activating its perma death thing on him when it struck him down."

Daniel's eyes got a little watery at the thought of losing his old friend once more. Quickly rubbing his eyes, he tried to think of something else to distract himself.

Way to seem like a cry baby, gah.

Alyssa patted him on the back as she soothed him, "Aww, well it sounds like you both made it out okay. Did you get an awesome quest reward?"

"Just a title, that was it."

"Ohh, everyone got a title."

Their conversation lapsed into silence as they finished eating. Alyssa and Jasmine both got pulled into side conversations and left Daniel to sit quietly by himself.

Once the lunch break ended, he swiftly excused himself and unobtrusively slipped into his afternoon class.

The rest of the day was rather uneventful and Daniel finished up his fitness quests before logging back in after school.

He didn't make much progress on his defensive soul essence form and he credited that to his distracted mental state. He kept reliving his conversations with Alyssa and her friends, internally criticizing his lameness as he mostly just sat there quietly, not talking to anyone.

The rest of the week ended up following his normal routine, with lunches in the library as he browsed online wiki's or read books, followed by after school workouts and soul essence practice.

It ended up taking him until the first week of February, until he felt ready to give the Arc Bolt another try.

Exuberance Of Youth

Daniel made his way over to the barracks where he'd first found Alistar. He was confident in making a successful attempt at properly blocking the Arc Bolt after his month long training session as a pincushion for the archers and spear throwers.

Alistar greeted him right away and they marched over to the Arc Bolt ballista.

"Let me know when you're ready, Daniel."

Word had spread about Daniel's last attempt and the ballista was given a great deal of space in the courtyard, in case another pair of swords went flying. The soldier he'd accidentally injured previously was fine and was even there today, cheering Daniel on.

The line in the dirt was still there and Daniel positioned himself in front of it.

Taking a moment to flush himself with soul essence, he felt it move around his body.

Holding his arms up with both swords making a large cross, Daniel created a dense circle of protection that floated out an inch from his hands.

He gave Alistar a nod, and the General gave the loaded ballista trigger a strong tug.

This time, as the bolt fired off, Daniel was able to stay on his feet, but two long lines were etched into the dirt as the force of the bolt pushed him back nearly seven feet.

He'd taken no damage, and was completely fine.

"Yeah!"

"Nice one!"

"He really did it!"

"No need to dodge a sword this time!"

"Woohoo!"

The soldiers in the courtyard all cheered Daniel's progress.

It was a strong confidence boost to have so many intimidating men congratulating him. A warm fuzzy feeling bloomed in his chest as his face flushed with excitement.

Alistar was already loading another bolt as he smiled over at Daniel.

"That was excellent, lad. You're almost there. The final step in establishing a truly insurmountable defense is to properly root yourself. What I do is use the same technique that you employ while making the front shield, to make two spears that extend from the base of your heels and dig into the ground behind you. Now give it a go and let me know when you're ready for another bolt."

Daniel got to work and tried imagining a set of spears poking out the base of his heels. It was difficult to maintain the front shield and the back spears, mostly because his mind was having trouble molding his soul essence into the correct spear shape. He kept feeling them solidify, but then they'd lose consistency right away. It was a delicate balancing act, keeping his focus split, but when he felt he had it, he gave a nod to Alistar.

TWANG!

Daniel was flipped end over end, landing hard on his face.

At the last second, the spear coming out of his right heel lost its form and the other spear somehow bent itself, causing him to do several backflips before landing on the ground, face first, a few feet away.

"Oww, that looked like it hurt!"

"How many flips was that?"

"I think it was three.. And a half."

"Nah, it was two and a half."

"Are you sure? He was spinning pretty fast there."

"What a grip! He kept both swords in his hands again!"

Feeling embarrassed, Daniel got back up and stood in front of the dirt line once more.

Alistar hadn't said a word, only loaded another bolt and stood at the ready.

In a fit of inspiration, Daniel asked, "Does it have to be spears? Or can I use swords?"

Alistar took on a thoughtful look as he considered it.

"Hmm. I think swords would work, might even be more natural for you. Give it a shot!"

As Daniel prepared himself for another bolt, he found it was significantly easier to keep a sword shape, similar to his own blades, with his soul essence. He had almost no trouble at all keeping them solid and digging into the ground behind him.

He nodded once more to Alistar and the man let loose another bolt.

A wide grin spread across Alistar's face as Daniel stood unmoving after taking an Arc Bolt point blank from a ballista to the chest.

The silence in the courtyard only lasted a few seconds before wild cheering began echoing off all the walls of the enclosed space.

Daniel couldn't stop his own smile from stretching ear to ear as he took in all the praise.

Nice! I totally did it! Should I tell Alyssa? .. Why did I just think of her? I should definitely tell Emmy though. Haven't heard from him in a while, hope he's okay.

"Well done, lad! I'm impressed it only took you this long to master the defensive sage arts."

As the cheering died down a bit, Alistar's face changed from radiating happiness to serious intensity. Daniel caught on to the shift in his mood and was focusing nearly all of his attention on the large man that stood before him.

"I suppose I ought to make this official then. With my authority as a Defensive Specialist Sage, I hereby recognize you, Daniel, as a peer. Congratulations on taking another step along the path of sagehood."

Quest Update:
The Hunt for Sword Sages
You have taken another step on the path of sagehood. You have successfully unlocked the Sage Rank in the specialization combat form and defensive combat form skills. Seek out the offensive specialist Sage to advance further. Alistar and Rose can be found in Vandean.

Reward: Sword Sage Training
Penalty for Failure: Loss of advancement
potential

Sweet!! Now I just need to talk to his wife, Rose, and I can hopefully get the offensive form, although the movement form seems pretty overpowered as it is. I can't even imagine an offensive focused strike or what that would even look like.

Alistar's face shifted back into a jovial relaxed look as he walked over and placed his hand on Daniel's shoulder.

"I spose you'll be lookin for my wife next. She's away from the city for another day and won't be back until some time tomorrow. Some kind of diplomatic mission to ease tensions with our Orc neighbors. Come find me after tomorrow and I'll introduce you to her. After she read that letter from Gwen, she's been dying to meet you."

"Oh, for sure. I'll come find you in a day or so then. Thanks so much, man! I really appreciate everything you've done for me."

"Myself and Rose would do nearly anything for such a close friend of Gwen's."

With a final clap on his shoulder, Daniel could feel the dismissal from the man who was used to ordering around soldiers all day. Alistar turned to the milling crowd and started barking out commands. The relaxed atmosphere instantly morphed into one of focused intensity as everyone seemed especially motivated in their respective workouts and sparring sessions.

Laughing to himself, Daniel turned and left the barracks.

As he started wandering around the town of Vandean, mostly for the first time since almost all his time had been spent at the nearby archery range, Daniel sent a message to Emilio to check in with him.

It took a while to get a response, but it turned out Emilio had been given a bunch of solo fetch and escort quests with a promise of a huge reward at the end. He was getting rather bored with all the faction grinding, but he claimed the rewards should be worth all the trouble.

Not finding all that much to do and with it being nearly his normal log out time, Daniel went to his inn and disconnected a bit early.

He found both his parents hanging out in their living room watching a news program, so he sat down and joined them.

They chatted for a bit and Daniel's apparent good mood became infectious. They decided to go out for a family dinner at a nice restaurant that evening.

As they were ordering their meals, a group of arriving guests that were being seated not too far away caught Daniel's attention. A familiar figure was taking a seat and locked eyes with him momentarily.

Alyssa!

Before Daniel looked away, Alyssa shyly averted her eyes for a moment, before shifting her eyes back towards him and giving a small wave.

He looked down at his table, briefly looked back up, gave a small wave himself, then looked back down again.

His face flushed a light pink as he felt an extreme bout of nervousness churn in his stomach. It felt like the side of his face was throbbing with each beat of his heart.

My heart is beating so loudly! Ugh, how embarrassing. I bet my mom can hear it.

To his utmost relief, his parents seemed oblivious to his current state and remained that way throughout their dinner.

Daniel did his best to remain as undetected as possible while he surreptitiously spied on Alyssa and her family. He could have sworn that he caught her looking his way on several occasions.

Leaving the restaurant with his family, Daniel couldn't help but feel a sad disappointment suffuse his mood. He had been fantasizing about going over and convincing her and her family to dine with his family and then letting his mind explore all the possibilities that could have led to.

Alas, my social anxiety is a force to be reckoned with. Not sure if I'd ever have the courage to do something like that.

As night turned to day and classes came and went, Daniel found himself presented with another unexpected encounter.

While out on his daily run to complete his fitness quests, he saw Alyssa doing some pull ups at a nearby neighborhood park.

His feet had a mind of their own as his run turned into a light jog that finally transitioned into a slow walk leading him straight to her struggling form.

As she landed heavily and slightly out of breath, she gave him a welcoming smile.

Giving a small wave, Daniel spoke up first, "Hey, .. how many did you do?"

Wiping her brow with her shirt sleeve, she turned to face him.

"This is my fifth set. I can only manage around six or so before my arms give out."

"Nice. I'm not much of a pull up guy myself. Luckily my fitness quests don't require me to do them often."

"Yea, I figured I could use this as an arm and back workout at the same time, knock off two exercises at the same time."

Daniel suddenly felt extremely aware of what every part of his body was doing. He kept thinking how weird his hands and arm movements must look and started fidgeting nervously.

Shit. What do I say next? Should I talk about that restaurant yesterday? What about school? Maybe I should talk about classes.. Ahh!

As Daniel was struggling mentally on what he should do or say next, Alyssa just calmly stretched her arms and back as she checked her neural net workout info. She was looking to see what her next exercise should be when Daniel blurted out something neither of them were prepared for.

"So, you wanna go out sometime?"

Oh. My. God. Wha–

"Oh.. Umm.."

With a dreadful sinking feeling, Daniel could feel her answer would be no.

"S-Sorry.. Daniel. I.."

As she slowly shook her head, Daniel started panic talking, "Hey, it's all good! No worries! Good luck on finishing your fitness quest. Get that Expee!"

Daniel had lifted his right hand into a fist and made a silly motion with his arm as he said the word expee.

Turning around, he fled down the street the way he'd come. Lamenting the entire way on how lame his silly hand gesture was and how awkward he appeared.

I can't believe I said that! What the heck! That was so ballzy. That bastard Emilio must be rubbing off on me. This is so embarrassing. I'm so proud of myself for even asking, but I really want to puke now.

In a state of utter shock, depression and rejection, Daniel burst into his house and ran right to his toilet where he hovered over the rim as his nausea spiked.

It took him a good half hour just to leave his bathroom.

Another hour passed of just him sitting on his bed, staring at the wall in disbelief while his proudness of his courage fought against the humiliation of rejection.

The depressive feeling of rejection ultimately won out and in a malaise of sadness he logged into Final Bastion Online.

Hunted Once More

With a numb emotional state, Daniel robotically made his way over to Alistar's barracks. He had fallen back to his old habit of dissociating and turtling up when everything became far too overwhelming for him to deal with.

Alistar could instantly tell that something was wrong as he walked up to Daniel despite the mask hiding his face, but he kept his concerns to himself. If Daniel had been more aware of his surroundings, he would have seen a strange flash of light travel across Alistar's eyes and a knowing smile creep up his face.

Instead, Daniel let himself be led from the barracks as he mutely followed along behind the large man. Alistar was able to confirm that Daniel was at least listening to him through his one word responses and for some unknown reason decided to take this opportunity to express his musings on love and relationships.

He referenced his own marriage and spoke a great deal about how he suffered from all kinds of rejection before he met the love of his life. Alistar kept up the one sided conversation about his many romantic failures until Daniel finally asked him a question.

"How do you get over them?"

"Hum, well, you never really do get over losing someone or ending things. They stay with you, forever changing you in some small way after leaving their mark on your soul. Don't remember them for how painfully they hurt you, instead let your mind and heart remember how happy they made you feel. Most people we meet aren't meant to be in our lives for all that long, it's the truly rare ones that stick around."

Daniel was like a sponge as he soaked up Alistar's wisdom. He started to try and come to terms with what had happened between him and Alyssa, focusing on how excited she made him feel and letting the sadness weigh a little less on his heart from the rejection.

He hadn't been paying any attention and was rather surprised to find himself standing at the back of a very large crowd. Alistar's presence seemed to give off a strong repelling vibe and there was a circle of emptiness around them.

As they stood there, Daniel gave the crowd a once over, noticing all kinds of races present. He saw dark elves and vampires chatting it up with dragonkin and many others all mingling together.

None of them seem like players. Is this just a massive group of non-player characters? What are we even doing here?

Before he could voice his question, a small commotion towards the front of the crowd got his attention.

A striking young woman walked out on the raised stage in front of everyone as a much taller guard wearing resplendent full plate armor followed right behind. What gave Daniel pause was the massive sword the guard had strapped to their back. It looked a bit comical, since it was extremely wide and thick, making it appear completely unwieldy.

As the young woman began speaking, Daniel spotted sharp fangs and pegged her as a vampire.

He quickly became uninterested in what she was saying as her first few words started with thanking the local citizens for being good citizens and then her kind words turned into some sort of political campaign speech.

"Why are we here?" Daniel couldn't help letting a little huffiness escape, his emotions were still raw and not under his complete control.

"Well, we're here to meet up with my wife. That's her on stage!"

"Wait. What? Your wife is a vampire?"

"Huh? No. Not Queen Fidel, she's the one standing next to the Matriarch."

That person with the ginormous sword?

"Oh."

Daniel didn't know what else to say.

Alistar elbowed Daniel softly as he pointed towards Queen Fidel.

"You see that necklace the Queen wears?"

"Yea. That glowing purple color seems pretty intense."

"Oh aye. It's got some incredibly powerful enchantments. It's widely known as the lover's heart gemstone. If you put it on, it will pull you in the direction of your true love's soul essence. And what's even crazier, is if they see you wearing it, they instantly fall head over heels for you. It has something to do with how it creates a sort of bridge between peoples soul essences. That's how Rose found me. The Queen lent her that necklace and it pointed her right towards me. We've been together ever since."

Daniel mulled over his story about the necklace as he watched the purple glowing gemstone sway slightly back and forth as the Queen became impassioned by her own words.

As a resounding cheer echoed out at the end of her speech, she departed the stage with Alistar's wife.

"This bunch will be getting rowdy for a while after all that, follow me."

Alistar led him through the crowd and past a security checkpoint that was manned by several heavily armed guards. They saluted him as he walked passed and Daniel made sure to stick close by as they scrutinized him intensely with their eyes.

It didn't take them long before they ran into Alistar's wife as she was giving orders to a contingent of guards.

Once she had finished handing out assignments, she turned towards her husband and removed her plate helmet.

"Alistar."

"Rose."

Their voices were full of steel and both of their countenances were hard as iron.

He made it sound like they were waaay more lovey dovey. What a lia–

Alistar broke first and started making kissing noises and Rose did the same.

Several guards standing nearby rolled their eyes so hard their helmets nearly fell off.

After their overly affectionate public display, Rose turned to Daniel with a questioning look in her eye.

"Is this him?"

"Yes, love, let me introduce you to the newest Sage. Daniel, this is Rose, the absolute love of my life. The beacon of my heart. The piece of my soul that I never knew I lost until she found me. I would climb–"

Laughing, Rose interrupted him, "That's enough Ali. It's nice to finally meet you Daniel. Gwen's letter was such a wonderful surprise to receive. Thank you for bringing it, it was good to hear from her again."

"Heh, hello, nice to meet you."

Daniel reflexively scratched the back of his head.

"Would you be willing to remove your mask? My husband claimed you were rather handsome."

"What? I said no such–"

"Shush."

Sheepishly, Daniel took his mask off and put it in his inventory.

"Sorry about that, I forget I have it on most of the time."

"Mhm. I know how you feel. The same thing happens with my helmet. Invisible worn enchantments sure are something!"

She tapped her helmet, then turned. Motioning the two of them to follow her.

"Well, let's put you to task, shall we? We have a large block of Adamantian Muramite at one of our training halls. Several of my students are striving to become Sages themselves. If you manage to cut that block, I bet they'd become green with envy. Might even motivate them a bit, something they sorely need."

It took them a little while to navigate their way down several twisty streets until they came upon a building very similar to Alistar's barracks. This building was a good bit smaller, but the overall design was the same. The inner courtyard she led them into was also much smaller and only had a handful of people in attendance when they entered.

"Attention everyone! I have a special surprise for you all today! Gather round, gather round!"

She motioned for everyone to stand near the large stone block that was the size of a minivan as she addressed them.

"Daniel here is an aspiring Sage."

She winked at him as she continued.

"Today, I will be showing him how to manifest and then project your soul essence into an attack. I know this is something many of you have all seen countless times, but pay attention and watch how he learns from my technique."

Stepping over to stand in front of the large stone, she motioned Daniel to come closer.

"Now, my students usually try to cut the stone directly with their chosen weapons, but for me and you, we will make our attack from back here."

She walked about ten feet back and drew a line in the dirt with her foot. Standing behind the line, she then manifested her soul essence as she unhooked her massive sword from her back. Shadowless light radiated out from the overly large weapon and she looked over at Daniel to make sure she had his undivided attention.

"This next part is important. Watch the flow of my soul essence. I'm not just cramming it into my sword, I'm recreating the sword with pure essence and forcing its existence into this reality."

Huh?

Daniel watched as he tried to make sense of what she'd just said. His eyes opened wide as he watched her sword grow to three times its original size. He could feel it emitting a pressure as if it generated its own force of gravity and pushed against him.

She lightly swung her sword downward and the massive weapon sliced cleanly through the Adamantian Muramite stone block.

Sheathing her back to normal sword across her back, she stepped aside and motioned Daniel to take her place.

"Your turn!"

Uhh .. how the hell am I supposed to do that?

Feeling zero confidence in himself and still emotionally raw, Daniel stood behind the line and withdrew both of his blades. It took him longer than normal to find the floating denseness that held all his soul essence, since his focus was a bit off. Mentally berating himself, he did his best to shove down his lingering emotional turmoil and dedicated all of himself to the task ahead.

He'd become quite adept at manipulating his soul essence to pass the defensive tests and found it took hardly any thought at all to focus his essence into both of the blades held in front of him. The next part was a bit of trial and error, but he focused on the words she had said to him.

Create the swords with essence, then make them exist in this reality. Make it exist.. Make it real .. make them carry weight..

He was able to create enlarged swords with his essence easily enough using the new techniques he'd just learned. As both of the swords stretched out overhead, now roughly four times their original size so they would reach the stone block, they began to flex and change.

It was very gradual at first, but everyone standing around the block could lightly feel a weight pressing down against them.

Daniel's focus intensified as he kept empowering the two swords with the heaviness from his soul until the pressure they gave off was similar to Rose's sword.

With more force than necessary, he violently swung his arms down.

A deafening boom rattled the entire courtyard and caused a mini earthquake to shake the surrounding buildings.

All the students had fallen to the ground and threw their arms up to protect themselves.

Rose had started frantically waving her hands around as Alistar clutched his stomach and began laughing uncontrollably.

"Woah, woah, woah! Not so hard! Did you not see how my swing was soft?! You'll destroy half the damn city if you're not careful!"

Seeing the block split cleanly into three new sections and a massive crack under the block itself, Daniel put his blades away.

"My bad."

Alistar was wheezing at this point, causing Daniel to smirk a bit himself.

Taking a deep breath to calm herself, Rose then turned to her rattled students and started quizzing them on what they inferred about the differences between her strike and his. This went on for a few more minutes as Alistar struggled to contain himself.

He seemed to finally settle down, only to start back up again when he saw the massive crack in the ground give way about an inch.

Rose had finally gotten annoyed enough to smack him on the back of his head and he quickly apologized as he wiped a few tears from his eyes.

"Well, it was certainly impressive that you managed it on your first attempt. Although, I'm not sure how much damage you may have inadvertently caused."

A worried look marred Daniel's face as he imagined the penalty for damaging a structure in a massive city such as Vandean.

Rose waved away his concerns when she saw his frown, "It's fine, Daniel. This building was getting rather rundown anyways and was already scheduled for repair work in the coming years. We'll just up the priority a little, which means I get to have a custom redesign of this entire training center."

A gleam of excitement flashed across her eyes as she envisioned all the much needed updates her personal training grounds would get.

Coming back to herself, she stepped over in front of Daniel and placed her right hand on his left shoulder.

"Time for a bit of seriousness. With my authority as an Offensive Specialist Sage, I hereby recognize you, Daniel, as a peer. Your path through sagehood is steadily progressing."

QUEST UPDATE:
THE HUNT FOR SWORD SAGES

YOU HAVE TAKEN ANOTHER STEP ON THE PATH OF SAGEHOOD. YOU HAVE SUCCESSFULLY UNLOCKED THE SAGE RANK IN THE SPECIALIZATION COMBAT FORM,

DEFENSIVE COMBAT FORM AND OFFENSIVE COMBAT FORM
SKILLS. SEEK OUT THE COUNTER SPECIALIST SAGE TO
ADVANCE FURTHER. ALISTAR AND ROSE MAY HAVE MORE
INFORMATION.

REWARD: SWORD SAGE TRAINING

PENALTY FOR FAILURE: LOSS OF ADVANCEMENT
POTENTIAL

"Tck. He was *already* a Sage?"

Rose had to take a moment to hide her smile from her students. Turning her face into a neutral mask, she whirled toward her students.

"Yes, Relithon, he was, but in no way does that diminish his exemplary performance here today. Each step along the path of sagehood only grows more difficult the higher you climb. Now go, think on the lessons you have learned today and get back to your training. Dismissed."

As the gathered students all dispersed, Rose and Alistar walked over to Daniel.

Alistar slapped his shoulder and asked, "So, what's next for you, Daniel?"

"Uhm. I guess I will go looking for the counter specialist sage. Do either of you know where to find them?"

As Alistar scratched his chin, Rose hesitantly spoke up, "The only person I sort of know the whereabouts of, would be Denton."

Alistar looked over in surprise.

"That ole bandit captain? What's he up to?"

"Last I heard, he was down south, out past the Dreadland Swamp. But that's all I know, that place is not fully explored and most of it is filled with deadly abominations."

Alistar was nodding along and added, "Not to mention The Dread Beast itself. Just making it past that thing is a harsh trial. Do you know much about those swamps?"

Shaking his head, Daniel responded, "Nope. I don't even know how to find them. I thought the Orc Tribes were in that massive desert to the south."

Rose picked up the explanation.

"That they are. I just got back from trying to placate those frustrating bastards. Not sure if it did any good, those Orcs still hate us something fierce. The only thing that kept them from cutting me open was knowing what would happen if they tried. The Dreadland Swamp is further south of their territory. There is a massive amalgamation of some kind that is simply called The Dread Beast. Every few months it wakes up from its slumber and tries to expand its swampy territory. We rely on huge adventuring parties to cause enough damage that the beast is forced back into hibernation and its territory shrinks back to its smallest size."

Alistar slapped Daniel's shoulder as he spoke up once more. "If it weren't for adventurers like yourself, that beast would probably grow so big it would consume both the Orc Tribes *and* Vandean. We spend a lot of money offering rewards through the Adventure Society any time we get reports of the damn thing waking back up. So, as long as it's asleep, it shouldn't be too bad getting through its territory, but the beast doesn't have a regular sleep cycle and it can wake up at any time."

As the two imposing figures lapsed into silence, Daniel hadn't picked up on exactly where this Denton person could be found.

"Okay, so, go south, past the Orcs, then through those swamps and finally, once I'm on the other side of that, where to next?"

Alistar looked over at Rose who just shrugged in response.

"If Alistar doesn't know anything more then that's all I've got for you. I only just overheard some conversation between a few Orc Chieftains that spoke about how they chased him out of their territory and all the way through the swamps before giving up. The wily bastard stole some artifacts from them."

Nodding to himself, Alistar spoke up next. "He was always up to all sorts of mischief. I asked him to join our city guard several times. He always refused, said it sounded too boring. I need to head back, I'll see you in a bit, my love. Good luck on your search, Daniel! Feel free to stop by and visit any time!"

Alistar turned and left, leaving just the two of them standing by the large fissure that was starting to grow a little bit minute by minute.

After giving the damaged courtyard an appraising glance, Rose motioned Daniel to follow her.

"Come, let me walk you out. I need to clear the building, just in case."

After saying a polite goodbye to Rose, Daniel opened his quest to see if the prompt had changed to reveal a bit more info to help point him in the right direction.

Quest Update:
The Hunt for Sword Sages
YOU HAVE TAKEN ANOTHER STEP ON THE PATH OF SAGEHOOD. YOU HAVE SUCCESSFULLY UNLOCKED THE SAGE RANK IN THE SPECIALIZATION COMBAT FORM,

DEFENSIVE COMBAT FORM AND OFFENSIVE COMBAT FORM
SKILLS. SEEK OUT THE COUNTER SPECIALIST SAGE TO
ADVANCE FURTHER. ALISTAR AND ROSE SUGGEST
TRAVELING TO THE FAR SOUTH IN SEARCH OF DENTON.
REWARD: SWORD SAGE TRAINING
PENALTY FOR FAILURE: LOSS OF ADVANCEMENT
POTENTIAL

Riveting. Guess I should go ahead and start walking. At least my magic map has a built-in compass function.

Pulling out his map, he zoomed out from where he was to get an idea of how far he would have to travel. The Orc territory was massive. Easily ten times the distance from Aeryenous to Vandean. He found the swamp area, which was fortunately only half as large as the desert, but still unbelievably massive. Just beyond the swamp was an area labeled as unknown desert steppes. This region of his map was as big, if not a little bigger than the Orc desert.

That is.. So damn far.. And how exactly am I supposed to find some wily bandit in such a huge place.

Feeling a bit defeated, he put his map away and despondently walked to the city gates.

He wasn't really sure if he should leave just yet, especially if he was going to have to camp out several times along the way. He needed to buy one of those player tents that his friend Emilio had. They'd used it while traveling from Aeryenous to Vandean and the tent made them basically invisible to everything, keeping their avatars safe out in the wilds while they were offline. It also had the very similar magic sigils used by Gwenithe when she had set their camp. Something to do with repelling monsters.

Daniel had more than five hours left before he needed to log off for the night, but he really didn't feel like doing anything.

The sounds of the city were starting to annoy him so he went for a walk out past the gates. Turning to his left, he kept the wall that surrounded Vandean a good hundred yards away as he kicked a rock along the ground.

At first, he thought about Alyssa, but that just made him super depressed, so he ended up not thinking about anything and just kept kicking a rock along the outside of the twenty foot wall.

He'd gotten some odd looks here and there from the soldiers and guards patrolling along the ramparts, but Daniel never even noticed them.

He was finally broken out of his zombie-like state when a small white rabbit tried to bite his left ankle.

"Ahh, what the heck!"

Startled, he jumped to the side.

That's.. What is a rabbit doing out here?

Daniel just stood there, staring at the tiny fluffy rabbit.

The rabbit stared intensely back at him.

Then it turned and hopped a few feet away, stopped, and turned to look back at him.

Confused and curious, Daniel took a step after the rabbit and once it noticed he was following it turned back around and bounced away.

It would stop on occasion to see if he was still following, and he was.

Daniel tried to inspect it but nothing happened. It was as if the skill refused to activate for some reason. He picked up a rock to test his inspection skill and it worked just fine. As he followed the rabbit, he tried several times to inspect it and it failed each time.

He followed it to an oddly placed rocky protrusion.

That looks weird. The rabbit is also weird. This whole thing is just weird.

The rock formation was like a very steep triangle.

Watching the rabbit hop up and run along the steep slanted edge towards the top of the strange formation, Daniel decided to follow it up.

It was surprisingly tall as Daniel surmised it to be roughly three times the height of the city wall.

When he got to the top, the bunny was nowhere to be found, so he walked over to the edge and looked down. It was a straight shot to the ground and it made him a little nervous to be up so high while standing on the edge of a sheer drop.

Not really sure what else to do, Daniel took a seat and dangled his legs over the edge as he looked out at the vast city before him.

Look at all the people. Doing stuff. Living their lives. I wonder if they ever realize they are just artificial intelligences. There are so many of them. How does FBO even create them all? That has to need a massive amount of energy and tons of processing power to create such life like people. I wonder how they do it.

As Daniel's eyes roamed around the city of Vandean, his vision focused in on a particularly tall structure that seemed rather close. The building was much more opulently designed than all the others around the city. He quickly surmised it must be the home of someone very wealthy.

As he was looking at a balcony that seemed to extend much further than it should in his direction, he spotted someone entering the room behind it.

The unmistakable glow of the lover's heart gemstone could be seen as it was placed on top of a bundle of cloth that was bunched up on what looked like a dresser of some kind.

Queen Fidel was wrapped in a towel as she put the pendant down and then disappeared from the room.

Daniel stared at the empty room and the glowing purple gemstone as a terrible idea flitted across his mind.

She had a towel on, so she was probably going to go take a bath or something, which means she will be gone for a while and that balcony is close enough to reach from here.. Should I do it? What if I put it on and nothing happens?

Daniel's mind was on the fence about whether he should jump over and put the necklace on or just leave it be.

A sudden burst of memories of Mirantil flashed across his mind and for a small moment, he wondered if it would lead to her.

Entirely unsure if he was making a good decision, Daniel got to his feet and gauged the distance from where he stood to the edge of the balcony.

A little over half my current aura strength ought to do it..

Letting himself slightly fall over the edge of the rock face, he surged his aura and catapulted towards the empty balcony.

His aim was off.

Instead of landing gracefully like a thief in the night, he slammed chest first into the balcony railing causing it to crack and partially fall inwards.

Scrambling to his feet, he rushed into the room.

Feeling slightly panicked from making so much noise, he rushed over and grabbed the wadded up cloth with the necklace still on it.

The door to the room suddenly burst open and two additional people were now in the room with him.

Queen Fidel stood there soaking wet with a towel completely covering her and a terrified, yet somehow also furious, look on her face.

Rose stood next to her with her massive sword held in both hands as she maintained a fighting stance.

The Queen was the first to speak, "No! Give those back!"

Rose spoke up immediately after, "Daniel?!"

Several thoughts bombarded his mind in that moment.

First of which was knowing his mask was sitting innocently in his inventory and also realizing that Rose had already identified him so there was no pretending that it was someone else who'd snuck into the Queens dressing chambers. He also needed to put the items in his hands into his inventory so he could escape and never return from the sheer embarrassment of what he'd just done.

Daniel pixelated the things in his hands, intending for them to go straight into his inventory, but to his confused horror, only the clothing disappeared.

The necklace shimmered as if it was resisting the pull and was then repelled across the room to smash into a wall and fall behind a large piece of furniture.

Rose instinctively struck out at him but with a surge of his aura, he slowed down time, sped himself up, turned and fled.

Out on the balcony he launched himself back towards the strange rock formation, only to discover it was nowhere to be seen.

Not only that, the building he leapt from was actually near the heart of Vandean. He was an awfully long way from any wall to escape over.

What the fu–

He slammed into a nearby rooftop and rolled to his feet.

Without pausing to think, he simply reacted.

Nothing was making any sense to him right then so he just ran. As fast as he could, he traversed the rooftops, leaping from building to building until he neared a wall and rocketed over it, landing awkwardly then turning to run away at top speed.

He didn't stop until he'd burned through half his health.

What the actual fuck was that?!

Looking around in absolute bewilderment, Daniel was completely at a loss for what had just happened. He wasn't even sure if it had actually happened or if it was all just some weird fevered dream. Something he'd imagined to distract himself from all his emotional trauma.

Checking his inventory, he pulled something out that caused the pit of his stomach to drop.

Queen Fidel's Ceremonial Underrobe
Effect: Will emit an ever increasingly large pillar of light when held by anyone other that the Queen
Note: These belong to the Vampire Queen Fidel Ast'Delerost. She has worn these underrobes to every special event in her life and they have

BECOME A SUPERSTITIOUS IDOL FOR HER. THEY ALSO
HOLD UNFATHOMABLE SENTIMENTAL VALUE TO THE
QUEEN AS THEY WERE GIFTS TO HER FROM HER BELOVED
GRANDMOTHER.

"Aww shit."

Daniel quickly put them away as they started to glow ominously.

He began pacing back and forth.

His racing thoughts were interrupted by a forced alert.

WORLD EVENT:
A VAMPIRE'S REQUEST

ATTENTION ALL PLAYERS! SOMEONE HAS DONE THE
UNTHINKABLE! THE VAMPIRE QUEEN FIDEL
AST'DELEROST CALLS UPON THE BLOOD OF HER SWORN.
THE PLAYER **DANIEL** HAS TAKEN SOMETHING PRECIOUS
FROM HER. AFTER PERFORMING THE RITUAL OF DEATH'S
VENGEANCE, ALL VAMPIRE RACES WILL BE ABLE TO SENSE
HIS GENERAL LOCATION. SHE HAS PLACED A BOUNTY ON
HIS HEAD FOR EACH DEATH INFLICTED ALONG WITH A
VAST REWARD FOR HIS CAPTURE. CHECK IN WITH YOUR
LOCAL ADVENTURE SOCIETY FOR MORE DETAILS ABOUT
VARIOUS REWARDS! THE PLAYER **DANIEL** IS NOW
PERMANENTLY BANNED FROM THE CITY OF VANDEAN AND
WILL BE CAPTURED OR KILLED ON SIGHT BY ALL CITIZENS
OF VANDEAN.

Oh. My. God.

THE END
FINAL BASTION ONLINE
Sages & Demons

Thank you for reading my book, and I hope you enjoyed the ride! More books are on the way!

Email: justinclarkebooks@gmail.com

Upcoming Titles:
- ➤ Final Bastion Online: Mentors & Shadows

Currently Published Titles:
- ➤ Final Bastion Online: Villains & Bullies
- ➤ Final Bastion Online: Sages & Demons